Mindbender

Avinash Naduvath

Publishing History

Hardcover Edition 1 / April 2022

ISBN: 9798803703327

Imprint: Independently Published

Paperback Edition 1 / April 2022

ISBN: 9798803700333

Imprint: Independently Published

Kindle Edition 1 / April 2022

Dedication

To my beautiful wife, bubbly son, and lovely parents

Acknowledgments

I want to begin by thanking you, the reader, for trusting me with giving you food for thought for the duration of time you read this book. I hope you enjoy the book and that it lives up to your expectation.

This book wouldn't be possible without the relentless efforts of my wife, Minu. Her persistent drive to make me complete the first draft was all it took to get me all pumped up to go further. The late-night chapter reviews wouldn't have been the same with anyone else. Thank you for being a part of this journey.

A big thanks to my brother-in-law, Vishnu, who has been instrumental with constant feedback on the story as well as the flow of events. Whether it's pointing out an obvious flaw or alternate ways of looking at what is happening, his feedback and trust in me are what got me moving forward.

I want to thank Bill Smart, who is not only a meticulous editor but also a very good pair of eyes for logic validation and copyright editing. He has been encouraging from the start and has been genuinely interested in making this book a success.

Finally, I thank God for giving me the idea and drive to complete the book.

Table of Contents

Mindbender

Avinash Naduvath

Prologue

I recall the psychiatrist telling my mom that it was possible for some people to confuse a dream with reality when they had just woken up from their sleep. He thought that I was not paying attention, so he continued his adult talk with Mom. As per the psychiatrist, it's very common for kids to start "lucid dreaming," whatever that means. I just remember waking up from my desk at school and punching Clive sitting next to me. Images flashed before my eyes, and I could see Clive crying in agony and Mr. Romero dragging me to the principal's office. The next thing I knew, I was visiting the psychiatrist.

On the way to the psychiatrist, I tried to explain to my mom, "Mom, I did not know it was Clive, I swear! I thought I was Batman, and he was the Joker. It was so real. I thought punching him was the right thing to do." My mother was aware I have had episodes like this but never at school and never physical.

She looked at me lovingly and said, "It is fine, dear. Calm down. You are not in trouble. We just need to get the doctor to tell us you are fine."

I did not want to argue with her. I loved spending time with her, and every moment with her was happiness wrapped into a nice cuddly blanket. I gave in, "Alright, but I want to have ice cream later."

She replied," Sure, but don't you think it's a little unfair that you punch your best friend and then get ice cream as a reward?".

Prologue

She was looking at me as though she was scolding me, but I knew she was not angry. I could feel her warm smile hiding behind her chiding façade. She used to fake anger often, and I loved being dramatic so that she would give me that extra attention. Mostly, all I needed to see was her smile, but this time I was comforted only when she said I was not in trouble because punching my best friend would have earned me her disappointment and her wrath. Father beating on me was bad enough, and I did not want Mom to get angry as well.

Fighting with each other was commonplace with twelve-year-olds, but I think most parents use "you are not in trouble" to get their kids to have a fake sense of complacence before they go nuclear on them. I was cautious not to let my guard down and reveal something I should not. This time though, she appeared different. She was looking out of the taxi window and was humming a tune I had never heard before. My angry mom wouldn't do that, which meant that she was not angry.

My father's mistreatment of Mom and me had only brought us closer. She always understood my concern. She sang without knowing that I was focusing on her voice. It was like a soft blanket protecting me and keeping me warm. She realized I was hearing her and quickly stopped singing and looked at me and smiled again. Her loving eyes could convince me that everything was fine, even if the world was ending.

My mental recap of the taxi ride to the hospital was shaken by the doctor continuing his diagnosis. I heard him saying that he might need to check to see if there was something more deep-rooted in today's episode but that he could not say for sure so far. There was an exchange of some words I could not even begin to pronounce, but he said it was rare in children. Good, that's good. That means I am not a freak. When he started explaining some more medical terms, I zoned out completely.

I liked the smell of spirit in hospitals. It was partially another reason why I did not throw tantrums when my mom wanted to take me to the doctor. I was keenly observing my environment and, more specifically, the psychiatrist. He seemed to be young and did not have the bald spot on his head like Mom's doctor at the public hospital. Glasses suited him well, and he also did not have a stethoscope on his shoulder like I have seen in the school textbooks. Since he doesn't have the scope, does that mean he is not a doctor? I don't know. I was scanning the room for anything remotely interesting, but all I could see were steel plates with some knife-like instruments and a lot of posters. I spotted a brain model sitting on his desk and got up to have a look.

He was busily elucidating the diagnosis to my mom about the possible repercussions of something I did not understand, but my movement towards his brain model seemed to raise his proximity alarms. He turned to me and asked, "Do you like the brain? It is the most interesting organ in the human body."

I replied in my matter-of-fact voice, "I thought the most interesting part was the face. That's the only part that people see first, and if mine is not good, then no one will be my friend."

The doctor chuckled and looked at my mom and then back at me," Kid, when you grow up, you will learn that the mind will stay on forever, even seven minutes after you die. All other organs wither away with age but not the mind. The mind stays strong if you exercise it often. So, keep studying and dream all you want."

I pondered over what he said for a while, and then I said, "I am afraid of dreaming now. I may hurt my mom when I sleep."

He responded with a reassuring smile, "You won't, kiddo. What you are undergoing is perfectly normal. When you sleep and have a dream and wake up, your mind basically is half asleep and half awake. Imagine you are at a cinema with your parents, and you go to sleep because adult movies are boring, right? You wake up just in time to see the action sequence, but you are still half asleep. You look around and realize your parents are not there. What would you do?"

Prologue

I was considering the question and secretly thought if my father was not around or left, I would just say, "Good riddance!" I knew my mom would not just abandon me because she loved me more than anything, but if I didn't see her, I would panic. I told the psychiatrist, "If my mom was not around, I would panic and try to find her."

The psychiatrist then said," Some people would just wake up from the dream, but you, as you said, would try and find her and change the outcome of the situation you are in. You would basically direct your dream. Sounds cool, right? This is called 'lucid dreaming.'"

It did sound cool, but I did not want to even consider the possibility of my mom abandoning me even in a dream. I just nodded my head, and the psychiatrist continued, "So next time you have an episode like this, try and get an outcome you like. You said you were Batman, and you were punching Joker, right? See if you can understand that it's a dream by asking yourself the question, 'Is this real?', and then try talking to him. Do anything except punch him and see where that leads you." He rolled his chair and turned back to mom, leaving me with this cliffhanger. He scribbled a set of medicines and said there was nothing to worry about. I liked this psychiatrist. He even gave me a chocolate before I left.

The next day when I told Clive that I could direct my own dreams using lucid dreaming, he said, "Whoa, that is wicked sick! Can you teach me?"

I replied, "The doctor claims it's fairly rare, and not everyone can do it, so maybe not your cup of tea." It was a harmless lie. Who doesn't like to feel special? I continued, "The first question you need to ask in the dream if you can, is – 'Is this real?'"

PERSPECTIVE POGO

(Life Is Unfair)

"For in every adult there resides the child that was, and in every child there lies the adult that will be."

~ John Connolly

Chapter 1
Is This Real?

"Is this real?" was my first reaction when I heard the scream. My eyes were still closed, and I did not want to wake up. The voice was clear and prolonged enough to be distinctly identified and yet not too long to be a wail. If this was a dream, then I wanted to figure out who was screaming. If this was not a dream, then I am sure Mom would have heard it as well.

My eyes partially opened to see the window. I did not see light outside the window, so I assumed it was still night. My mother had spent a good chunk of her lifetime training me to wake up when there was sunlight in the room and subsequently on my face. There was no reason for it to be any different today. No light means more sleep, but I had to check.

"Mom, you there?" I got no response. I turned around groggily and saw an empty space on the bed. I was too sleepy to realize that the bedsheet had not been used, and there was no blanket or even a pillow. I thought, "Ah well, Mom probably went to the restroom. More sleep for me. Even if this was a dream, I wasn't in a mood to direct it. Mom would handle it tomorrow.

I turned around and buried my face into the pillow. Sleep was at my doorstep, but I was aware of a looming thought at the back of my mind. Who had screamed?

*   *   *

My eyes were half open now, and I was catching a glimpse of the ceiling at regular intervals. The air around me was pregnant with the aroma of pancakes and scrambled eggs. I was leaning towards sleeping another five minutes and waking up two hours later, but the aroma wouldn't take no for an answer. This specific combination of pancakes and scrambled eggs was my favorite, and I did not need any more incentives to wake up if this was being cooked. My mom used to make them almost every day.

Today must be a Sunday because Mom was not all over me with her steel spatula in hand, brandishing it like a highwayman's sword. The threat was usually, wake up now or feel the spatula on your thigh, though we both knew it was an empty threat and would never come to pass. If today was a Sunday, there was nothing to do except laze around and play in the garden. Maybe I could coax her to take me to the beach. What does a twelve-year-old have to do during the day, anyway, except for playing or going to school?

The thought of school initially brought a sense of aversion. Like most kids, I do not like school. I was not popular in school and had only..., wait..., I don't know. I could not remember my best friend's name. It was at the tip of my tongue, but I could not remember it. What's going on? I tried to remember the name of the school I go to but couldn't remember that either.

If I was on the fence about waking up, I was now awake with sleep long gone. The icy hands of fear began to grip me, and I sat straight up on the bed with a jolt. Did I just lose my memory? I tried hard to think of a name, but it was as if my memory had been erased by one of those Men-in-Black thingamajigs.

I looked down at my dinosaur-themed pajamas. They were my favorite pajamas with mini-dinosaurs across my shirt and pajama pants. I seemed to remember my favorites, so that's a good thing. Why was this happening to me?

Chapter 1: Is This Real?

My hands began to tremble. I wanted to pull the blanket over my face and let out a huge shout, but I couldn't do that. If Father was here, that would be the end of me. I tried to remember the last time Mom and I went out, but I couldn't remember that as well.

I was awake already, so I decided to brush my teeth and proceed downstairs. My room was on the top floor of a two-storied home. I glanced at my room and realized that it was not exactly cluttered but was not as neat as a nail either. The room itself had a certain charm that I always liked to imbibe before starting my day, except when Mom threatened me with her spatula. I had a habit of just getting up from bed and staring at the ceiling for a long time. I didn't seem to have lost all my memory but only certain parts of it, so I remember this is indeed my room.

This time I stared at the ceiling, hoping a portal would open and someone would jump down and explain what was happening. My bed was in the far corner of the room. My parents were not rich, and so it wasn't a big bed or a race-car-themed bed as I would have liked, but they did what they could. The best part of the bed was that it was flanked to the left by the window. My mom's strategy was to wake me up when the first rays of light came in which was an ingenious one that began when I was much younger, not that it was needed today. Facing a window while sleeping or waking up almost felt like a part of my consciousness had expanded, and I almost always felt pleasant and complete. Today I felt none of these. What I felt were fear and doubt. I needed to speak with Mom and ask her if she was facing a similar dilemma.

I turned to look at the room. On the right side of my bed was a small table where I placed my glasses, which I could not find today. It had some crumpled papers and a plastic toy soldier I used to love when I was around six. It was just a sea-green plastic soldier taking his aim and shooting at another soldier who was in a falling pose.

Wait! What? I thought I had lost this toy when I was around eight. Fear and surprise were playing a ping-pong match in my mind. Where exactly did these come from, and how and when had I found them? I needed to know if it really was my lost toy soldier, not that I really wanted it back, but this toy was dear to me because Mom had got them for me behind Father's back despite having only a little money.

I reached my hands over to pick the toy from the bed, and as I was about to pick it up, I howled in pain. Looking down, I saw that I had stepped on my spectacles. They must have fallen while I was asleep. The pain was not excruciating but was more of an unwanted discomfort. I hopped on one leg until I reached the edge of the bed and then slumped back. It took me a while to twist my leg and figure out where the point of discomfort was. How much more bad vibes can the room throw at me?

When my pain subsided, I extended my hand carefully, looking down to make sure I didn't step on something else and picked up the plastic toy soldier. Immediately I saw a flash of light.

*

I looked at myself, and I was no longer in my dinosaur pajamas. I was wearing my nursery uniform, and I was with my mom. We were coming back from the nursery, and I saw a street hawker selling small plastic toy soldiers. There was another kid who had bought a toy from the hawker and was showing it off to his circle of friends who stood around him awestruck. I could feel my emotions welling up. Jealousy and dismay are a bad combination, and that was the exact mixture brewing inside me. I wanted to be like him. I wanted to have a lot of friends, and I wanted to show them cool toys so they would stay as friends with me, and I knew that would almost never happen. I tried to say something, but it wasn't me. It was almost like I was just a spectator watching the six-year-old me talking to my mom.

Chapter 1: Is This Real?

"Mom, can I have that toy soldier, please?"

"No, Munchkin, I'm sorry, but we cannot afford this toy now. Can I get it for you next month?"

"No, Mom, I want it now. I want it now!"

The mixture was brewing well, and I had just put in a pinch of anger, pouting at the fact that this toy couldn't be mine. My mom could see the smoke rising from my ears, and I knew my mom couldn't and wouldn't let me ever be distraught like this. That is why I loved her so much. She just couldn't let me be sad, but neither could I. I could see the change of expression on her face. She was probably thinking of all the bills she may have to forego to be able to afford the toy. Her silence was deafening, and I couldn't bring myself to play with a toy that burdened the family. She rummaged through her purse for some money and went to get the toy from the shopkeeper. As she was leaving, I stopped her.

"Mom, I changed my mind. I don't want the toy."

"It's okay, Pogo. I know you really want it."

"No, Mom, I don't want it. It looks like it might break easily."

My mom looked at me, initially skeptical but now more confident that I wanted it. "Pogo, you don't need to be burdened with the finances of the house. How your dad and I manage money shouldn't affect your desires. If you want something and its reasonable, I will get it for you."

I was at a loss for words. I was so lucky to have Mom. I wondered in silence how Mom even got married to Father. She walked to the hawker, who was now happy to make another sale. She picked out the toy soldier, brought it back to the car and placed it in my palms.

"Here you go, Pogo. I love you so much!"

"Thanks, Mom. I love you too." I was shining brighter than the sun above us.

*

I was back in my room. My dinosaur pajamas were wet with my perspiration. "Scared" was a mild word to describe my current mental state. I was rooted to the ground and couldn't think properly. An eerie cold surrounded me as if this episode sucked the warmth that the pancakes and scrambled eggs had brought into the room. What I had experienced was a memory, but the possibility that it just happened was beyond my understanding. I doubt it was within the understanding of any adult, let alone a kid. Maybe this was a dream. Is this real? The psychiatrist's words came back to my mind. I made a mental note to ask Mom.

Opposite to the foot of the bed was my book rack. It was a dilapidated rack and was almost crumbling. I recall that this rack was where I stocked all my storybooks. Some of my favorites were there like *Snow White and the Seven Dwarves, Little Red Riding Hood,* and more recently, *Harry Potter and the Prisoner of Azkaban.* Ants were beginning to form a disciplined line behind one of the books. It must have been a while since I read them.

My book rack was something I prized as I was always fascinated by books. It was easy to escape into a storybook when I heard my father beating Mom. I just couldn't bear to hear her screams, so reading books gave me an escape, but if the books hadn't been used recently, that means there was no beatings, which is good.

What caught my attention was the bicycle that was now placed beside the door. Its unannounced presence surprised me. This was my bicycle, of course, as I distinctively recall its yellow-and-green-colored handles and the metal basket in front. Many a time, I have enjoyed rides on this bicycle, but what I did not remember was that how it came to be here in the room. I do not recall bringing it here and was scared if it was Father who placed it here. I observed the bicycle in detail. There was no dirt on the wheels, so I can only infer that I did not take it out. The basket was empty, which means I did not buy anything. The bicycle was clean, and the yellow and green were reflecting the sunlight above the bed, giving the bed a glowing arc above it. Yet again, a sense of dread crept into my mind when I thought about who could have used my bicycle and then put it back in my room. I had to ask Mom before I go crazy!

I walked slowly past the bicycle and moved into the bathroom to brush my teeth. My mom had taught me how to brush, and she was especially proud of me the day I brushed on my own. We had gone out to have a burger just to celebrate the first brush. Father was not in that day; otherwise, that trip would have ended with another beating.

The bicycle was just inside the room beside the door. I did not want to make father angry. If I get down late for breakfast, he gets angry and would beat me. When my father beats me, my mom wouldn't be able to take it, and she would protect me from his wrath. I was not sure why I was consistently reminded of my father as that is one memory I wanted to forget, but it seemed that this memory was a deep-rooted part of my mind, and like chewing gum sticking to the sole of my shoe, I couldn't get rid of it. I love my mother and despise my father.

I opened the door and left my room. The smell of pancakes wafted through the air bringing with it a familiar warmth. Fear was now replaced by hunger. I still couldn't remember what school I go or who my best friend was, but I was comfortable that at least I was at home and Mom was making pancakes.

I was not sure where Father went, but if he was around, the atmosphere at breakfast would be completely different. He read the newspaper and drank his coffee without uttering a single word. Mom would try and have a conversation, but he would just ignore her. He was like one of those dementors in Harry Potter books sucking the happiness out of any situation. I always felt sorry for Mom and even asked her, "Mom, does Father really love us?"

She seemed surprised and a tad angry that I even asked. "Yes, Pogo, he loves us both."

I dared to follow up, "Then why does he beat you and me every time?"

She seemed distraught. She turned her face away and said," He loves us and provides for us in his own way. We must respect that'"

I thought to myself, 'What kind of love demands hurting others?" When I glanced back at Mom, I thought I might have seen tears, and I scolded myself for making Mom cry. Curiosity is not worth Mom's dismay.

I was now excited to go down and have breakfast and especially looking forward to the pancakes and scrambled eggs. Being completely confused by what was happening presently, I was looking forward to speaking with Mom to either confirm the incidents I had just observed or tell me all was well.

My room was on the extreme end of the upper story and faced an old worn-out wall. Walking along this wall would lead me to the beginning of the staircase, which would then lead me down. I began following the smell of the pancakes out of my room and onto the corridor towards the staircase. Above me was an extendable attic which I dare not go into for fear of being beaten. As I was being led by the aroma of pancakes, I realized that all my senses were awake now, and every small nudge in the environment set me off. My mom was generally like this when she was around Father. I was ambling for a couple of minutes when I thought I heard a sound from my room. I turned around only to see the light green door to my room was still ajar exactly as I had left it. I thought to myself that I must have imagined it, but the urgency to tell someone about all of this was increasing as I walked to the staircase. I needed to speak to Mom; otherwise, I was going to explode.

I looked ahead and saw a light blue door. I do not have fond memories of my parents' room. I noticed that the door was still closed, and there was a rusty lock on its bolt. The location of the keys was always a mystery to me. Sometimes when I see them dangling at my father's

Chapter 1: Is This Real?

hips, they appear to mock me as they were closer to him than I would ever be. He rarely even gave them to Mom, but when it was missing from his hips, I have never been able to find them. Surprisingly, the locked door did not rouse my curiosity, but instead, I felt much safer.

I recall briefly that had I had once curiously wandered into the room while I was playing after discovering that the door was ajar. There is a sort of excitement in being in an adult's room and that moment was no different. I felt a mixture of accomplishment and satisfaction in making it into the room. I carefully started observing my surroundings.

The bed was at the center of the room, with a mosquito net on all sides. There was a dressing table on the opposite of the bed with all forms of cosmetics. To the far right was their bathroom and beside their bed was a table which mostly had my father's wallet and his glasses. To the left of the bed was a cupboard which currently was wide open. It piqued my curiosity. I opened the cupboard and started searching for an unknown treasure which would be my cherry on top.

The Gods had favored me, and I found something intriguing. It was almost six inches and had a smooth trigger. The butt fit perfectly into my hands, and at that time, I was exhilarated. This was an actual gun, like the ones we see in the alien movies, just smaller. I held the gun in my hand and began enacting all the heroes I had seen in movies.

With my arm stretched out as far as possible and the gun in my hand, I tilted my neck and closed my left eye. My right eye was directly in line with the rear sight of the gun. I placed my left hand below my wrist and was tracing a semi-circle across the room with a loaded handgun. Before I could complete the semi-circle, I saw a large figure standing at the other end of the gun. He did not seem daunting at first and put his arm halfway up and said, "Kid, you don't know what that is. Slowly put it down onto the floor and slide it towards me. It's okay. Daddy will not hurt you." What a lie!

His voice did not project anger, so I believed him and slowly placed the gun on the floor. As I was doing so, he observed my hand with great intensity. He probably did not trust me enough to place it down on the floor without firing a shot. When I kicked it towards him, that's when I saw relief spread across his face. I don't know if there was a shadow of a smile because if there was, it disappeared instantly, and I could see the red in my father's eyes. He closed the door and turned to me, "So you want to play with a gun? Do you think this is something a child should play with? WHY ARE YOU IN THIS ROOM?" His voice echoed in the room like thunder.

I was now trembling because I knew what was next and did not see Mom anywhere around to protect me. In retrospect, I should have just taken the opportunity and pulled the trigger. I was a big boy. I would be able to take care of Mom. There are a lot of jobs for kids my age, or so I thought.

I was considering running a gaming center when I felt the first hit from the belt. Pain shot through my body like juice spreading on a paper napkin. The mirror on the dressing table was the only witness to the ferocity of the whipping that I received from that belt, and he knew that the mirror won't talk.

My mother did not realize this until later during the day when she saw the belt marks on my feet and skin. I could see the rage and helplessness in her eyes. She gave me some pasta to eat that night and looked at the bruises and cuts for a long time, hoping her gaze would fix the gashes and make me feel better. She then got up and went to speak to Father. I could faintly hear their discussion escalating. As I moved towards the door up the staircase, the conversations became clearer.

"How dare you touch him? Is it not enough that you beat me?"

"I don't care. He was playing with my gun."

"Why do you have a loaded gun in your cupboard? Do you want to kill me, Marko? Do it now then and end it."

I did not want her to feel helpless and I did not want them to fight, but I was just in time to slide the door open just enough to see a slap land on her soft cheeks. She covered her cheeks to prevent any blood from dripping on the floor, which she would eventually have to clean. Her frills covered her face, and thankfully she did not know I was behind the door. Father left her there alone like a discarded piece of crumpled paper.

As I recalled the experience, I reassured myself that it was better this room stays locked.

I made my way down the stairs. When I reached the bottom of the stairs, I could see our main door slightly open. Oh golly, was Father back? I really did not want to have breakfast with Father. I hoped with all my heart that he wasn't back, and Mom was just making pancakes for me.

To my right was the living room where Father sat most of the time. Mom feared calling him lazy, but deep down, I knew that's exactly what he was. Ever since he lost his job at the construction site, he constantly drank and beat Mom. Once he was done beating, he would get some beer from the refrigerator and sit on the couch and watch TV all day. A shiver ran down my spine even thinking of peeping in to see if he was in the living room. My destination was to my left, and all I cared about now was talking to Mom and eating pancakes.

My footsteps announced my arrival into the kitchen. The sweet fragrance of honey and pancakes were all over the kitchen, topped by scrambled eggs. Ah, this is how food heaven must smell like.

There was a small extension of the kitchen which had a table with an old plastic tablecloth that we could afford and four chairs. I did not see my father and heaved a sigh of relief that there would be no awkwardness. The scrambled eggs were on the table, and I saw the pancakes sitting beside the stove.

I immediately noticed that someone was at the stove flipping eggs, probably making omelets, but not wearing the usual white skirt and blouse. This person was wearing the kitchen apron but did not have the same build as my mom. Did she lose weight? I began to wonder if I was in a coma for a year or two because the individual was wearing socks with holes in them. I could make out that the feet did not look like my mom's feet. I could not feel Mom's presence, and I was getting scared. I wondered what more this day would hit me with.

Taking a leap of faith and hoping against all hope, I asked, "Mom, can you please pass me some of those pancakes?"

I lifted my head to look at Mom and was shocked to see that it was a boy I had never seen before.

Chapter 2
The Boy with the Beanie Cap

I was surprised to see a boy standing there beside the stove with a spatula in his hand. Apart from being eight to ten years older than me, he was quite tall and wore a black beanie cap on his head. I felt it was an odd choice to wear a beanie in the kitchen where one would have to deal with a lot of smoke and perspiration. I couldn't catch a glimpse of his hair because of the beanie cap. Mom was very strict about combed hair, and if she was around, I am sure he would have had an earful for using a cap at home. He appeared malnourished due to the overly loose Iron Maiden t-shirt that he was wearing, and to top it off, a small section of his jeans, especially those around the knees and along the feet, were torn. The tears looked almost intentional, and I wondered why he was wearing them in the first place if they were torn and unusable. I saw him wearing the same socks that Mom had bought for me some time ago, but these looked extremely worn out with holes in them. The brown shade of dirt over the white stripes was getting darker.

His presence was a mystery. He wore my mother's red apron across his waist. If I was not actively fighting the urge to scream at him and ask where Mom is, I might have found his current dressing sense funny. It was rare that you see an adult wearing a loose t-shirt with worn-out pants and socks cooking breakfast with an apron. I was not sure what my mind was going through. There was sadness and uncertainty regarding not seeing Mom, and then there was an intense curiosity about who he was.

I was not sure if he was even a teenager, but he definitely looked and dressed like one. I wasn't saying anything because of the emotional rollercoaster whirling around in my mind.

I sensed multiple emotions suggested by his behavior as he studied me as well. One was of surprise, but somewhere behind that waterfall of surprise was a hidden cave of recognition. I must have imagined it, but I was certain I caught a glint of recognition. He was probably undergoing the same confusion as me, but I was sure it was something else and not just the surprise of seeing me.

We probably had stared at each other for a long time because now both of us smelled burning food. He realized that he had almost burnt the omelet he was making and quickly turned around and flipped it. I was expecting Mom to barge in any minute, but that never happened.

I don't know how much time passed, but he finally flipped the omelet out of the pan, placed the spatula aside, switched off the stove, and looked at me. There was that flicker of recognition again! He placed the apron on the side of the kitchen slab where a small hook was present and walked across the room towards me. I had still not sat down or even moved from the kitchen entrance, and I was now aware of his presence near me. He looked at me, extended his palm, and said, "Hello, my name is Joshua."

"Who are you? Where is Mom? How did you enter our kitchen! Why are you cooking?" I was rapidly firing questions at him to mimic the tumult that my mind was in.

"Easy, Pogo. Don't stress out. Your mom knows I am here."

"How do you know my name? Where is Mom? Why is she not here?"

"Let me answer one question at a time. Your mom said you would be alone at home, and she had to go somewhere urgent. She asked me to sit with you and give you company."

"You mean she wanted you to babysit me? I don't need babysitting, so you can leave now."

Chapter 2: The Boy with the Beanie Cap

I did not mean to be angry or mean to him, but I did not feel comfortable having a stranger in the house and not having Mom around to deal with it, especially with all the weird stuff that happened in my room. He did not seem to take offense and smiled, "That's not how you speak to your elder brother, Pogo. Even after all that we have been through?"

My head was spinning now. Brother? Did he say BROTHER? I am twelve years old, and I have no recollection of having a brother. I remember my parents very clearly, so why do I not remember my brother? I was now face to face with a stranger who has entered my home and claimed to be my brother and made me my favorite pancakes and scrambled eggs. My brain was getting scrambled now.

Those thoughts brought me back to another pressing matter, which was my hunger. My entire day was led by the anticipation of having those pancakes, and my primal side was taking over. I walked past him to the stove and picked the pancakes. I slowly moved to the side of the table, pulled out a chair, and started eating the pancakes. He turned around and walked to the far end of the kitchen towards an obscure kitchen cabinet. He opened it and fetched a half-used bottle of maple syrup and placed it on the table beside the scrambled eggs.

I asked him with my mouth half full, "How do you know my name, and how did you get in?"

"I told you, Pogo. Your mom asked me to be with you while she was away. She gave me the keys. Here, you see?"

He edged his body forward a bit and lifted his Iron Maiden t-shirt to show me the bunch of keys dangling at his waist. Seeing them dangling like that sent a shiver down my spine, almost like seeing Father again.

"Do you know where Father or Mom is? Did Mom tell you where she was going?"

"I don't know. Your father wasn't around when your mom called me. I just assumed that he left early. Aunty just said she had to go to the city for something urgent. She did not give me a lot of details. She just asked me to take care of you and make you your favorite pancakes and scrambled eggs when you wake up."

That was a relief. I was already in a confused state, and I did not want the presence of my father to complicate it any further. I thought to myself that Joshua knew exactly where the maple syrup was, and he also knew the recipe of the scrambled eggs and pancakes, similar to how Mom makes them. It cannot be a coincidence. I was now thinking out loud.

"How come I am twelve years old, and I do not remember us living together under the same roof?"

"That's because we are cousins. Your mom is my mom's sister. I live close by, which is why your mom asked me to come here."

"Have we never spoken to each other frequently? How come I have no memory of you?"

"Well, I know you. I'm not sure why you don't remember me. Do you remember the day we went out with your bicycle, and I was walking along with you, and you were constantly looking back to see if your mom was following you? You fell down that day, do you remember? You were around eight at the time, if I recall correctly."

I did remember this incident, but I did not remember him being there. Why would I go cycling with a cousin?

"Was your mom there as well? I don't remember her either."

"Yeah, she was talking with Aunty, and I was with you."

The incident and memory were true, but somehow that was not what I remember. I clearly recalled my mom asking a pedestrian for help, and that was neither him nor his mom, but I saw no point arguing the details because it was some time ago when I was eight years old, so I may not remember the exact details. Joshua stood there waiting for me to acknowledge the memory, but I had my mouth full of pancakes. I was considering all possibilities about this bike incident, most of which seemed farfetched. Either I was in shock on the day of the accident and didn't remember him being around, or somehow my mind had deleted

Chapter 2: The Boy with the Beanie Cap

this entire individual and my memories of him. He knew my parents. He claimed my mom had a sister, but I never really went into the details of my mom's family tree. He stood there now with his Iron Maiden t-shirt smiling at me.

"Can you tell me something else which only our family would know?"

"Pogo, I know how your father treats your mom. I have been here sometimes when he has mistreated her."

"Mistreated"? What an understatement! If he had been anywhere close to what I have seen, he wouldn't be using the word "mistreated."

I felt a pang of anger. I lashed out, "If you have seen the way he treats her, why did you not help her? She gets beaten every day, and I am not big enough to get her away, but you're older than me and stronger. Why couldn't you save her from my father?" I could feel tears welling up. I was angry at myself and my own helplessness. It was unfair to take it out on Joshua, but it was just not right.

"I'm sorry, Pogo, but I did. I took care of the problem to the best of my abilities. You will not know it now, but you will know it later. Your mom may choose to tell you, or you will learn it yourself. Rest assured, I can tell you for certain that you had a major part to play in fixing this for your mom. I am sorry I cannot tell you anything more". He walked up to me and embraced me.

Tears ran down my eyes and joined with the maple syrup dripping down the sides of my mouth. I did not mean to cry but thinking about Mom and the way my father beats her and me, I couldn't control it anymore. I had not imagined in my wildest dreams that I would be crying in the arms of a complete stranger.

Joshua did not seem a stranger anymore, though. When he told me that the problem had been fixed, I felt lighter. Maybe I was not directly involved, but the issue was fixed, and that's all that mattered. He hugged me even more tightly and said, "There, there, Pogo. It's okay to let it all out. I want to let you know that you are not alone. Don't be scared. Your mom will come back soon, and it will all be okay."

I looked up, and when I saw him, it was as if Mom was smiling at me. It was like her tender smile was assuring me that everything would be alright. At this moment, I decided to trust Joshua. Maybe he was always there to help, but I just did not pay attention. If my mom trusted him enough to let him in the house and give him the keys, then I trust him as well.

He pulled away, and I continued with the pancakes, which now had a new taste to them. It was like my own inhibitions and doubts had reduced the taste of the food itself. Every piece of maple syrup-laden pancake now felt rejuvenating and reminded me how well Joshua had made them. I could feel my mom's warmth through this food, and most of my focus was now diverted to the food itself. While savoring all the flavors of the delicious pancake, I realized that I had not offered him the food. I beckoned him to sit down on the chair opposite me.

"Why don't you sit down and eat with me?"

"Thanks, Pogo, but I had some already while you were asleep. Did you like the pancakes?"

"Oh yes, I did. I thought me gobbling them up was a dead giveaway."

That seemed to have tickled him. He looked at me and said, "I don't see any bread at home, and I wanted to make sandwiches for later. I don't recall the neighborhood exactly, but we can find a supermarket close by and get some bread. You wanna join me? If you think of anything else, we can buy that as well."

I had just woken up from sleep, had been sucked into a dream-like memory, and had been introduced to a cousin-brother who I have no recollection of. Considering the emotional rollercoaster I had just been through, I thought it would be a good idea to take a trip outside. "Anywhere but here!" is the first thought that came to my mind. Joshua also considered me as someone who could help him out. Father never takes me to the supermarket to buy stuff, and mom says it would be too boring. In a way, I have never been considered as someone capable of taking responsibilities until now, and I respected Joshua for considering me as an equal partner. It was great to feel part of something, and at least being asked an opinion was a good first step. Maybe him showing up here unannounced was for the best.

"I don't know if there's a supermarket close by. Mom used to go without me."

"That's okay. There is bound to be one close by. We will go together. Listen up, Pogo, I saw the lawn outside, and it's pretty messy. I'll start mowing the lawn. You finish your food and then join me, okay?"

"Mmm…" was all I could mumble. My mouth was full of pancakes, so I doubt he heard a clear affirmation, but he seemed comfortable with the answer and left me to my pancakes and silence.

I heard him open the door and then his valiant attempt to resuscitate the lawnmower. When it came to life, the sound of its constant roaring chewed away my silence. I did not enjoy solitude and was eagerly waiting for Mom to come back. Pancakes were tasty and a welcome diversion, but I couldn't help thinking about how different this morning was. Joshua seemed to be a nice person, but I did not have a full picture of what was happening, …and then there was the scream. Had Joshua heard it as well? After having breakfast, I decided to join him. I may not remember him at present, so I thought I might be able to uncover my lost memories of him through conversation. With all the pancakes and eggs consumed, the atmosphere became dry and gloomy, and the buzzing of the lawnmower was the only sound keeping the spirits up. I took my plate and placed it in the sink. The slow dripping of water from the tap was competing with the lawnmower to grab my attention and was clearly failing. Mom will have to fix it once she is back. I opened the door and walked out into the patio.

The patio outside was small but beautiful to look at. Colorful flowerpots flanked a cement path from the road up to the patio and then continued to the door. The path divided the front yard into two parts. From the patio, I could see Joshua, shirtless now, pushing the mower across the left side of the lawn overlooking the blue and yellow flowerpots. He seemed lost in thought and was on autopilot with the lawnmower.

There was a huge fence around the house and a gate to exit the yard. The gate had a large bell carving on it. I noticed a foldable chair to the far right of the lawn just where the house edges out to the sides, so I walked slowly across the front yard and picked it up. It was heavy, but lifting and moving it was doable. While crossing the front yard, I noticed the overgrown grass and concluded that it needed trimming, but I was not confident using the lawnmower or any other garden tools. I hated this feeling of being a liability. I needed to clear some of the anomalies I had witnessed with Joshua, so I placed the chair across the left side of the lawn and sat on it. I could see the fence to the left of the lawn covered with creepers. Dragonflies were visiting various blades of grass, blissfully happy. A whole other world was brimming in and around the lawn. A fly buzzed past me, trying to get a reaction from me, but I did not budge until it flew right into my eye.

"Ow, damn!"

That seemed to have broken Joshua's train of thought. He quickly slowed down and asked, "You okay, Pogo?"

"Yeah. I just smacked my face because of that stupid fly."

He smiled. I took this opportunity, "Hey Joshua, when you woke up today, did you feel anything weird? Like, did you forget something you wanted to remember?"

His face turned pensive. It was like he was considering the events in the morning before I woke up. He was still mowing the lawn but was slow, and I did not need to strain to talk to him. I observed the subtle changes in gait and speed. After a while, he said, "Well, in the morning when I touched your cycle, I got a memory of you falling. It was weird because it was like I was living your memory. I don't think your mom saw it, but she asked me to leave the bicycle in your room. I thought that was a bit strange. It's not every day that you get objects on the floor with memories attached to them."

I felt a large burden lifted off me. Joshua had experienced a similar memory vision, and it was he who placed the cycle in my room, which explains how it got there. Maybe if I had touched it there, I might have got a vision as well. I told him, "I had experienced something similar as well. I touched my toy soldier, and I got the same effect. I lived the memory of mom buying the toy for me as if it were happening right there in reality. I also do not remember a lot of information like your existence, for example. Do you know what city we live in? Or our address, or even our street?"

Joshua gave me a blank stare and said, "No."

The sound of the lawnmower which once titillated me, was becoming an irritant. "Do you remember how long we have been here? I know this is home, but I don't see any familiar houses around. I don't know if it's different houses or just that I don't remember. It's hard to tell now."

His movements were erratic now. "No, actually. Now that you mention it, I cannot remember how long either. I remember we had old neighbors with an old house. I don't think that is the house they had." He was pointing to the current house on the other side of the fence. He then continued, "I also don't think we have been here for more than a year because we haven't celebrated your birthday."

I was observing Joshua while he answered my questions. Joshua was now moving the lawnmower forward at a steady pace. While returning to complete the circle, he would stop and extend his sight across our fence to see further down to map out the area. Joshua's statement about the birthday made me uneasy. I do not recall celebrating any birthday, and the only person happy about my birthday was Mom. Did Joshua make a blanket statement to end the topic? The celebration I always had was some alone time with Mom at the park. We would sit on a bench and feed some pigeons. When I would see other parents with their kids, it would trigger my grief, almost like an unseen force extending deep within me and pulling out my underlying sadness. Mom would then pick up on the emotional change in me and quickly hug me and say she was sorry I had to live like this. I never understood it, but I felt happy when she hugged me. Logically, Joshua's statement could have been based on the limited understanding he had of my family, but I knew he was as lost as me. I wanted to trust him, and I wanted to give him the benefit of the doubt. I could understand that he was also undergoing the same confusion as me. I had no one else to trust, and considering how close he claims us to be as family, I asked him, "When is your birthday, Joshua? Mine's in August."

"Mine is in January, kiddo," he replied

I sat on the chair thinking about a lot of things. Most of all, I was waiting for Mom to come home. I missed her. Her warm hug and light kisses were some of my most cherished memories. I did not know why she left without telling me. A stray thought crossed my mind: What if she just left me because she wanted to live with my father? I did not want to even consider that option.

We both went into a period of silent contemplation. I was waiting for Mom to open the gate any moment and come in. Flies and bees reminded us that we are still a part of the greater Earth. While contemplating my mom's heroic return, the scream revisited my train of thoughts. I wanted to bring this up with Joshua, but no sooner did I try to broach the subject than I heard a female voice.

"Hello boys, I saw you from my window, and I guess we haven't formally acquainted ourselves with each other. I am Sarah, your neighbor, and I would be thrilled if you could join me for cookies later today. I am planning to bake the cookies with my mother's secret recipe, and I am sure you will not be disappointed."

Chapter 2: The Boy with the Beanie Cap

Joshua and I both turned to see who our neighbor was, and we both had the exact same expression on our face.

We had never seen this woman in our life.

Chapter 3
A New Acquaintance

My English teacher had once taught us a phrase, "When it rains, it pours." I couldn't remember her name, but she explained the phrase in the context of a situation when a lot of bad or weird things happened together. I began to really appreciate that phrase, considering all these anomalies popping up at the same time. My reverie was interrupted by the silence when Joshua stopped mowing.

I did not feel acrimony towards Sarah since I had just met her, but there were too many coincidences that I was unable to fathom. I remember our neighbors used to be old. I couldn't remember their names, but I did recall their faces, and it was definitely not Sarah. Sarah, though, was not young by any means. She had a pleasant, amicable face. Streaks of grey hair lined her wavy tresses, and her face showed early signs of wrinkles and dark circles below the eyes. Contrasting her physical blemishes was her beaming personality, and I could somehow sense her happiness. She wore a long pink skirt and a dark blue blouse with sleeves covering her elbow. The floral patterns seemed somewhat similar, but I was unable to place them. Maybe it was something Mom wore? I wasn't sure, and I wasn't going to question where she got her clothing from.

Deep down, she reminded me of Mom, but at this point, I would have attributed this observation to my desperation to find her. I was acutely aware that anything I said or did would bring me back to Mom and her not being here. I wanted to get over this feeling but was unable to do so. That's why her cookie offer was so enticing, and she seemed friendly enough to invite a couple of complete strangers over. She stood there now looking at us, or to be precise, Joshua was her focus of attention. She waited there for an answer.

It seemed like an impasse where we were all just awkwardly staring at each other until Joshua finally broke the ice. "Hello, Sarah. My name is Joshua, and this is my brother Pogo. We would be glad to join you for cookies."

I thought to myself, "We are?" Joshua stole a glance at me to assure me that he knew what he was doing, and I did not want to negate his decision. I sat on my chair and just let the events play and let fate take its course. I was also noticing a change in Joshua. He was, of course, brotherly and loving towards me, but his reaction to Sarah was not one of doubt but of a deepening attachment. It felt as if Joshua was accepting her offer a little too quickly.

"Perfect! See you in a bit then, Joshua." She then turned towards me and said, "Pogo, is it?"

"Yeah. I'm Pogo, his younger brother."

"Well, it was nice meeting you both. See you in some time."

With this, she turned and started to move back to her house. Joshua kickstarted the lawnmower and was mowing again. I got lost in my own train of thoughts. We have a neighbor we do not know, who is in a one-horse town that we do not know where. That's when I recalled the scream. I still remember it piercing my sleep like a pin pricking a balloon. I took this chance to broach the scream subject with Joshua.

I was now straining to speak and hear him over the cacophony of the lawnmower. I literally shouted, "Joshua! I am not sure if I was imagining things, but I heard a scream last night. I barely woke up and then went off to sleep again. Did you hear any such scream?"

Joshua did not respond, and I shouted back, "Joshua! Did you hear me?" Joshua appeared uneasy at first but quickly gathered his bearings.

"Scream? What scream? I did not hear any scream." He increased his mowing speed.

Out of nowhere, Sarah waved her hand to get our attention. She shouted out, "I did hear a scream yesterday."

Joshua stopped the mower again. She paused for a while, let us digest this information, and then continued, "I am sorry for eavesdropping, but I was just leaving when I heard Pogo ask this question. It was a bit frightening, but I definitely heard it. I am not sure where it could have come from, and I do not recall any other buildings in the area. Honestly, I thought I was going crazy, but if you boys have heard it as well, then I think we need to know what was going on." She looked over at me, and I was clear to show my displeasure that she hijacked my conversation.

Joshua asked, "Sarah, do you know anyone in the locality we can ask about this?"

Sarah replied, "Unfortunately, I cannot remember, and I have not stepped out of the house for a very long time, so I might be the wrong person to answer that question. It might sound weird, but I just seem to have a lot of gaps in my memory since I woke up today. I do not remember where we are or who you are, which is why I wanted to meet you and understand what's going on."

Yes! So, this was not just us. This selective remembrance was concerning. I started to say, "Yes, that's exactly...", but Joshua cut me off.

"That's interesting, Sarah. Did anyone else in your house hear the scream?"

Sarah responded, confused. "My husband and daughter are not at home. Unfortunately, I don't recall his name. My daughter, as far as I can remember, is not someone who would wander off alone, but I don't remember her name as well or where she could be. It's strange, but I am assuming this memory thing is temporary, and it will come back to me soon, but I am getting concerned about where they could be and why they are not here."

Joshua continued, "There are several inexplicable events that are happening now which we have no idea about. This scream could be one of them. Hypothetically, if what you and Pogo heard is true, I would be very curious about where the scream could have come from. While mowing the lawn, I was observing the buildings that are present within the gate's visible radius. There are only five buildings here as far as I can see. Two are our houses, one is clearly a diner, and it is just a couple of steps from your house. One looks like a supermarket, but I'm not sure unless we go there. Pogo and I are planning to visit the supermarket after I mow the lawn. Apart from these, the only other option where the scream could have come from would be the skyscraper across the highway, which I have only a faint view of."

I could sense that Joshua was uncomfortable about this topic, almost as if he had something to hide. He started the mower again, and this time, he was moving faster and almost toppled a flowerpot near the central path. He seemed disturbed by this topic which made me wonder if there was more to his denial than he was letting on. He was mowing eccentrically, and we were observing his inner conflict. He stopped abruptly and offered his opinion, "We should probably let the police figure out what that scream was about. There is no point speculating what it was. It could have been a car-wheel screeching or maybe a high pitch howl from a werewolf. I don't know, but it is none of my business."

Sarah was not convinced, "Don't you want to know what the scream was about? What if we are in danger?"

"What if we get into danger if we snoop around in other people's business?" Joshua seemed to have charged up the conversation, and I did not want it to go south. We hadn't even had cookies yet. Thankfully, neither Sarah nor I took it further.

Sarah quickly glanced at me and then said to Joshua, "Yes, you're right. Better stay safe than snoop around and get in trouble or worse.

I'm old, so I get curious about everything. See you boys in a while," and she disappeared into her lawn and then to her house. I looked at Joshua, and though he was standing still, I was certain his mind was sprinting.

I decided not to give it too much thought. I tried to look at the sky, and the sun blinded me. I covered my eyes and looked up again. The sun had not moved an inch since morning, and it was hot and bright as ever. I tried to recall if I had seen dawn, but all I recall was sunlight in my room, and the next time I saw sunlight was when I followed Joshua into the lawn. I was feeling thirsty due to this oppressive heat and wanted to get a soda. I turned to Joshua and asked, "Joshua, can we go to the supermarket and get some soda as well before we go to meet Sarah? You said you wanted to buy bread, right?"

"And milk. Yeah, we can get the supplies before we meet Sarah. Pogo, can you put the chair back and wait near the gate for me? I will wash my hands, get the cash, and be right back." Saying so, Joshua disappeared into the house.

My body was on autopilot now. I folded the chair and moved to the edge of the house where I had found it. My feet automatically took me to the gate, but my mind was still thinking about the scream. A large mango tree grew beside our gate, its branches spread wide, and its ripe fruit was almost ready to fall to the ground. My mind was exactly like this fruit. It had so many thoughts being processed and so much to explain to Mom that I was ready to burst. My emotional rollercoaster was just a catalyst to the current state I was in. A slow breeze brought me the fragrance of roasted coffee beans. I wondered if they were coming from the diner.

Joshua finally reappeared after spending much more time in the house than needed for washing his hands. When he hugged me in the kitchen, I was inclined to trust him, but now I felt there was something he was hiding, and I wanted to know what it was. He opened the gate and said, "Ladies first.". I gave him a sarcastic look.

"Ha, ha. Very funny."

Together we made our way to the supermarket.

Chapter 4
Nothing Is What it Seems

Closing the gate to our home felt like leaving behind a part of myself. Though we had started off together, Joshua seemed preoccupied and walked much faster. I quickened my pace to catch up with him, but he was quite a way ahead of me.

"Wait up!" I called out, but he did not stop. He seemed to be lost in deep thought. "Hey, Joshua," I shouted, hoping he would hear. "You sure we should be leaving the house? What if Mom comes back?"

He shouted back, "Well, she did leave you alone. I'm sure she can handle herself when she's back."

His acerbic reaction startled me. I did not press him further but continued observing the path we were on. Soft blades of grass covered an otherwise muddy path. The mango tree behind us swayed ominously, almost as if it were waving goodbye. Surprisingly, there were no animals. I could hear various insects and even saw a monarch butterfly fluttering past me, but I did not encounter any small animals like frogs or cats. What kind of place was this? I was pretty sure we had been kidnapped and just left to die until Mom pays to get us out, but then Sarah did not fit the profile. Why kidnap us and leave us in a house with an oblivious neighbor?

Joshua was silent all this time. After his outburst, I did not want to trigger another meltdown. Catching up with Joshua seemed a bad idea now, and I slowed down my pace a bit to give him some space. The sun was still stationary, and as I looked up again to verify, I was considering the ludicrous thought that the earth had stopped spinning. This almost brought a smile to my face, but it did not last long. I began thinking about Mom again. What could have been so urgent that Mom had to leave without telling me? I hoped she told Father, otherwise, that would just be a reason for another beating.

The fluctuations of emotions were getting tiresome and frustrating. I was so angry that I kicked the first stone my feet could find. I prepared myself for pain to rain down on me, but it did not sting. Maybe my pain of missing Mom overcame all other pain I felt. The stone clattered and landed at the base of a wall. There was a large gate beside this wall above which was a large neon sign which read "DINER" in blue and pink.

Joshua had already reached the diner while I was still passing Sarah's home. I could see her garden, and I could sense the entropy in there. From the path, I could see overgrown trees and grass. Her house was barely visible from the angle from which I was looking, and all I could see were the orange tiles on the roof. I began to imagine Sarah cooking those delicious cookies in the kitchen of this largely untidy home.

I must have been daydreaming about the cookies because when I snapped out of it, I realized that Joshua was far ahead. I think he didn't even notice that I was lagging. So much for being a loving brother!

I was now exactly opposite the diner, and it seemed to be crowded, from the looks of it. Seeing the usual hustle and bustle of the diner gave me some relief. At least there were people we could talk to, and it's not some ghost town we are lost in.

A lady was standing at the door waving at me. I looked around, confused. Was she waving at me? She nodded as if she was reading my mind. I waved back but immediately got embarrassed and looked for Joshua. I wanted to call out to him and ask if we could go into the diner and ask the lady about our current predicament, but he was not within hearing distance to respond. The lady seemed welcoming, and standing in front of the diner gave me an intense urge to enter the diner and have some food, but I decided against it and hurried towards Joshua.

I caught up with him in just a short while and saw him standing opposite to the supermarket. I stopped and bent over to catch my breath. I couldn't really blame him for leaving me and running off, so I just stayed silent.

I was beginning to stabilize myself when he asked me, "Pogo, do you feel odd about this building?"

The building had a large gray face. I had expected to see some parking spaces like Walmart or Costco, or even like the diner, but this building was brazen. It reeked of intimidation. There was a small door right in the middle with some stickers on them and some flyers. I thought maybe some of these flyers would have a date and tell us what time we were in because this looked like a *Mad Max* movie minus the crazy people.

There was a slight walking space between the building and a large wall, and we could see a road on the other side extending in both directions. At least we have a road to somewhere.

I looked at Joshua and replied, "Honestly, this place gives me the creeps. I am unable to make up my mind whether to enter or not. Can we skip this and go to the diner?"

"Pogo, what are you scared of the most?"

Father, of course, but I did not respond to him with the answer. Instead, I asked him, "Why did you ask me that question? It's completely irrelevant."

He looked at me perplexed. His eyes were looking around as if whatever possessed him had just left his body. "I don't know why I asked you that. I was thinking about entering the building, and as soon as I thought about taking a step, I got this compulsion to ask you what your worst fear was. I am not sure what caused it. I really don't want to know what you fear because I already know."

How could he know what I feared? He did say he had been around when he saw Father misbehaving, so I wouldn't be surprised.

I decided to get in and take what we came for and get out of this spooky building. The soft breeze had now become a howling wind announcing our arrival. Clouds seemed to rapidly form around the building threatening a heavy downpour. It was almost as if the environment began to affect anything immediately outside the supermarket, forcing anyone wandering outside to behave abnormally.

"Joshua, have you ever considered what your last thought would be before you died?"

What? Why did I just ask that? I did not want to ask that, but I think this was the compulsion that Joshua was talking about. Joshua was surprised but seemed to understand that it was not me asking the question. Before he could answer, we heard a shout.

"Hey kids, are you going to stand outside all day, or are you going to buy something? C'mon in."

I looked at Joshua. He nodded his head, which I assumed meant that he was fine. I was fine as well but scared. I had a feeling that this building was not a supermarket but a horror ride.

"Yeah, we're just coming in. Thanks," Joshua muttered.

As we reached the door, we got a closer look at the flyers. One of them was a 65% discount on Australian apples, and another was a 50% discount on all dairy products. It was clearly not attractive enough since I did not see any customers.

Joshua and I walked in and were immediately welcomed by the cool breeze of the air-conditioner in the supermarket. I observed the inner supermarket and was spellbound by the sheer size of it. I had once visited a supermarket with my mom when I was around seven, and that supermarket was not anywhere near to how big this one is.

As I entered, to my right was the cash counter. ONE single cash counter. Was this town so low in population that the supermarket was built to have just one cash counter? I threw a quick glance at the supervisor behind the counter, who was now smiling at us.

The supervisor appeared to be a man probably in his mid-thirties. I was not sure of his age, but he was wearing a flawless white shirt and black trousers. He wore a red apron over his shirt, which extended to his knees, making him look like one of the advertisements on TV about men supporting the family or something like that. I couldn't recall exactly, but Mom used to love them. I wondered why a supervisor really needs to have an apron. Shouldn't he have staff to do the work for him? I thought it might be logical for him to take up all tasks in the supermarket considering the dearth of not only customers but staff as well.

The supervisor had jet-black hair and a small, caterpillar-like mustache over his mouth. He seemed almost like a military dictator standing and observing us immigrants in his motherland. He did not seem anything like the supermarket supervisor I had seen when I visited with Mom. I did not trust him at all, and I was sure Joshua felt the same.

The supermarket itself did not seem complex. There were a set of racks to my left that had chocolate bars and other sweets and snacks. After a brief space for guests to walk and enter, the aisles began. I looked down and saw a queue of empty horizontal lines originating from the cash counter and ending somewhere far at the other side of the supermarket. There was a small statement above each line that said, "MAINTAIN SOCIAL DISTANCE OF 1 METER." I wasn't sure why this was even needed.

I looked at Joshua, who was already looking for something. "Hey, Joshua. I am going to check out the soda aisle to the right. You are going to get the bread and milk, right?"

Joshua answered," Yeah, I am going to search for some bread and milk on the other side. This place gives me the creeps, and I want to get out of here as soon as possible."

As I turned toward the soda aisle, I considered my options with the presumption that the building was out to get me. One option was to walk alone in the creepy building to find some soda, and the other was to stay close to someone I met some time ago, hoping that the building would back off.

"Actually, Joshua, I think I'll join you. We'll go and find the soda together later."

He obliged, and we started walking together, looking at the aisles and their content labels on top. It was an extension of the racks, and each rack had a content heading which was basically a small board with the name of the contents of the rack hanging from a metal hook. The black ink and the curvy font almost looked Elizabethan. We began searching for the bread section and soon came across *"English bread."* I was honestly not sure what *"English bread"* was but was even more confused when I saw *"Australian bread"* and *"Dutch bread."* The naming convention seemed odd to me, but I ignored it for now because my need to escape this establishment was much more important than my need to investigate yet another anomaly in this world.

My purpose of following Joshua was purely selfish, and it was safety in numbers. I was just following him wherever he was going. He seemed unfazed by the naming and quickly stopped at an aisle which read *"BREAD."* So, we finally found a bread which was from nowhere. It seemed fitting, considering that's exactly where we were.

We were still at the aisle entrance, and he was observing the aisle itself. That's when I looked to my left. The end of the aisle was nowhere in sight. I saw no end to my right either. We had only walked for a short frame of time, but the cash counter or the supervisor was nowhere in sight. The rack of chocolates was gone, and all I saw was darkness at the end of the aisle extending beyond my sight. I tried to call Joshua and turn back, but he had already entered the aisle marked *"BREAD."* I could see him disappearing down it and did not want to be alone, so I quickly followed him.

No sooner did I enter the aisle than I realized that I shouldn't have done so. I could see Joshua ahead of me, looking at some of the bread.

Chapter 4: Nothing Is What it Seems

I walked behind him and observed the aisles. There was bread on both sides, but the left side had the bread sliced and stacked in plastic. The right side had large chunks of bread with unclean cuts and just set out in the open like in a bakery. Was this even allowed in a supermarket? I picked one of the plastic-covered bread and was signaling Joshua ahead of me to return, but he was moving forward too fast.

I called out to him, "Joshua, slow down." He seemed to slow down. As I approached him, I saw a wall light beside each aisle. Dim yellow light spread across an already dark aisle, and I realized that this light acted as a divider between two columns in a rack. It was now becoming obvious that the aisles were basically never-ending. I turned around, and I couldn't see its beginning as well. All I could see was an infinite aisle of bread.

The aisle itself was as dark as midnight, with the wall lights reminding us that there was bread and not some other substance. The imagery of the bread remained the same. Even the half-cut bread to my right was cut in the exact same spot with the same number of crumbs scattered around it. It was almost as if someone copied an image and pasted it multiple times.

As I reached Joshua, he stopped and said in a low voice, "Pogo, there is something wrong here. I do not see a beginning or an end to these aisles, and we need to get out of here as soon as possible! I was moving fast to find an end, but the faster you go, the farther it expands." His voice was shivering, and I saw the color leave his cheeks. He was no longer looking forward or backward but was looking for a way out.

"Joshua, do you know how to get out of here?"

"Let me think…"

I did not want to think. I wanted to get out. Joshua had just mentioned something that moving faster expands it further, but I wasn't paying attention. I needed to escape, and all I could think of was to traverse back the way we came. I did not wait for Joshua to finish thinking. I turned around and ran as fast as I could. I could hear Joshua shouting, "Pogo, wait! Don't run! This will just keep expanding!" but I did not heed his advice.

I kept running until my feet gave out. I couldn't see an end to the beginning or a beginning to the end. I turned around and saw emptiness. Tears ran down my cheeks. All I wanted more than anything in the world was to be with Mom. I cried, knowing very well that no one would hear me, "MOM! Why did you leave me here alone? WHY?"

No one answered.

"Don't you love me anymore? Why did you leave me with these bad people?"

Not a sound.

"I don't want to face this anymore. Please come take me home."

I curled my feet and bent my body into a fetal position on the floor. There was no point in fighting. This was the end. All the time I missed with Mom, I would spend with her when I meet her in heaven.

I had given up all hope when a flash of light caught the attention of my left eye. I could hear muffled voices. Was I already in heaven? The voices gradually became clearer.

"Pogo! Pogo! Can you hear me?"

"Yes." It was more of a windy croak than a shout, but I think Joshua heard me.

"Pogo, follow my voice. If you can hear me, you are close by."

"Joshua. Can you come and pick me up? I cannot move. My feet are numb.

"Okay, hold on," is all I heard. I couldn't bear the stress any longer, and I passed out.

* *

A bright light awoke me. I was surrounded by a gooey liquid, and it was almost as if I was underwater. When I looked down, I realized that it was only my head that was submerged, but my body was not. My body seemed different, well-built, and adult. I tried to move my hands and legs but was unable to do so. What was going on? How was I breathing? I could feel some extensions attached to my neck which was rising and falling with rhythmic, harmonic motion. I tried to tilt my head to the side, but something was holding my head straight like a helmet. I tried to peer forward and was sure I saw Sarah sitting on a chair with a similar helmet on her head. Or was she Mom? I wasn't sure. I had just seen her in her garden some time ago, and now she and I are tied up in a chair with goo buckets on our heads.

I heard voices in the distance.

"Did he wake up?"

"Yeah, he did not take the supermarket well. Should we send him back?"

"He has not fully woken up. Increase the dose and send him in. He must come back only with Kobi."

"Yes, commander."

"It's hardly been two minutes since they have gone under, and we already have one of them surface? Everyone stay vigilant. Our VIPs should not be allowed to see such errors!"

"Yes, commander"

More watery liquid sprinkled on my face, and that's when I woke up.

*   *

I stared up to see a vividly frightened Joshua and a straight-faced supervisor. Joshua held my hand, lifted me up, and hugged me. I needed a hug after what I had been through.

When we broke our embrace, he asked me, "Pogo, are you okay? I thought I lost you there for a while."

I looked at him, tears welling up in my eyes, and asked," Joshua, I don't know where I was. I was in a water helmet and on a chair, and maybe Sarah or Mom was there too with the same helmet. It wasn't clear because of all the water around me in the helmet. I heard someone say I woke up. I don't know what happened. Was Mom here? Did she come back?"

"No, Pogo. She wasn't. Why do you ask?"

I was fighting to control my tears. "I don't know, Joshua. Maybe the lady opposite to me was Sarah, or it could have been Mom. It was so real. I just wanted to run away but couldn't. I couldn't move my hands, arms, legs, or anything! Why did I see her like this, Joshua? Is she dead?"

He looked at me sympathetically, knowing very well there was nothing he could say or do which could calm me down. "Pogo, you passed out. The supervisor found me and helped me get out, and when I couldn't find you, he helped search for you and bring you out.

"Klaus, you can call me Klaus," said the supervisor in a matter-of-fact tone.

Joshua looked at him and then back at me. "Pogo. She is not dead. Like I said, she has just left for some urgent work and will be back. Hasn't she done this before?"

"No. She hasn't. She always tells me where she is going or takes me with her. Father doesn't allow her to roam around much, so why did she go now?"

"Pogo, I am not sure, but we'll ask her when she's back, okay? Come on, get up and let's get out of here. I've got the bread. We will buy milk and soda some other day."

He extended his arm, and while I grabbed it and was getting up, I said with dread, "Joshua. Something was wrong. I tried to…"

"Shh!, Pogo. We will talk about this later. This is not the right place to do that. Let's just buy our stuff and get out of here!"

"Yes, let's get out of here. I don't want to be here anymore. There is something sinister here that I don't want anything to do with."

"Are you able to walk, or do you need me to hold you up?"

"I can walk." It was a lie. I was spent. I would have happily been carried out of the building in a gunny sack if I was allowed to be, but I did not want to show weakness.

Seeing me in a livable state, Klaus, the supervisor, probably was relieved that he wouldn't have to deal with a dead body in his supermarket. He walked off ahead of us to the cash counter nonchalantly. He was completely calm, acting oblivious to our visibly shaken faces. He either knows about this aisle or is party to this evil presence, and I was sure he had something to do with what we had just faced.

Joshua walked up to the counter, and I followed closely. This time, he did not leave me behind and kept waiting for me to catch up. When he reached the counter, he placed the bread on the counter and waited for the supervisor to tell him the cost. The supervisor picked the bread and began the mundane task of scanning the product. While doing so, he asked us," By the way, kids, where are your parents? Did they send you alone?"

Joshua quipped," How does it concern you? Just give me the bread, and we will be out of here."

The supervisor seemed surprised. "No, you're right. It's none of my business, but I was concerned about your safety considering the scream last night. Did you kids hear it?"

"No, we did not." was Joshua's immediate reply. I was not surprised that he did not want to continue the conversation. Why would someone bring up screams in a supermarket when you're buying bread?

"Hmm, I think this scream came from the hotel across the highway. I overheard you telling the smaller one that his mom left for something important. She could have been working at the hotel. It was deserted but is going to reopen soon. The manager was looking for some locals to work there but couldn't find the right staff. I am helping them by taking care of the rooms at night. She might be helping with the logistics or something. What does she do for a living?"

Both of us were silent. I had partially zoned out but was still listening to Klaus. What he said could be true. Maybe Mom had gone to the hotel and was in trouble. Maybe it was something she couldn't tell us, which is why she left without saying anything. My head was about to explode, and the recent aisle experience had left me traumatized. I just wanted to leave.

The bread had long since been scanned, but Klaus asked us, "I haven't seen you around here often. Are you a local? What are your names?"

Both of us did not utter a word.

"Okay, no worries. You want to keep it a secret. I understand. Its $7.95 for the bread."

Joshua finally said, "I am Joshua, and he is Pogo. We live in a house along the road, close by, in fact." I noticed he did not give the exact location. I was glad. I did not want a Christmas card from this supermarket.

The supervisor responded with new vigor, "You know if you kids want to stay there and get a feel of a five-star hotel or even go look for your mom or dad, I can facilitate it for you. All free, of course. You can bring along anyone else if you like. Just let me know in advance."

Joshua responded with lightning speed, "No thanks, we don't really care. Can we get this bagged up, please?" Impatience was reeking through all his pores. His brow was constricted, and he was tapping the table with his finger. I was now a bit more settled and calmer. I began considering the supervisor's idea. It seemed to be a good idea since we might be able to look for Mom and see why she left. Maybe she needs our help, and if we complete what she needs to do, we can go back home early.

I pulled his shirt, but he looked at me and said, "Not now, Pogo. Let's get out of here, then we will talk."

Klaus then said, "Sure, kid. Don't reject the offer right away. Think about it, and if you change your mind, let me know. That'll be $7.95, please."

"Yeah, sure." Joshua handed a $10 note and said, "Keep the change."

Unimpressed, Klaus said, "Thanks for shopping with us."

Joshua took the bread from Klaus and handed it to me. He then tugged me out of the supermarket door as if I was a leashed puppy. I could understand, though. I wanted to put some distance between us and that weird supermarket.

We exited the door and reached the grassy footpath. I felt as though a large weight had been removed from my chest. We stopped for a while, and after spending some time catching our breath, we stood up and turned to look at the supermarket one last time. Then we started to walk back home before we got more murderous thoughts in our heads.

As we were walking, I asked him, "Joshua, I'm sorry I ran away in the aisle. I was scared out of my wits, and I can imagine how you felt, but I just couldn't take it anymore. I was sad and missed Mom, and so much has been happening today. I couldn't think of anything else except escaping that place and seeing Mom." I paused for a second. Joshua wasn't saying anything.

Finally, he broke the silence," Did you notice that this person was very interested in our parents? I found that a bit strange. He was able to find me and you in that aisle, and we both know that aisle is not normal, which means he doesn't see the aisle for what it is, or he controls it. I am assuming the latter."

I pondered and responded, "Yeah, and he wasn't happy when you tipped him, which seems weird. What service-industry professional doesn't like getting tipped?"

"Yeah, there is something else going on here. We need to find out what it is once your mom is back."

My eyes lit up, "That's why I was pulling you aside in the supermarket. Don't you think we should reconsider the offer the supervisor gave us? We could find Mom and help her out in whatever she is trying to do. Maybe she needs our help."

"Yeah, we can think about it, but Pogo, I do not want to take you to a place which could be dangerous. I already feel there is something strange about this world, and I do not want to put you in danger. Your mom would never forgive me. Anyway, let's go meet Sarah and have some of those cookies, okay? I think we might need them a lot more now."

He was scared; I could sense it. His demeanor seemed to have a ripple effect on mine as well. "Okay, let's go meet Sarah." I thought to myself that cookies always brighten up my day. Even Mom used to bake them.

We stood close to the diner to catch our breaths. Once we had calmed down, I turned around and gazed at the hotel in front of me. I imagined staying at the hotel and consuming all its five-star services. It wasn't such a bad prospect. I had never stayed at a hotel of that sort and was now intrigued by all the soft linen and mattresses I had seen only in the movies. I could leave the TV on and go to sleep. I could open the window and view the entire city. Of course, my biggest motivation was the possibility of Mom being there in the hotel, and I could go and help her so that we could be together again. Then I remembered the scream and the supervisor's face and was inclined against staying there. Of course, if Joshua goes, I will follow him, but only if he decides to go.

The rest of the path, we walked silently. The grassy path welcomed our footsteps back to Sarah's home.

Chapter 5
All Alone

Looking at Sarah's home once again reminded me why she needed a lawnmower and someone to mow her lawn. The yard or mini-jungle, both usable interchangeably, was to the right side of the mango tree, and I was able to see some mangoes splattered close to where her fence touched the tree. No efforts had been made to clean out the mango pulp from the yard. We surveyed the unicorn-themed gate with two unicorns facing each other. Joshua lifted the bolt from the gate, and it made a loud clang announcing our arrival. Minutes later, Sarah was already at the door waiting for us. It was almost as if she was doing nothing else but waiting for us, but we weren't complaining. The smell of fresh cookies was wafting outside, and my nostrils picked them up.

Sarah called out to us from the door, "Hey, boys, come on in. The cookies are ready. You're just in time."

I was struggling to find the path and was relying on Joshua to lead us through this foliage. Joshua was able to find the path to the door, which was covered by a thin layer of grass. There was no bifurcation of the lawn because grass had grown all over. The wetness of the grass stuck to the back of my calf. There were some shades of color from the local wildflowers, but none of the charm that was in our home. I was reminded of my bald neighbor's home as I entered Sarah's yard. Unfortunately, I couldn't remember his name. He had a lovely wife with blond hair, and I recall she would always invite Mom and me over for milk and cookies. Sarah reminded me of them, and I did not discount the theory that she might be related to them. I thought of asking her about that later when we were having cookies.

Weeds and tall grass up to the waist had taken over most of the garden. It was less of a garden and more of a grassland. Flowers and leaves were almost falling off their stalks. There were dried leaves below most of the larger plants, and some of them were even decomposed. I was not at all comfortable with the way the garden was maintained.

The consistent chirping of crickets even during the daytime caught my attention. I have heard crickets chirping at night, that is the cliché we all know, but why are they chirping during the day? It did not feel right, just as the long list of everything that has happened today. I stopped, picked the nearest stone, and threw it to the far end of the yard to see if that would disturb the chirping. It didn't, and it was scarily consistent. Joshua had to pull my hand to get me to move toward the door.

Sarah still wore her pink skirt and blue blouse, though she seemed a bit more glowing. She ushered us in and asked us to sit down on the sofa set. The sofa set was a two-seater facing a large, cushioned chair. It was, at first glance, a lightly furnished house with only a single floor. She probably did not have any guests at all, considering the way the garden was maintained and the house was furnished. The house seemed cozy enough but was very simple. The dining room was combined with her living room, and I could barely visualize her kitchen and bedroom. I saw two doors to the right. The main sofa set faced a room that most likely was a bedroom and the dining room probably faced the kitchen, but it was hard to tell. She had a medium-sized dining table with four chairs. The chairs were plastic and not very inviting. Completely out of place was a vase at the far corner of the room near what I believed to be the kitchen. I couldn't see it clearly from the sofa, but I wondered what made her place the vase at that location. It was out of place and clearly attention-grabbing.

Chapter 5: All Alone

Her placement seemed odd and quite different from Mom. If Mom was around, she would have made sure that the room was well furnished with a television and maybe a carpet at the center. She would have put in a couple of hanging portraits of us and would have got some decorative plants. Now that I thought about it, there was no television here, which was odd as well. The house was, in general, bland. Mom would have spent a lot of time making this house a home.

I was excited, though, to meet and speak to someone else who was not throwing relationship bombs on my face like the first person I met who claimed to be my cousin, who I don't remember at all. Immediately, I thought it was unfair to pin the blame on Joshua. It wasn't his fault that I could not remember him. He was trying his best to be with me all this time while Mom was away. Joshua is like a brother to me, and I felt bad slandering him even if it was only in my mind. I looked at him and smiled. He looked back squinting, lips pressed together, silently asking me what I was smiling about.

Sarah sat on the chair facing the window. I walked past the window and realized that our house and the lawn were completely visible from here. This is probably how she realized we were her neighbors in the morning.

I walked past the window and sat on the sofa facing Sarah. Joshua joined me there as well, almost dropping his weight on the sofa. I could see a bedroom behind her but couldn't get full visibility. Across from me was a small glass table at the center of the room with curved wooden legs. There were some magazines about home and décor under the glass, which I was not interested in at all. Once we settled down, there was an awkward silence for a few minutes when Sarah wasn't making eye contact with either me or Joshua and was gazing at the vase.

Joshua decided to break the ice. "Sarah, do you need some help cleaning the lawn? It seems to have just been unattended for a while. Maybe I could mow it later tomorrow with our mower."

Sarah seemed unfazed. "Oh, thank you, darling. That's okay. I never really cared for the lawn anyway. I don't get a lot of folks or guests here, as you can see. You guys look spent. Where did you go?"

I was quick to respond, "We went to the supermarket to buy some soda and bread, but that place is pure evil. Joshua did not like it as well, and we barely escaped. The supervisor there is a bit off. I am going to make my Mom report him."

Sarah caught on to the supervisor bit of the conversation and asked, "'Off' in what sense, honey?"

Joshua explained, "What he meant was that the supervisor was not very forthcoming with the prices and discounts highlighted at his store. He did not seem to be trustworthy." I was a bit surprised why he lied about the supervisor, considering both of us had the most harrowing experience there.

Sarah responded obliviously, "Well, all shopkeepers keep their best interest in mind. They go about saying the customer is always right and then just devise more methods to part us from our money." She then looked at us, almost embarrassed, and said, "Silly me! Let me get the cookies for you." She left to get the cookies, and we sat there observing her home and taking in as much information as we could. Joshua seemed at ease, but I was still not comfortable and wouldn't be until the cookies arrived.

The smell of freshly baked cookies completely took over my inhibitions, and I am not ashamed to admit that I was ready to be the first to try the cookies. I've seen adults being polite and asking the other person to be the first. Not me!

Something was taking Sarah a long time, and I was thirsty after all the running in the supermarket. I never got a chance to buy soda, so I asked Joshua, "Hey, can I get some water as well. I'm dying of thirst." He seemed to understand," Yeah, Pogo, me too. Let me get some water from the kitchen. Not sure what's holding up Sarah. I'll see if she needs some help."

Chapter 5: All Alone

Joshua left to get some water, and I continued observing the house. Sarah would have sat on her chair and watched us mowing the lawn in the morning. I wonder where her husband and daughter were. The house, though, wasn't impressive, and I was getting impatient. I started making circles with my feet on the bare floor and fidgeting with my nails. The magazines now looked inviting. Anything to pass the time between now and the cookies showing up.

Finally, I decided to give up the task of watching paint dry. Joshua, who went to help Sarah, had now disappeared as well, and I was very thirsty. I decided to make a move and ask them if I could have the water, at least. I got up and slowly made my way across the dining room to the kitchen. I passed the vase, now clearer with a purple floral pattern which made it look aesthetically plain. As I reached the kitchen door, I could hear that Joshua and Sarah were talking. I was within earshot of Joshua and heard him saying, "I don't know, in all honesty. The only people Pogo really cherished were me and his mom, and unfortunately, she's dead. I cannot imagine how surprised and sad she must have been when her own husband killed her. He must have felt ashamed and depressed as well because after the act, he ran away, never to come back."

"That's so sad to hear. I'm sorry I brought it up." Sarah said sympathetically. She continued saying something else, but my ears had stopped accepting any more information. I couldn't believe what I was hearing. What does he mean Mom was dead? It can't be true! It can't! I couldn't really control my emotions.

I could feel the bile rising inside me and my nostrils flaring. A variety of thoughts were forming in my mind. When did his happen? How does Joshua know? Why did he lie to me initially? I couldn't stop to think. The rug had been swept out from under my feet, and now I was unable to think or do anything. I do not know what happened, but the next thing I remember was my hands extending out and pushing him.

I shrieked, "No! No, Joshua! You are lying! You're a liar! I don't want to see you anymore!" He jerked and lunged forward, tripping Sarah as well.

The freshly baked cookies fell off the plate and hit the floor, crumbling to pieces. The cookies breaking into pieces accurately represented my world now, which was crumbling around me. Sarah was on the floor in shock. The glass from Joshua's hand fell, and a large chunk ricocheted to the other side of the kitchen. He was on all fours now but was quick to recover. "Pogo, what did you hear? I'm sorry! It's not what you think!"

I did not want to see him. I did not care if his hands were bleeding or if Sarah was sick or hurt. I did not hear his shouting. The betrayal was killing me. How could he not tell me this? The very thought of my mother coming back to be with me was my driving force in this place. Every roadblock in this place was overcome with the expectation that Mom would come back and fix everything. Now that I know she will not come back, I couldn't fathom doing anything else. I don't want to go to the hotel. I don't want to eat. I don't want to be around anyone anymore.

I ran as fast as I could. I hoped Joshua would not follow. I ran to our gate, swung it open, and probably broke a couple of pots. I didn't care. Let them break. I closed my eyes and hoped I would make my way to my room without tripping or hurting myself. I kicked open the door and ran up the stairs, opened the green door to my room, and swung myself onto the bed.

Everything in the room was exactly as I had left it. I buried my face into my pillow and shouted as loud as I could. If there was someone in the house, they might have heard a muffle, but I had to let it all out. My mother, my sole source of light, was dead, and my life was now in darkness. I had cried when my mom was being beaten up by my father. I cried when my father used the belt to beat me as well. I cried when my mom was proud of me, and now, I cried when I realized that my mom had died. My pillow has witnessed all my sorrows and here it was, bearing witness to yet another breakdown of a twelve-year-old who just lost his will to move forward.

After a while I heard the front door opening and someone climbing the stairs. I knew that Joshua was coming. My head was turned towards the window, and I was still crying. It was not as muffled, but he probably knew that already. He walked in slowly and asked, "Pogo, buddy, are you okay?"

"Go away, Joshua! I don't know you! I do not remember you! My mother is not dead, and you just imagined it all. Why did you lie to Sarah? Why did you come to this house.? I HATE YOU!!"

I don't think Joshua had any form of animosity towards me. He patted my back and said, "Kiddo, I'm sorry you had to hear it this way, but that is the truth. Your mom is dead, and your father has fled. I know how much she means to you and how much you wanted to see her. I knew telling this to you would affect you more than any of the anomalies we are seeing today, and I did not want to expose you to that kind of pain."

"I don't want to hear anything! GO AWAY!!" I just couldn't take it anymore. I slapped his hand away. He realized I couldn't be reckoned with and pulled back.

Before leaving the room, he said, "I'm leaving now, Pogo, but know this – that I love you, and you will always mean everything to me. You are a part of me, and I will do anything, and I mean anything, to protect you. All I was doing was shielding you from something bad, but I think there is something much more sinister going on here. I will figure out what is going on and get back to you. Until then, stay here and stay out of trouble. Remember, I will come for you."

I did not respond. I think he stayed for some time, and I soon heard footsteps receding.

That was the last time I saw Joshua.

*   *   *

I don't know how much time I spent buried in my pillow. The tears had dried, but the wound stayed. My mom was not coming back, and there was nothing I could do about it. Why was I in this state? I have always wondered why I was dealt such bad cards in life. I had a wife-beater father, a loving, but now dead mother, a cousin who I had no idea existed, who lied to me, and an unknown anomalous world.

I began contemplating suicide. There was no need for me to go on, so I decided the best course would be to end it. My mind was set, but there was a storm of emotions inside that left me undecided. Joshua lied to me, but I still couldn't forget him. He was just as alone as me in this world, and he had only been supportive. He might be alone out there fighting something he may not be prepared for. Joshua might need me.

I sat up and was battling my own thoughts when I heard the doorbell. Was Joshua back already? Why was he ringing the doorbell? He could just walk in as he had done before. I was thinking of reasons why he was not entering when I heard a knock on the door. I got down from my bed and moved across the floor towards the staircase. As I was slowly descending the stairs, I heard a second, stronger knock that was more like a thud on the door. What was Joshua doing? Was he in trouble?

I reached the door and opened it and said, "Josh…" but I immediately swallowed my words when I saw the guest.

This was not going to end well.

PERSPECTIVE
SARAH

(Nothing Is More Powerful than Love)

*"For it was not into my ear that you whispered
but into my heart. It was not my lips you
kissed but my soul."*

~ Judy Garland

Chapter 6
Whiplash

A light shout was enough to wake me up as I was highly sensitive to loud noises. I was sitting up sweating all over because this scream I heard was almost a shriek. It was succinct enough to jolt me out of my comforting sleep. I was not a stranger to hearing screams from neighboring rooms, but I was finding it difficult to identify the source of this one. It must have been the orphanage that normalized my apathy to screams at night.

I stared at the ceiling, childishly looking for hidden ciphers about this scream, but failed miserably. I was none the wiser and wide awake. I glanced around to make sure that I was not back at the orphanage, and there was no Madam Costa around. Putting aside my blanket, I got down from the bed. The satin camisole on me felt very loose because I had lost weight over time. I put on my nightgown and walked to the washroom. My most honest partner, the mirror, revealed to me how much time had weathered my face. For a fifty-four-year-old lady, the wrinkles were just another signboard to the final destination. I looked at myself and stepped back so I could get a better view in the wall mirror, which was now showing only half of me. I adjusted my tummy and tried to force my tummy out, but the mirror was unforgiving, and I looked starved. Who cares, anyway? I only came here for the sleeping pills.

I opened the mirror cabinet and took out the sleeping pills. I had trouble sleeping for a long time, and sleeping pills were a part of me now.

I opened the yellow container and popped two pills. Hello, sleep, old friend. Embrace me and take me into your loving arms. I just made that up; it must be the sleeping pills acting out. I walked back and sat down on the bed. Looking to my side, I saw a neat, well-made half with a pillow that hadn't been used. Two pillows mean I have a significant other, but where could my spouse be?

I laid my head on my pillow and closed my eyes. The pills were taking effect, and I hoped that all my issues would just vanish tomorrow when I woke up.

*   *   *

I was woken up by the roaring of a lawnmower, half expecting to see Madam Costa near my bed, ready to whip me for waking up late. It seems as if I left the orphanage eons ago, but I was still troubled by that hell. I couldn't overcome these muscle memories and hearing a loud sound in my sleep immediately put my brain into a defensive mode.

I did not know my parents well, and they were not my concern. I did not wish to pursue it any further, but what I remember was that I was left in the orphanage at the age of five and ever since have been part of Madam Costa's kingdom of helpless girls. I remember the first day when I had joined the orphanage. She seemed to be very caring and motherly until the time she asked me to have dinner. I had not been introduced to table manners, so when I just picked the bread with my hand and began to chew it loudly, she took the wooden ruler and smacked my hand. It wasn't a light tap but a very hard whack! The bread fell on the floor along with some of my tears, and I remember her clearly saying with devilish anger, "You need to grow up to be a woman of class and dignity! We will try this again tomorrow."

Who says that to five-year-old? A monster.

Tomorrow became close to fifteen years of torture. She would show up at any sign of imperfection to "fix it" in her own words. If the bedding was not folded to perfection, she would be there to "fix it." If girls were not punctual for prayer time, she would be there to "fix it." If there were girls playing truant or talking to boys outside the orphanage, she would apply more permanent fixes.

"Fixes" ranged from whacks with a wooden ruler to mental and physical torture for more serious offenses. I was surprised that an organization like this was even legal. Wasn't the law supposed to protect children from abuse? This hell was so perverse that probably even the law did not want to dirty its hands. We were in hell, and she was the queen here.

I snapped out of my daydream. I remember I was able to escape this netherworld, but I couldn't recall when. Was it with another family, or was it after marriage? I do not recall the finer details, but I know I had escaped it.

I sat up, no sweat this time. My satin nightwear rubbed across my skin, and its softness made me want to sleep again. I looked to the right of my queen bed, and it was still empty and neatly made. The bed itself was tucked safely in the corner of the room beside a window. Surprisingly I was not able to see much through this window, and it was black as if something was covering the glass. There was a small table with nothing specific, and opposite to my bed was my wardrobe.

I lazily got out of bed, put on my plush slippers, and walked to the bathroom. A mild headache got me yearning for some coffee, so I moved on to brush my teeth and start making breakfast. In general, it felt like a lazy day, but my curiosity never died. Who was that other half of the bed made for? Why were there two pillows? What was the scream I heard about last night?

I brushed my teeth and opened the mirror cabinet to look for medicine for the headache. When I couldn't find any, I just cursed my luck and decided to rely on coffee to do the trick. If I had to describe my feeling in this house, it would be "safe." If one solution does not fix your problem, you will always find another one. There was no tyrant waiting to make me do the days' chores exactly the way she wanted. I did not have to hear screams of agony when my friends did not do what she wanted.

The house itself looked familiar, but I did not remember how. I was getting on in years, and my memory was failing me, but what mattered most was that with Madam Costa was out of the picture, and now I could do whatever I wanted. I wonder how long she had been in my life before I got here. Irrespective of the time, the feeling of not having to be perfect all the time was…for lack of a better word…perfect.

I left my bedroom and moved outside into the living room. From the looks of it, this house was single-storied, just as I would have liked it. I did not like large houses because maintaining them would be very tough. Having to be perfect for years in the orphanage brought a compulsive minimalism in my adult life. I lived with bare minimum requirements in a controlled environment. It had dented my psyche beyond repair.

The living room was part of a larger space and had been extended as a dining room as well. The dining room opened into the kitchen, and there were visibly no other rooms. In totality, there were three occupiable spaces in this house.

Even though it was sparsely furnished with just a couple of couches in the living room and four chairs in the dining room, it was home to me, and I felt comfortable here. I did not feel threatened or lost or sad, but the feeling was more of a happy and safe one. I know this house is close to my heart, but I was unable to remember why.

My train of thought was disturbed by the uneven roars of the lawnmower. I just realized it had never stopped since I woke up but had now lost its rhythm, probably due to lack of fuel, and that uneven cacophony was what caught my attention. This was another side effect of being forced to be acutely self-aware in the orphanage.

I walked past the single chair and moved to a soft sofa set, behind which was a window. Through the window, I spotted two kids across the lawn in the neighbor's house. The orphanage had killed my need for social niceties and interactions. As a result, I wasn't a very amicable person. I rarely got out of my house, and I honestly did not recall who my neighbors were, so my assumption was just that these brothers were my neighbors and their parents were probably off shopping somewhere.

There were two. One looked like he was in his early twenties. The perspiration on his shirtless body was making him gleam in the sun. He was still wearing his beanie cap. It was a bit odd, considering that would just make him feel warmer. His pants were torn at the knees as well. Their family must have a weird sense of recycling to be wearing such shabby clothes. The younger one was sitting on a chair near the door entrance wearing pajamas. I couldn't make out what pajamas they were, but they did seem to have some design. Did he just wake up and walk down?

Watching them gave me an idea. There was no Madam Costa to disapprove if I walked over and started talking to them. It has been so long since I spoke to another human, and I was now, for some reason, interested in getting to know the taller one. What better way to incentivize kids than to bake cookies? I quickly decided to make cookies and invite them over to get to know them a bit more. I did not need to suppress my curiosity anymore. It felt almost rebellious against a non-existent tyrant.

I waltzed across the room to reach the dining room. I began to have a new sense of purpose. Once I got this purpose, I realized that this is exactly what I generally missed in my life. All my life, I was directed by this source of pain to be exactly how she wanted me to be. Not acquiescing to another human was liberating. For a while, my purpose in life had become maintaining a routine, and I was now keen on breaking it.

As I entered the kitchen, I spotted a vase at the corner of the room, which seemed disarranged. My inquisitive nature kicked in, and I wanted to check it out more closely. I was not sure when I had received this vase or who gave it to me, but I was sure this was out of place in this room and wanted to move it into the kitchen so that it didn't ruin the aesthetic of the room. The vase stood as tall as my waist. It was not fancy and had simple floral patterns with a tint of purple and white. I stared at it while trying to understand why I placed it here, and after failing to remember, I reached forward to pick it up. I was immediately surrounded by a blinding flash of light…

*

I was not at home anymore but was walking with a man. He was walking to my left and was holding my hand. I had a feeling that this man had a considerable significance in my life and was not just an acquaintance. This location didn't seem to be our local street but looked more East Asian, crowded as ever. A couple of locals were trying to sell me all kinds of exotic statues by thrusting them in my face, but I was not interested in any of them. This man seemed to know the local language and was able to keep the hawkers off me, but the heckling was getting disconcerting. He could sense my discomfort as we meandered through the sea of hawkers, and with great dexterity, he maneuvered me to a less crowded area.

He held my hand and said, "Sarah, You can buy whatever you want from this market. Let me know, and it shall be yours. If you want to do something else, I am okay with that as well, darling."

I thought for a while and then pointed to a shop on the far end of the street that we had just passed. We had passed this pottery store some time ago, but the heckling from other hawkers did not allow me to consider an option to buy, so I left. I was looking for that one vase that had caught my attention and was constantly in my mind. Going back to the shop would mean jumping back into the sea of people and wading through them to safety all over again, but he showed no sign of dismay. He led me through the hawkers, who were now less aggressive since they knew I did not want to buy anything. We reached the pottery shop faster than before, and I stared for a while, searching for my target. I finally pointed to a specific vase in the far corner of the shop and said, "This vase had caught my attention. It's simple and yet distinct. Could you get that vase for me?"

The man did not flinch. He immediately extended some local currency notes and got the vase, smiling at me all the time. It was a purple floral pattern on a white background. When he gave me the vase, he said, "May this be a bottomless vase into which both of us can pour our love."

I don't know what he meant, but he said it so warmly that I accepted it gladly. The memory faded out like a fast-forwarding cinema reel, and I recall making love to him later in the evening. He was a selfless lover and what I felt with him was safety and security. As my head was cradled on his chest, I could hear the thumping of his heart and the slow rhythm of his breathing.

I was about to look at his face when I was transported back home...

*

I was now staring at this vase beside the kitchen. I was flummoxed at what just happened and thought I was in one of those artificial worlds or virtual reality simulations like from the *Matrix* movies. Why was I not able to remember the name of this man who appeared to be close to me as my significant other?

I was now sweating again and was unable to focus on anything specific. Loss of control got me worked up, and I needed to know if this was just me or if others felt this phenomenon too. Interaction with more people from here would help me understand what exactly constitutes this place. I thought the best course of action was, as planned, to meet the boys and, while having a conversation, figure out what exactly this place is and decipher what I had just experienced.

With the resolution of what needed to be done next, I navigated into the kitchen and started rummaging all cupboards for the ingredients. This was based on a recipe that I learned at the orphanage, and since we had to make food fast and with limited supplies, this recipe needs only three ingredients – flour, sugar, and butter. I finally found them at separate locations around the kitchen, and I placed them lined up on the kitchen counter, ready to be utilized for the backing process later.

The kitchen was not tidy, but who cares? There was no Madam Costa to "fix" me. At face value now, I was beginning to think that I was more attached to the house itself than the people in it. The way entropy has taken over the house, and the satisfaction that it doesn't need to be the epitome of perfection were two of the keen factors why I felt safe and comfortable in the house. I was enjoying this feeling of anarchy.

With the ingredients sorted, I decided to wear something light and not too flamboyant when going to meet the kids. I walked back to the bedroom and opened my wardrobe. I was looking for a specific pink skirt and a loose blue top. I always thought I did not have any fashion sense, but these are basically kids, and I had no need to impress them. I was flicking through my clothes when I noticed a pink frock. It did not look my size, so I wasn't sure whose it was. I ran my fingers across the pink frock and was immediately surrounded by another blinding flash of light.

Here we go again...

*

I was now with a teenage girl who was happily holding my hand, pulling me towards a shop in a mall. She looked very pretty and vaguely familiar. Her jet-black hair was bouncing to mimic her personality. She wasn't looking at me but was definitely pulling me towards one of the shops. Finally, she reached a shop, and we stopped momentarily. While I tried to gather my balance, she disappeared into the shop only to return a couple of minutes later with a pink frock.

Chapter 6: Whiplash

I could sense the excitement in her voice as she stood there breathless after all the running, "Mom, can I get this frock, please. I want to wear this for this year's Christmas party."

"Okay, sweetie. It's yours! Let's go buy it." I replied.

"Thanks, Mom. You're the best!"

She ran up to me and kissed me on the cheek. It was the best feeling I ever had.

I have had a plethora of emotions most of them being based on fear and anger. It was a pleasant surprise to feel warmth and love, especially from a young girl. My heart was elated, and I hugged her. She hugged me back with the frock sandwiched between us. My hand involuntarily held her head as she rested on my shoulder. I knew she loved me, and I loved her. This had to be my daughter. She looked back at me with a twinkle in her eyes, and I could rest well that day knowing I had made my daughter happy beyond measure.

She hugged me tightly, and I said, "Careful, I am pretty old, you know." She laughed and ran off to look for other stuff to buy.

I wanted to savor every moment of it, but unfortunately, I was now back staring at my wardrobe...

*

I now realized that I have a daughter as well. This revelation led to a new fear. My mind was now directed to the scream I heard last night. Could it have been my daughter? She wasn't at home, and anything could have happened to her.

Fear now began to grip me. I needed to speak to the boys even more than before. I was still struggling to recall the name of my possible husband and my daughter. My purpose now was to identify why I cannot remember anything in my life, and what was the phenomenon that I had just encountered with the vase and the frock. I quickly removed my nightdress and put on some clean underwear. I slipped into my pink skirt and blue top and walked briskly to the front door.

When I exited the front door, I was greeted with even more unkempt plants. The garden was clearly not taken well care of, but secretly, I loved it. I stood there to take in all the entropy. I made a mental note to trim and improve the garden at my own pace. It was less of a perfectionist move and more of making sure the yard, which is the face of the house, is in good presentable condition. Maybe I'll get this done another day.

I walked across the yard, careful not to stamp any of the already degenerating flowers but inevitably stamping some of the long grass over the now invisible walkway. The grass was wet, and every step left drops of water on my skirt. As I reached the fence, I looked around and saw rotting mango pulp at the edge of the fence and was disgusted by the flies around it. I needed to clean that out, at my own pace, of course. I then stood at the fence and called out to the two boys explaining in simple terms that I had no idea they were my neighbors, and I would be glad to have them over for cookies to get to know them better.

I lied about my cookie recipe though. I don't know why I did, but I told them it was my mother's recipe, which it definitely wasn't. I just did not want anyone to know that part of my past. I did not want them to judge me or pity me as an orphan.

I instantly felt comfortable speaking to Joshua. I felt a sense of oneness communicating with him which was weird considering he was a young boy, and I was a fifty-something lady. I did not pay attention to the younger one, who clearly seemed to dislike me. Joshua instantly accepted my invitation, and I know he also had the same spark. The younger one, Pogo, was a bit more apprehensive, but in the end, they agreed, and I got what I wanted, so I turned to leave and make the cookies.

The lawnmower was as loud as ever, but I was still within earshot when I heard Pogo asking Joshua about the scream. Hearing it from someone else made it real. Somewhere in my mind, I was hoping that I had imagined it, but now it was real, and I needed to know what they know about it. It could very well have been my daughter, and I was on a mission to find out.

I retraced my steps and interrupted their conversation to confirm that I had heard it as well, though I was surprised and curious when Joshua denied hearing the scream. If he did not hear it, he was either deaf or lying. Why would he lie? I explained to them that I had heard a scream, but I could not pinpoint where the scream came from. I was internally debating whether to tell them about the vase and the frock and decided to start small and explain about the gaps in my memory. Pogo immediately caught that train of thought and was about to explain something when Joshua stopped him and started asking me about my husband. I interpreted this as a diversion implying that Joshua did not want me to know details of what happened to them. That was when I learned from Joshua that there were only five buildings in the entire complex, and that the most plausible suspect for being the source of that scream was the hotel across the main highway.

Joshua seemed suspiciously defensive about the entire topic. Especially about finding out the source of the scream. What if someone needed our help? How could someone just ignore all that and not act on identifying where the source of the scream was from? Maybe it was his age, but he did not seem to be insensitive. I don't know how, but I was sure that Joshua was a nice person. He made valid points of involving the police and the topic was clearly making him uncomfortable, so I decided to leave it alone and maybe broach it later when we have cookies. He seemed to be more interested in getting the police to check it out and was repeating with conviction that he did not hear it. There was no point flogging a dead horse, so I turned and left to make the cookies.

I went back home and was alone, but this time I had a little more information. I knew that someone other than me had also heard a scream and that there were only five buildings where we live now. I was excited to learn more from them when they came over.

I moved to the kitchen to start baking the cookies. I was my own master now.

Chapter 7
What Is in a Name?

There was a big void in my memory. I couldn't recall the last two decades of my life. As soon as I came back from meeting the boys, I went on autopilot. My legs took me to the kitchen, and my hands were making the cookies, but my mind was far away. Where was this mystery man from my memories? What was his name?

I don't know how much time passed, but I was now sitting on the couch thinking of the same topic. Had something bad happened to my daughter? The vase made its way into my mind, and though the memory was vivid, I did not recall that man's name. Nothing made sense, and worst of all, I was alone having to deal with all this information.

I also thought about the two kids from the next house. I remembered Joshua very clearly with his shirtless body and beanie cap. I had a strange sense of affection towards Joshua. I felt safe and enjoyed the little company I had with him and felt it was pleasant to converse with him. I don't think I would call it an infatuation; it felt a bit more complicated than it was. It was eerily similar to what I had felt with the man in my memory – safety and warmth. I forgot the little one's name, though. It was related to a stick or something. Yes, Pogo – that was his name. Pogo was a cute kid. I liked both of them, and I was glad I decided to speak to them, but everything happening was so confusing that I had to stop my activities and close my eyes to think.

*　*　*

My train of thought was interrupted by the clang of the gate bolt, and I knew it was Joshua and Pogo. I reminded myself that the main motive now was to understand how we fit into this world, how we can explain the anomalies, and how I could possibly find my husband and daughter. I walked to the door and opened it, only to find them struggling to find the path to the house. I ushered them in and asked them to sit wherever they felt comfortable, and they both sat with each other on the sofa.

I was observing them and realized that they seemed to be good kids. Joshua was wearing his Iron Maiden t-shirt and looking much more presentable, and I felt the urge to give him a hug and tell him that everything would be okay. What I also noticed was that they were extremely tired, as if they had run away from a mad dog. They were sitting on the sofa waiting for me, so I closed the door, walked across the chair, and sat opposite them. When I looked at Joshua, I remembered the mystery man again and his body over me in the memory. I could feel his hands tracing the contours of my body, and it sent pleasant shivers down my spine. I turned and looked at the vase, hoping that the memory would become more clear and more vivid, but it did not. That was when Joshua brought up the lawn.

They must have really had to spend some time navigating the lawn because Joshua seemed keen to mow and fix the overgrowth. I definitely wouldn't mind, but I did not want his parents to feel I was taking advantage of him. I asked them why they looked tired and spent. Pogo mentioned his trip to the supermarket and seemed pretty frightened by the supervisor at the supermarket. I may have to visit him at some point, so I made a mental note to remember this. I was going to ask more questions about their experience when Joshua cut him off and changed the subject.

I felt Pogo was going to give some specific information, but Joshua cut him off, and this was not the first time he did something like that. Joshua appeared to be concealing his true intentions and emotions. My affection for him was not reduced, but I wanted to know if they were in some sort of trouble and help them out.

I realized that I had forgotten the cookies I had baked, and I could see Pogo was getting impatient. I excused myself and went to the kitchen. I put on my oven mitts and took the cookies from the oven. I placed them on the table and started looking for the milk. I recall having placed the milk on the table before making the cookies, but I couldn't recall where I placed it after cooking. I began opening all the cupboards and drawers, but I couldn't find it.

I think it might have been a while since I was gone because I saw Joshua entering the kitchen. He walked in and asked me with concern, "Hey, Sarah, is everything okay? You have been gone for a while, and Pogo was asking for some water."

"Oh yeah, sure. Sorry I was looking for the milk. I cannot recall where I placed it." I looked around and found a bottle of water that I had filled earlier. I picked a glass tumbler from one of the open cabinets and poured in the water. He was waiting intently, and I added, "Here you go."

"I can help you look. Do you know where you kept it last?"

"I had placed the milk on the slab here before I made the cookies. I was a bit preoccupied, and I forgot where I put it back."

"Okay, let's see if we can find it." He started looking around the kitchen, and I started searching as well. Our two-man search party was going well, and I took this opportunity to get to know him more.

"What are you two planning for lunch? I'm planning to roast some chicken. You can join me if you'd like."

Joshua replied, "I don't think we have anything specific in mind. We can join you if you are comfortable with us being around."

I was thrilled! "Of course, that would be great. I hope I don't misplace the chicken like I did the milk," I replied with a chuckle to lighten the mood and get him to become more comfortable.

We continued searching and were getting nowhere. Surprisingly Joshua now initiated a question, "Hey Sarah, where did you get this vase? It seems out of place from the other furniture."

I had felt the same in the morning, which is why I touched it and got my memory of the mysterious man. Of course, I had no idea who he was, and it was obvious that anyone who sees it could see how out of place it was in the room. I gave him the only reply I could, "It was a gift from my husband. I don't know where he is or if he will come back today or tomorrow, but I think he used to love these milk and cookies." I could see he was getting tired. "Hey Joshua, you don't need to help me here. You and Pogo both look tired. Take this water to him and have some yourself. I will bring the milk later. Take these cookies too."

Joshua left the cookies but took the water. He seemed to open up a little more, "Look, Sarah. I'm sorry we look a bit tired. We have been experiencing weird things lately, and the visit to the supermarket is kind of the thing that tipped us over the limit. The supervisor there said he had heard a scream as well and Pogo got scared. We have been on edge, and weirdly, the supervisor offered us a free staycation at the very place where we thought the scream originated from."

Now things were getting interesting, and there was a lot of information here for me to process. One worthwhile piece was that the scream was heard by a lot more people than just me and Pogo. The second piece here is the staycation offered by the supervisor. I was somehow elated at the prospect of staying at a hotel. That feeling was doubled if it was a hotel where something was going on and needed to be investigated. Maybe this is what mid-life ennui feels like!

This entire train of thought got derailed because I realized Joshua had not asked me to accompany them. Another prospect came to my mind, a deeper one that did not match with Joshua's initial revelation about the scream.

"Joshua, you said the supervisor heard the scream as well. Are you sure you did not hear a scream?"

He seemed a bit hesitant to answer but finally did. "I'm sorry for lying, Sarah. I did hear the scream. I just did not want to get involved in anything about that for Pogo's sake, and now I am scared for him. The supervisor seems to be keeping secrets.

"He said the hotel was deserted and was being reopened to the public. It seems a bit convenient that we heard that scream, and the hotel is now opening to the public. He mentioned he wouldn't mind throwing in a free night for me, Pogo, and anyone we would like to take with us to visit. They do not have enough hotel staff, so the hotel manager asked the supervisor to do the general room logistics until they find someone permanent.

"How is it that the hotel will then cater to guests like us? Everything seems to be conveniently laid out for Pogo and me to visit the hotel, which I think is weird. Pogo thinks Mom is working there for some reason and wants to go and check if we can help out."

I picked the cookie tray and pondered over what Joshua had just said. I did not know what to make of this information. I was interested in joining them, but I wasn't sure if their parents were interested as well. I had not seen his parents around, so I asked him.

"That's great. Why don't you and your parents accept this offer and go stay there? You said Pogo thought his mom might be there, so take your dad and meet her there."

Joshua was filled with dismay. He looked down to the floor and then to the side. I thought I saw a glint of moisture in his eyes. His lips were twitching as if he was trying to control his urge to cry. He finally said, "Our parents are not here, Sarah. It's complicated, especially for Pogo."

It was heart-wrenching to see him open up like this about his parents. I could see where this was going, so I tried to be a bit pragmatic and sensitive about this topic. If he was uncomfortable, I did not want him to relive something he did not like. I told him, "It's okay, Joshua. If this is something you don't want to say, it's fine."

He replied in a shaken voice, "I don't know, in all honesty. The only people Pogo really cherished were me and his mom, and unfortunately, she's dead. I cannot imagine how surprised and sad she must have been when her own husband killed her. He must have felt ashamed and depressed as well because after the act, he ran away never to come back."

I knew something explosive was coming, but this was a whopper! I was taken aback by this revelation, but at the same time, I wanted to protect him and make him feel comfortable. I did not want him to feel the sadness and emptiness I feel now without my husband and child. I wanted to get closer and hug him, but I restrained myself.

"That's so sad to hear. I'm sorry I brought it up."

Joshua was almost in tears now. "I did not know how to explain this to Pogo, but now he wants to go and look for his mom in the hotel. I don't think I can do this alone with him. Sarah, I was thinking since our parents are not here, would you mind joining us at the hotel? I would like to understand what that scream was about as I feel it has something to do with why we are here and why we have this large set of memories missing."

This was unexpected. I was glad that Joshua opened to me and asked for help. I also was keen to explore and observe anything at the hotel and figure out the source of the scream and its possible relation to my daughter. Before I could give him my consent, all hell broke loose.

The next thing I knew, the cookies were falling on the floor, and Joshua had lost his balance. He tried to hold me for balance but ended up nudging me, and I fell on my back. The cookies were already on the floor and messed up. The glass from Joshua's hands had been scattered across the kitchen. Thankfully Joshua was not hurt, and he got up and brushed the cookies off his t-shirt.

He turned towards the dining room and screamed, "Pogo, what did you hear? I'm sorry! It's not what you think!"

He then turned back to me and said, "I'm sorry, Sarah. I'll go see if he's okay. I think it is better if he stays out of this for now because he has probably heard something he doesn't understand. He is too fragile at this stage for any more secrets, and I am sure there are many more to find. Let him stay at home. I will check on him and come back here. Is that, okay?"

I strained to see past him and saw Pogo running away. I just got up and my legs and back were already in pain. I was barely able to stand but I knew Pogo was in a much worse state, so I got my bearings and spoke. "Okay, I will visit this notorious supermarket supervisor and try to get more information about this offer he was giving. "I believed that was the right thing to do because as Joshua had said the offer was too good to be true and I thought an adult needed to investigate this further. My back was killing me, but I would just have to live with it.

"Alright, thanks Sarah. We'll meet in a while then. Try and take some rest, and I'm sorry about this entire fiasco. You don't look so good. You don't need to go to the supermarket if you're not feeling up to it." He paused for a while and said, "Anyway, I'll leave. Hopefully, Pogo has not done anything drastic." Saying so, Joshua left the house, and I was alone again to plan my next course of action.

My back was still hurting, but when the pain had subsided a bit, I decided to go to the supermarket. The kids had gone there alone, walking, so I assumed it was an easy walk. I stepped out of the house and made my way across the lawn through the waist-high grass to the gate. The smashed mango was now beginning to rot, but the count of flies stayed the same. Too much had happened, and there was no time to reminisce about fallen mangoes. I stepped onto the grassy path and made my way to the supermarket.

I had only one motive and that was to really confirm what Joshua had mentioned about their visit there and see if I could gather more information about this supervisor and his hidden agenda, if any. The road seemed deserted, but as I passed the diner, I saw a lot of people in there. The diner lady was waving her hands and asking me to get in. I began to have a strong urge to enter the diner, but I snapped out of it and focused on my mission. I waved back to the diner lady, walked past the diner, and moved on to the supermarket. I wanted to be at home before Joshua got back.

* * *

The supermarket was now standing tall before me. The door itself was a small one, but it looked ominous, and I was scared by its presence. Maybe this was what Pogo was referring to. I tried to enter, but for some reason, I was unable to do so, almost like an invisible force field was blocking my way. I was wondering why this would be the case, and I realized I had just walked backward. I was getting scared out of my wits now, but I saw the supervisor watching me, and after a while, he waved his hands and asked me to enter.

I entered the supermarket and almost immediately saw the weird naming convention for the aisles. I had never seen this type of aisle arrangement, but I wouldn't consider this enough to qualify the place as evil. There had to be more to this place for Pogo to call it evil. It put me on my guard, and I was extra sensitive to everything around me.

As I was observing the neatly architected racks, my thoughts were interrupted by the supervisor. "Hey lady, are you going to buy something?"

This was when I got a chance to see the supervisor. His Hitler moustache was the most unique attribute of his face. He wore a white shirt and black trousers like one of the waiters at fancy restaurants, except he was also wearing a red apron. I almost smiled until I looked at his stone-cold expression. Of course, I was ready for this question.

"Oh yeah… No, I was not planning to buy anything. I actually wanted to clarify some information I received from a kid who just visited today. His name is Joshua, and he was here earlier with his brother Pogo. Do you recall meeting them?"

"Oh yeah, I do remember. Not a lot of business these days, as you can see, and we are short-staffed as well, so I was here all the time.

80

Chapter 7: What Is in a Name?

Interesting kids. They seemed to have got lost in one of the aisles and were screaming when I found them at the aisle – visibly scared." He quipped.

I shuddered to think what the kids might have had to endure at this place. I maintained my calm demeanour hoping the storm inside me was not visible. "Yeah, Joshua mentioned you had offered a staycation at the hotel across the highway. Is that correct? I was curious why that was the case. You wouldn't blame me for thinking if this was some sort of elaborate scam to get us to buy something, right?"

He was prepared as well, "Oh no, no. This is definitely not a scam, I assure you. I know the hotel manager there. His name is Kobi. He was looking for some local folks who have completed hotel management studies to support the new reopening of the hotel. He was unable to find any, so he asked me and some other folks to help him out. He said I am authorized to offer a free stay to anyone who is interested as long as they will use the services and provide feedback. This will not be an official stay or anything, but you can use all of the hotel services for free as long as you give constructive feedback."

I thought to myself that it was indeed a valid reason to give out free stays. It was clearly a rehearsed answer, so I tried to stump him a bit. "Why haven't you placed fliers or put an advertisement for this in the papers?"

He seemed taken aback and clearly did not expect me to ask a follow-up question. He was fumbling for an answer and finally said, "I assumed there were not enough people to see a flier considering the small population, and we do not have a printing press here, so newspapers were out of the question. We had to ask people and then get them to spread the offer by word of mouth, which is why I asked them and subsequently you."

He evaded my question well, and assuming that he would be a glib liar, it wasn't a surprise. I asked, "Do you know why this hotel is being reopened now specifically, despite being closed for a while?"

He was even more taken aback. He finally had to admit, "I'm sorry. I am only a messenger or more of a worker, to be specific. If you want to clarify this offer a bit more, then I would suggest meeting Kobi. He is the hotel manager and is at the hotel. You could ask him if you go there."

I found it weird that a town with such few people needed such a large supermarket. Additionally, a hotel wants to reopen in such a small town with negligible advertisement. Even more strange was that there was no newspaper in the town. This guy was clearly hiding something.

"Thanks. I just wanted to know what it was about. We will most likely be accepting your offer and will be visiting the hotel later today to set up the logistics."

I was starting to leave when he called me from behind. "Hey, sorry to bother, but aren't you Sarah Miller from across the street near the diner?"

"Yes. Have we met before?" was my immediate reaction.

"No, we haven't, but Marko had talked a lot about you. Where has he been?"

Marko? Why was I familiar with that name? No sooner did I hear the name than I felt a similar blinding flash of light engulfing me, and I was now certain I was going to see a memory. This felt a bit different, though. I was feeling all sorts of emotions as well with this memory – anger, love, lust. It was like I was feeling him all over me…

*

I was immediately transported to a hospital. I was on a metal bed, had all sorts of medical equipment scattered over me, and I was in extreme pain. I could see three doctors asking me to push, and Marko was on my left holding my hand. Bright hospital lights were glaring into my face.

"You can do it, Sarah. Push as hard as you can."

I couldn't explain what I was feeling. I was feeling anger and fear. I was clasping his hands so hard that I was scared I might hurt him, but he looked at me with loving eyes, and I knew we would get through this together.

"You're doing well, Sarah. Keep going."

I don't know if I kept pushing or not. One moment I was feeling extreme pain, and the next moment I was pausing to catch my breath. After harmonic inhalations and exhalations, I pushed with all my residual strength and finally felt a huge relief. I was completely spent, and my eyes were groggy, but I could hear the first cries of our child.

Marko brought the child closer to me and said, "She is beautiful, Sarah. She has your eyes..."

*

I was quickly transported back to the supermarket. I must have stood there for some time rooted to the ground because I saw the supervisor putting back the knife he had picked up. I gave him a belligerent look. Did he just try to murder me?

He seemed to understand my apprehension and said, "I'm sorry. You were shaking vigorously. I thought you got a seizure, and so this was the only thing I could get my hands on that was close by for you to hold. Are you okay?"

I replied, stunned and perplexed, "I'm okay." I was able to remember now. Marko was my husband, and we had a daughter together. She must have been the one I was with in my previous memory.

I turned towards the supervisor and asked, "Why do you want to know about Marko? When did you meet him? Why did you ask me about him out of the blue?"

"He came in yesterday looking for some rope and a meat cleaver. I did not know what he wanted to do with it, but after hearing the scream, I was not sure what to make of it. That's why I wanted to know where he was."

All this worried me. Marko was here yesterday looking for items that could, under specific circumstances, be used for murder. Where was I yesterday, and why did I not remember? Could he have lost his sense and have done something violent? I did not know how to respond, but I knew that he was a good man. I did not want to reveal any more information without knowing more. I need to find Marko and my daughter, and this hotel will be the first place I search.

"So, do you know where he is?" the supervisor persisted.

I did not like the way the supervisor was nosey about Marko. Even if I knew, I wouldn't tell him, and thankfully, I did not know.

I replied, "No, I don't. Sorry. I'll leave now. I'm not sure if Marko had anything to do with the screams. He is a good man, but I will leave the rest to the police. They will investigate and make sure the truth comes out. Thanks for confirming the details of the staycation."

I did not wait for his response, and I just left.

On the way my mind was assimilating this new information. I knew Marko was my husband and was missing since yesterday if I was to believe what the supervisor just said. I have a daughter, and she is probably a teenager now. I can touch objects or hear names to retrieve memories about them. My neighbors are two boys whose parents are not here. Marko was suspiciously looking for a meat cleaver and some rope and has since not been seen here, and I heard a scream at night while he was missing. It seemed pretty incriminating.

I did not know what to make of it, but with all these facts, it seemed that Marko had something to do with the screams, which I couldn't accept. I knew he was a calm and sensitive man. It was impossible that he would be involved in something sinister. This was even more reason to get to the hotel soon. I hurried back home; Joshua hadn't returned yet. I sat down on the chair and closed my eyes. If sleep came knocking, I would gladly welcome her.

* * *

Chapter 7: What Is in a Name?

I woke up to Joshua shaking me vigorously.

"I'm sorry, Joshua. I dozed off. How's Pogo. Is he alright?

"Yeah, he's going to be okay, but he's a kid who has just learned that his mom is dead. It will take some time."

I turned to the window and spoke while looking out at the yard, "Yes, true."

I paused for a while and then continued, "I visited the supermarket supervisor, and his reasoning seems legitimate superficially, but I am sure there is some hidden agenda, and he does seem a tad shady. They want to do a test drive with the hotel, and we are the guinea pigs. I think we should go. Not for the free stay but for another reason. I think this hotel has more to it than meets the eye. It seems to be the center of this mystery, and I want to find out what it is. I know my husband and child have something to do with that hotel, and I need to find them."

Joshua agreed with me. "You're right. I think we should go there, stay a night, and explore the hotel to find any clues about the scream. The source of this scream is most likely going to give us more insights into this world and, more importantly, why we are in it." He then seemed to have realized something, and he said, "You mentioned you wanted to roast chicken for lunch. So, are we going to the hotel in the evening after lunch?"

I had other plans and did not want to spend any time waiting for events to take their course. The secret to this world was waiting, and I had to find my husband and daughter. I would have wanted Joshua to tag along with me anyway, and I could see us building a symbiotic relationship. He needed me as moral support, and I needed his presence as a confidence booster.

I said, "I was thinking of skipping the cooking and just going to the diner. We can have our lunch from there and then just move to the hotel."

"I think that's a good idea. Let's go if you're ready."

"Alright. Wait for me near the gate. I will wash my face and hands and be right back."

I stepped away to the kitchen to drink some water and wash my hands. This was the real deal now. The small ounce of drama in my almost boring life was slowly taking shape. I was now the protagonist in my own story, and I was going to save my husband and daughter. I did not know how it would end but thinking of various prospects of the hotel journey excited me.

It excited me so much one would consider it almost criminal.

Chapter 8
The Diner

The diner was a stone's throw away from my house, but the trip itself felt like ages thanks to my aching back. I was dragging myself and frequently touching my lower back to isolate the source of pain, but after fifty, any pain is a major pain. Joshua was silent most of the trip. He was probably still thinking about Pogo and how he would be coping with the death of his mother. I gave him his space and thought about various approaches to exploring the hotel and its implications.

To begin with, I needed to validate the hotel manager's credentials. I have not heard of a single scenario where a hotel is about to reopen, and they gave free stays to anyone available. Hotels are known to send out free stays for high-tier members but not the public.

Secondly, I need to figure out a way to get access to either the hotel guest-register or be able to possibly access all rooms to look for signs of Marko or my daughter. It sounded absurd to go looking into each room, but maybe I could get help from the hotel manager. I was trying to remember his name, and the pain in my back was making it very difficult.

My train of thought was changing tracks like flipping a record on a record player. I shifted my attention to Marko. Why would my husband kill anyone? The biggest fear I had was the safety of my daughter. I did not know where she was and what she was doing, and the lack of knowledge was killing me.

I couldn't really gauge what Joshua was thinking, but I knew it wasn't easy on him as well. His brother was distraught, and he was confused about his place in this world with no parents. I wanted to make sure I was always with him and keep him comfortable. If he had been my son, that's exactly what I would do, and I hope that someone was making sure my daughter was safe as well.

The solitary walk was helping him as well as me to gather our thoughts. The grass seemed fresh as always, welcoming all feet with the same vigor. I walked at a slow pace, and soon I was facing the pink and blue neon lights of the "DINER" sign board. I could see Joshua making his way into the diner's car park with the entrance in sight.

The diner, contrary to the supermarket, had a pleasant feel. Even from a distance, I could see the hustle and bustle of people inside the diner seated at their tables. I immediately felt warm and comfortable. Joshua was already across the car park and walking towards the door. I followed him, still observing my surroundings.

This was a large car park and could hold at least fifty cars. There were at least thirty people in the diner, but the car park had just one car, a sea-green Subaru, which stood out. Did all the people in the diner come here by walking? The building itself seemed inviting, but I had a foreboding feeling about not just the diner but all the buildings in the neighborhood. It was surprising that I couldn't remember any of these buildings. Except for the hotel, none of these buildings look like they had been renovated recently. The lack of my memory was not justified unless I had never stepped out of my home for a long time, which was possible, considering my aversion to comraderies.

The building was single-storied but widespread, covering a lot of land. It had a large presence, but unlike the supermarket, it radiated comfort and warmth. The diner building itself was painted with a light pink shade which led me to believe that a woman's touch was involved. It could be the diner lady.

Chapter 8: The Diner

We crossed the car park and a meandering road to reach the main door. The door itself was a small one with metal borders, but the diner lady was already at the door waiting for us. She gave us her best smile and said, "Come on in. As you can see, we are almost full today. Do you need a table for two?"

I caught up with Joshua just in time to hear her. I said, "yes, please, table for two."

"Sure, and you folks are lucky we have the last one available there in the corner. Follow me."

I had just got a glimpse of the diner lady, and she was beautiful. Complimenting her beauty was her warm and welcoming personality. She was surely younger than me, maybe in her mid-thirties, and my hunch was corroborated by her flawless skin. She had wavy blonde hair which extended down to her shoulders, and every time she smiled, her perfect white teeth smiled as well. She was dressed in the standard light blue blouse and white skirt with a blue and red checked apron. Remembering the conversation with the supermarket supervisor, I figured that she was short-staffed as well and was doubling down as they cook, which seemed a large feat considering the crowd here and the quantity of food she may have had to make.

As we entered the diner, we heard a "ding" from the bell above the door. For some reason, I was titillated by the anachronism of a doorbell above the door.

The lady led us past some customers to a corner of the diner and showed us to our seats. There were all kinds of people sitting and having food. It seemed to be a busy lunch day. I could see an old man in his fishing clothes with his younger son, chewing on a hamburger. The kid seemed to be enjoying the burger. As I was passing the penultimate seat, I almost kicked someone's sneakers off. I gathered myself and looked to the left. It was a middle-aged woman in her jogging attire. She was having what looked like a frappé sitting with her partner in a similar attire observing me. I smiled and told her, "I'm sorry. I wasn't paying attention."

She looked back and said robotically, "Welcome to the diner. Nice to meet you."

I was confused by that response. She sounded like one of the voice bots in the telecom industry when you call a nonexistent number. I turned to her partner and told him, "I'm really sorry. I did not want to upset you folks. I'll let you guys enjoy your food in peace."

"Welcome to the diner. Nice to meet you," was the only response I got in a similar monotone. I was taken aback by the response. I was going to ask more about it when Joshua pulled me to the side and brought me back to the diner lady. She pointed to a table and mentioned, "Here is your table."

She already had two menu cards in her hands which she passed on to us. We sat down opposite each other, and she said, "Once you're ready to order, let me know, and I'll come over." She then left us to ourselves.

Joshua seemed to have lightened up a bit when he sat down opposite me. I think it had something to do with this place itself and its effect on us. These were not the best of seats, but mine felt new as if the cushion was not frequently sat on.

Despite having so many customers, the seats were clean as a whistle, and the diner was spotless. I couldn't see any drops of food on the ground or spare change fallen from pockets. For a diner with no staff, it showed that the diner lady was very efficient at what she does. Despite my wandering thoughts on the anomalies at this diner, the atmosphere was perfect to have a nice meal, almost as if the diner wanted me to relax and loosen up.

I was looking at the menu. The tuna sandwich looked inviting, but I was debating between the tuna and the chicken sandwich. Joshua was relatively calm looking at the menu. He then looked at me and said, "I think I'll have a chicken sandwich and an espresso. How about you?"

Chapter 8: The Diner

Looks like him selecting the chicken sandwich helped me make up my mind. "I'll have the same as well." I smiled and turned around to summon the diner lady. She was standing behind the counter with her apron and waiting for someone to call her. She immediately made her way to us and stood beside us with a huge smile.

"So, what can I get you folks?"

"A chicken sandwich and an espresso for me, please," said Joshua. The diner lady turned to me.

"I'll have the same, "I said.

"Okay, so two chicken sandwiches and two espressos. Got it! Coming right up. You folks stay safe."

Stay safe? Had Marko done something here as well? I was a bit concerned that she said, "stay safe." I decided to ask her what she meant when she brought the food. I focused on Joshua since he needed to have someone to talk to or maybe just vent.

"Hey, Joshua. I'm sorry about Pogo and everything happening to you now. It will be alright. Let's just see how all of this plays out."

"Yeah, there's nothing you can really do about it, Sarah, so no need to be sorry. You said you learned something about your husband. What exactly was it, if you don't mind me asking?"

"Oh, that's quite alright. I am happy I remember him now, but I want to find him as well. He seems to have landed himself into some problems. The supervisor said he was there at the supermarket yesterday looking for a meat cleaver and a rope. Considering this scream that we heard, it doesn't look good for him."

Joshua looked at me and then said," What about the scream? Did the supervisor say anything else about the scream? Did he say your husband was involved somehow?"

"No, he did not. He asked if I knew where my husband was. I was uneasy at the way he was interested in my husband, so I left it at that."

Joshua looked outside for a while as if gauging his surroundings. He then said, "I was thinking about the placement of these buildings. I am not able to understand why there is a hotel just opposite a diner and a supermarket. That seems odd, and it's also exactly at the edge of the road."

I was curious to know why. He seemed to read my mind and said," Well, to begin with, a hotel just on the road's edge would mean that it doesn't have sufficient distance from the main highway, which is at least ten feet. This is not the case here, and the hotel is exactly at the edge of the highway road. You can cross the road and reach the hotel immediately without having to walk a couple of paces. That seems odd. I'm surprised the construction company got approval for placing it there."

I wasn't an expert on buildings, so I had to take his word for it.

"Well. It is possible, though, right? I'm sure they had their reasons, or maybe they bribed the officials." I offered these thoughts although I could think of no other reasons.

"Hmmm." He went back into his pensive thought.

"Joshua, there is another thing. I haven't really spoken about my daughter. I don't know where my daughter is, and the scream was definitely a woman's. It might be possible something has happened to her, which is another reason why I am desperate to go to that hotel."

"I understand. Do you remember how old your daughter is?"

"In all honesty, I don't. My last memory of her was when she was somewhere in her teenage years. In my memories, she looks roughly fifteen. I haven't seen her since morning, so I'm worried for her as well."

He was empathetic to my cause. He held my hand and said, "We will figure it out. Let's get to the hotel and see exactly what's going on."

We both did not talk for a while, and then he said," Sarah, there is one more thing I haven't told you. Pogo is not my brother. He is my cousin. It was his mom that died and his father that ran away."

I was shocked. I wanted to know more but tried my best not to show the expression on my face. There would have been excitement as well as surprise. "What about your parents? What were you doing in Pogo's house?"

"I don't remember how or why I was at the house. When I woke up due to the scream, it was dark, and that's when I realized that this was Pogo's house, but it looked very familiar because I had been at that home to visit Pogo multiple times. I just went back to sleep and woke up to make breakfast before he got up."

Something was strange about his statement. No one can just wake up at a random place unless they were kidnapped or drugged. Who would do that to them?

"Do you know anyone who had any enmity with you or Pogo's parents?"

"Not that I know of."

"Where are your parents?"

"Something similar happened to them as well. I don't want to talk about it."

I backed off. It was enough that he was telling me so many details about his life. I looked outside and decided to give him some space.

Our silence was broken by the clang of plates being brought in by the diner lady. She was dexterously carrying two plates in one hand and two espressos stacked in the other. She reached our tables and placed the espressos first. The smell of coffee touched my soul. I immediately felt a need to have my food and drink the coffee. The place was perfect for gossip, and all the other patrons were busy chit-chatting. The diner seemed extremely busy. The diner lady brought us our order and said gleefully, "Here you go, folks. Enjoy your meal. Is there anything else I can get for you?"

"No, thank you," I said.

She then turned to Joshua and casually asked, "Hey, where is that cousin brother of yours, the smaller one? I remember you had a smaller companion, right?"

I was immediately on my toes. There is no way the diner lady knew that Joshua had a brother. My ears and senses just doubled their reception. I asked her," How did you know he has a brother?"

She was calm and said, "Oh, I saw them passing by the diner earlier. The little fellow even waved at me. I saw them going to the supermarket and thought he would be joining you here."

Joshua was unnaturally silent. I was getting irritated by her presence. She seemed to be harmless, but I felt a bad aura around her. I told her, "He was not feeling well, so he decided to stay at home."

I could see that the diner lady was feigning surprise. She said, "Oh, apologies if I am stepping over a boundary, but I would be very careful leaving kids alone at home, you know, because of the scream last night and the events that have happened afterward. There seems to be something weird happening in the hotel. When I went there today to clean the rooms, I overheard the manager talking to someone asking for a large shipment of bleach. On a normal day, ordering a large amount of bleach for a hotel is normal, but after the scream last night, I am not so sure."

I had half bitten into my sandwich. Joshua was still silently slowly biting into his food, and the diner lady was waiting for me to swallow mine, which put me under pressure to finish the mouthful. After I swallowed my food, I asked her, "So, you work there?"

She responded, "I'm not a permanent employee there, of course, but the hotel manager, Kobi, asked me to help out during the day while Klaus, the supermarket supervisor, takes care of the place at night. This arrangement was agreed to continue until he gets someone to permanently take ownership of the hotel and find a good team of housekeepers."

She seemed pretty pragmatic about it and explained it in a matter-of-fact manner, "Klaus actually gave me a ring to let me know that if I have some time, I could take you to the hotel and get your bookings in order since I have to go there anyway."

Chapter 8: The Diner

Interesting. I was still thinking how were they planning to open the entire hotel without any staff? Yet here I see her running a diner without any staff and am genuinely mesmerized. I saw Joshua eating the last morsel of the sandwich. He hadn't said a single word since he got the food. He sipped his coffee and probably did not like it as he grimaced and asked the diner lady, "I'm sorry, where is the restroom?"

"Sure, go down this aisle, turn left, go straight. It's the last room to the right."

"Thanks."

After Joshua left me with the diner lady, I looked outside directly at the sea-green Subaru. To my surprise, the diner lady sat on Joshua's chair. She held my hand and said, "Listen, Sarah, I'm sorry I did not bring this up, but I did not know who the kid was, and I did not want to ask personal questions in front of him. Do you know where Marko is? The last time I saw him, he was not at a good place mentally."

Here we go again! I was close to losing my temper. Why was everyone chasing Marko, and how did these people even know about him? I asked her, "How could you possibly know Marko?"

Here was that feigned surprise again. "Come on, Sarah. You and I have been friends for a long time, and I was scared to see Marko last night all worked up. He came here at four in the morning. I was sleeping soundly, but he barged in the door, and the bell woke me up. He was completely drenched and sat on that table there." She pointed to the first table close to the door and then continued, "He asked for some coffee, and when I got him the coffee, I saw blood on his shirt and the hilt of some cutlery in his jacket."

She said all of this in one stretch, and I was assimilating this information with trepidation, but thankfully I was so sure that Marko couldn't have done anything that I was desperately looking for holes in the story. It just couldn't be true that Marko was a monster.

"You said you heard the scream as well, right? Didn't you wake up and check if it was close by?" I asked.

"I did, actually, but I saw no one. Just darkness. So, I went back to sleep,"

"You're saying that shortly after that, Marko came over?"

"Yeah, but I wouldn't say 'shortly after' because I had actually been able to get back to sleep again."

"Why would he do something bad, spend some time elsewhere, and then come to the diner, of all places, when he knows I'm at home?"

"That's what I wanted to ask you. Did you guys have a fight or something?"

"I honestly don't remember our last conversation. The scream woke me for a bit, but I immediately took some sleeping pills and did not see him. When I woke up, he was not there as well."

"What about your daughter? Have you seen her? You kept telling me a lot about her, and now I know so much it's almost like she's my own. Why didn't you bring her?"

All my bravado was now vanishing. The diner lady's questions were bringing me back to the depressing reality that I was alone now, and there was literally no one to help me. Joshua was around, but he was not family, and yet again, I felt lonely. I looked down at the espresso and started circling my finger around the rim of the cup. I just responded, "No. She isn't at home as well. That is why we are going to the hotel to find them and see if the scream had anything to do with Marko and my daughter."

She was silent for a while, probably because she understood I was in pieces. I felt this entire conversation was more of a mild interrogation, and she basically got no information from it, so she's giving me her finishing punch line.

She stopped her line of questioning and said, "Listen, it is imperative you tell someone if you speak to Marko. I know you love him dearly, but he could possibly have done something wrong. Klaus told me that he was in the supermarket earlier yesterday looking for a meat cleaver and a rope. This morning, he lands here with bloody clothes. If you see him or anyone close to him, let Klaus or me know. Okay?"

She wasn't even trying now. I could see right through her lies, but for some reason, I did not want to confront her. I wanted to just pour out everything in my heart to her. I asked her." Why not the police? Can't I just go to the police and tell them everything so that they can do the needful?"

The diner lady was fidgeting with her thumbs now. She did not expect a change in the script. She stuttered and said," W…Well, the police are mostly useless down here, and they don't even have a station, so looking for them in this town is mostly futile. You know that already, don't you? Your best option is to let one of us know."

What did I really know or remember? Internally I had sensed a change in her behavior already. I knew from what Joshua said that there were only five buildings. I couldn't remember a police station, so maybe it was behind the hotel or something, and she did not know about it, or maybe she was telling the truth. My mind was getting scrambled. I asked her," You said you and I were friends, and you even know Marko. How is a thirty-something girl friends with me? What do we talk about – menopause?"

For the first time, she seemed truly surprised and hurt. Maybe she was good at faking those emotions." Oh my, Sarah. Are you alright? You and Marko used to come here every morning and order honey pancakes and orange juice. That's your usual here. You are frequent visitors, and we have had a lot of conversations about you, Marko, and your daughter. I feel hurt."

Her face changed to a light pout combined with a frown, and silence was her weapon now. I was not going to be able to continue this conversation further and wanted to end it soon, so I told her, "Look, I'm sorry. I don't remember you. I really am, but there are a lot of things I don't remember, like why I'm here or what I had spoken to Marko before he left. I met Joshua and Pogo a couple of hours ago. Before that, I had no idea who they were or that we were neighbors. So, I am not exactly in a good place to really remember you or anything else. I've got so many questions to ask, and I don't know who can answer them. I don't know where my daughter or Marko is, and the lack of knowing anything is killing me."

She seemed to empathize with my situation, held my palm, and said, "It's okay, dear. We all go through tough times. Like I said, I work the day shift at the hotel. Let me take you guys there and make sure your stay is smooth. I'm sorry I brought anything up."

On cue, Joshua came back. I finished my sandwich and sipped my coffee, but I was not able to finish it. I turned to the diner lady and said, "I'm sorry I unloaded it all onto you. If you're okay, can we go now since Joshua is here as well."

"Yeah, sure. You guys get going outside. I will close up and be out in a minute." It was a speedy exit, and she disappeared to the back of the diner.

Joshua did not seem to have changed his no-talking rule. He just nodded, saying he was ready to go, and I took a last sip of the half-glass of espresso and walked out of the diner. The people there seemed to be lost in their own world. They also seemed to have forgotten they had food on their plates. The fisherman's son had taken just one bite from the burger. I was sure we had stayed at the diner for quite some time, and this looked out of place.

Joshua and I walked outside the diner and into the car park area and I realized that my back pain was much better. It was present but bearable, but I began to immediately feel cold. It was like someone close to me had left. Somewhere inside me, I wanted to go back to the diner. Finally, we passed the parking lot and reached the grassy path that witnessed all the anomalies happening here.

Chapter 8: The Diner

In a couple of minutes, the lady came out wearing her light blue blouse and skirt. She seemed to have left her apron in the diner. She joined us under the DINER sign and said," Alright, folks. Are we ready to go?"

Joshua finally broke his silence and extended his arms to shake her hand, and said, "Hello ma'am. I'm Joshua."

The diner lady's face reddened. She said, "I know your name already, Joshua. Sarah told me about you. I'm not that old for you to call me 'ma'am.' Just call me 'Tonks.'"

We began our walk to the hotel. Tonks was walking faster than us, and I was slow because of my back pain which still reminded me how old I was. I turned to look at the diner one last time.

There were no people in it anymore.

Chapter 9
Fender Bender

Tonks, Joshua, and I were an unnatural trio. We were musketeers but from different phases of life. Joshua was young with a lot of life ahead of him. Tonks was an enigma, and then there was me, completely lost with no idea where my husband and daughter were. We walked past the supermarket, which I clearly had blacklisted in my "places-to-visit" list. I could sense the dread when I passed the entrance. Tonks walked fast, but Joshua was walking ahead steadily.

We did not have to walk a lot before we reached the highway, but surprisingly there were no cars or signals. As a matter of fact, there was no zebra crossing or traffic. It was just a road which was the first entry point to the hotel. Tonks had quickly crossed the road and reached the other side, but Joshua stayed back on this side.

I stopped focusing on the anomalies because I wanted to know what was happening in the hotel, which had become my priority. The hotel finally was in view, and I read its name for the first time. In fancy fonts and pink color was written "*The Bender.*" What a weird name for a hotel, but that was beside the point. The hotel was a skyscraper. Even from across the road, I could see its never-ending spire forming a stairway to heaven.

I held Joshua's arm, turned him towards me, and said, "Joshua, what happened? What's wrong with you? You have been silent for quite some time, and you spoke only to introduce yourself. Was it something I said?"

Joshua turned to me and asked nonchalantly, "Sarah, did you notice that there is no traffic at all on this highway. Do you know of a highway that has zero traffic?"

"I don't know. Maybe it's the afternoon, so not a lot of highway cars."

"There is no zebra crossing as well."

"Yeah, I had noticed that."

"There is more. Do you see something weird about the hotel?"

When I first looked at it, I did not observe anything specific. I squinted my eyes to examine the external façade of the building. It did not look any different, but I was now observing small cracks in the beautiful five-star picture that this hotel had painted. There were windows all around the building, and I just lost count after a while. The spire design was very plain and was painted dark purple on the outside, with a streak of black running through the entire length of the tower as far as I could see. I couldn't see people, but at this distance, it would be impossible to see them anyway. I turned to Joshua and said, "No, I'm not able to find anything different."

"Notice the distance of the hotel from the main road. It was exactly on the road when I went to the supermarket earlier today. Now it has moved some distance from the road. I am sure that its ten feet from the road now."

He was right, but I did not feel bad about not noticing. I was a simple woman with simple tastes. I observe the obvious but not stuff like Sherlock Holmes does. I responded, "Yes, you're right."

He then continued, "Do you remember what Tonks had asked us after she gave us her food?"

I thought for a while, then replied, "Yeah, she asked where your brother was. I felt it weird that she knew you had a brother."

Chapter 9: Fender Bender

He looked forwards and shook his head. "No, she asked where my cousin was – 'cousin.' No one knew that we were cousins. Not even you except for five minutes before she brought our food. I am sure there was a bug on that chair, and she was listening to our conversations."

When he started connecting the dots for me, that's when I realized what had happened. My eyes wide, I said, "So that's why you were silent? You did not want to give away any information?"

"Yes precisely."

"But why does she need to listen to our conversations?"

"I don't know but considering the interest that both the supermarket supervisor and Tonks have shown in your husband, I would assume it has something to do with that."

"Wouldn't the people there have done something if they were tapped as well?"

"I saw the reaction of that jogger pair when you kicked their feet. They said something mundane instead of 'It's okay.' That is not normal. I don't think those people were real."

He was right. When I left, I had noticed that the people just disappeared a short while after Tonks left the building. A new fear dawned on me. I realized the blunder I had made and cursed the moment I thought of visiting the diner. I began perspiring, and Joshua looked at me and caught the visible change on my face. It was not anger but apprehension. I told him," Joshua, I think I made a big mistake. After you went to the restroom, she sat with me and told me that she and I were old friends. I still did not believe it was true, but I told her who you were. I also told her about my husband and my daughter and that we were going to explore the hotel for information about them."

"What did she say about that?"

"She said that if I knew information about my husband, I should either report it to her or Klaus. Klaus is the supermarket supervisor."

"I know who Klaus is. From her reaction, since she did not bring up the police or stop you from going to them, I believe she wants us to go and check out the hotel. This has piqued my curiosity even more, but we must keep our distance from her. She seems to be a master manipulator."

"Yes, you're right."

He then turned to Tonks and realized that she was out of earshot. He asked out loud, "Hey Tonks, do you know where this road goes?"

She replied quickly. This was something she had probably rehearsed many times. "I don't, actually. I spend all my time inside the diner. I have no idea where this or any road would go. Come on, now. Don't lag."

Joshua turned to me. "How will we lag if there is no traffic signal? Obviously, this road goes nowhere and was constructed especially for this location. No car or bus will traverse here because the concept of vehicles isn't here. I had expected that she wouldn't know where this road went. This only strengthens my suspicion about her involvement in all of this and the hotel itself."

I nodded in agreement like a kid nodding at her teacher in spite of having no idea about what the teacher was teaching. He began walking forward, and I followed him solemnly. I realized that he was right and that there was no traffic and no traffic signals. The road was pristine clean with not even dirt on it. The white road-paint still looked fresh.

Ahead of us, Tonks had already opened the hotel door and was calling out to us, "Hey, you guys are lagging. C'mon faster."

"Okay, coming... Sheesh!" Joshua was clearly frustrated by this pressure and increased his pace. I followed him briskly into the hotel.

At the entrance we saw a big cardboard placard which read...

WELCOME, PLEASE ENTER

It was as grand as a hotel could be. The center of the vestibule had a beautiful fountain. Streams of water extended from the central fountain to both sides of the hall. The fountain and the streams were flanked on both sides by golden pillars to create the illusion of a shiny, gold boulevard. Decorative plants added aesthetics to the entire hall. The floors were spotless, and sofas and chairs seemed adorned with costly velvet.

There was a man at the far end of the room at a short distance from where the water extensions terminated. He wore a three-piece black suit with a purple tie. As we walked closer to him, I could see that he had well-combed hair and a well-maintained beard, almost like Clint Eastwood. He seemed happy being there and had a positive aura around him. I was careful now since I had felt the same feeling when I had entered the diner, and here was another person who looked amicable but could be shady.

Tonks had already reached the table and was talking to this individual. We strolled leisurely, imbibing the entire domain. As we reached the table, Tonks turned to us, then back to him and spoke, "Hey Kobi, these are the two guests I told you about. Klaus had extended a free stay to them to be able to help provide feedback on the hotel services."

Surprisingly this hotel had no computer. Kobi, as Tonks had called him, was busy noting something down in a ledger. His fountain pen probably was directed towards impressing an older crowd to make the hotel look like a historic relic. He looked at Tonks and said, "Thanks, Tonks. I'll take it from here."

That was Tonks' cue. She nodded her head and left saying, "See you, Kobi. I am going to the kitchen to prepare the meals for the guests."

So, there were folks here already, meaning more people. I did not trust anyone now. If they did not respond like a human, I was staying away.

Kobi seemed normal enough, though. He brought two of his fingers to his head and gave a salute to Tonks in acknowledgment. He then turned to us.

"Hi, My name is Kobi, and I am the manager here at The Bender. You'll notice we are a bit short-staffed, which is why we are getting help from Klaus and Tonks, but rest assured, the service you will receive here will be the best. We are re-opening the hotel to the public very soon, and you are beta-testers for us in a way. With your feedback, we hope to be able to improve our services."

This time Joshua quipped, "For a hotel that is focusing on hospitality, how many rooms have you set aside for this beta testing?"

"There are around four hundred rooms as of today with guests in them. We are getting continuous feedback on various aspects of the hotel."

"Who gives them room service?" I ventured to ask.

"Well, since Tonks is here, she does during the day, but she doesn't stay overnight, and Klaus is supporting the night shift until we get someone permanent. Can I have your names please?"

We gave him our names, and I followed up with another question. "Can one person support four hundred people? What is the trouble getting someone more permanent?"

Kobi was now looking at his register, "You know how the labor market is. No one really wants to work as a bell boy or even in the hotel management industry. Everyone wants to be an architect or an investment banker on Wall Street. It's tough to get folks to support this industry, and the pandemic made it even worse. So how many rooms are you looking to book?"

"Two please," I said.

"Very nice. Will you be joining us for just a night, or do you want to stay for one more night? I can throw in a free night as well if you'd like to stay for more time."

"For now, let's stick to one night. I then asked him in earnest, "Can you tell me when you were posted here?"

"I'm afraid I must admit that I was allocated to this hotel a month ago, and I just joined today. Coincidentally, so did a lot of our guests. Do you have any luggage you would like us to bring to your room?"

Chapter 9: Fender Bender

Joshua said, "No, we just came to have a look at the rooms. Once we are comfortable, we'll come back later." He then raised another concern, "We are not members of your hotel's loyalty. We did not even know your hotel existed. On what basis did you instruct Klaus to get guests for your hotel?"

He was now shaken and faltering, and he looked at us directly so that we would not see his pen making random scribbles. "We usually extend it to members only, but this time we needed more concrete feedback from the public. That should have included a test group of people who had no idea about the hotel, which is probably why Klaus offered this to you.

Somehow, I was not surprised. Kobi turned and called out to Tonks before we could ask anything else and asked her to take us to our rooms if we were ready.

"Tonks does the morning shift, so she will take you to your rooms. What about the smaller guy? Klaus mentioned you had a brother as well."

One thing was certain, Klaus, Kobi, and Tonks talk to each other and know more than they are telling us. I did not want to give any more information to him, and so I said, "He will join us a bit later in the evening. For now, we'd like to see the rooms before we bring him here."

"That shouldn't be a problem. Tonks will take you to the room. Your rooms are 2110 and 2120. When your brother is ready to come, Klaus can pick him up if you want. It's not safe, especially with the scream that apparently many heard last night. I feel it would be better if he had an escort."

I leaped at the opportunity to ask him about the scream. "We were all wondering if the scream came from the hotel. Considering that the hotel is receiving strangers and that it's still going to get new people, it's possible that something untoward happened to someone. Do you know if something really happened in the hotel?"

His face suddenly became serious, as if we had asked him to give us his family jewels. He nodded his head and said grimly," Unfortunately, I cannot give you more information, but the police have been here this morning. A girl was found dead in one of the rooms. I am not sure which one, but Tonks was the one who was with the police helping them with anything needed from the hotel side. I was not here yet, so I did not have knowledge of the room number or any more details. From what I know, we don't even know who she is or what the motive was. You could ask Tonks when she takes you to your rooms."

A chill ran down my spine. I had witnessed acute torturing in my life by Madam Costa, but never death as raw as a carcass. The thought of a dead girl shook me to my core. I was breathing heavily when another thought came to my mind.

"Kobi, can you tell me if the girl was fifteen years old?"

"No, she was twenty-one. Tonks mentioned this before she left for the diner earlier today."

I looked at Joshua, and he was back to not speaking, thinking about what to do next. I wish I could do that, but I had been so lonely all my life that I needed to speak my mind to be able to ponder and consider solutions.

Kobi then seemed to read the situation and made a failed attempt to break the ice. "Don't worry, folks, you won't need a lift operator to reach the twenty-first floor; it's easy to use. For room service, you can always dial 9, and either Tonks or Klaus will help you.

"Follow me, folks. The twenty-first floor has the best view in the house."

Tonks showed up out of nowhere. Was she there all along? If she was the one helping the police with this murder, why did she act innocent in the diner as if she did not know what happened? Tonks was hiding something.

I was a bit relieved that the girl was older than my daughter, but nevertheless, a girl had died. Joshua seemed to relax as well when he heard that a twenty-one-year-old girl had died. He was still silent, but I thought I caught a smile on his face before he reached the elevator.

We were still breathing slowly as we followed Tonks to ascend into the heavens, hopefully not literally.

.

Chapter 10
Is this the End?

The path to the elevator was not a long one. Tonks led us from the hotel manager's desk across the main hall to a small winding corridor into the heart of the hotel. An audacious symbolism of wealth was what I could think of when I saw the golden walls. Tonks led the way as usual, and Joshua and I were slow and absorbent of our environment.

We finally reached the two elevator doors, one of which was already open by Tonks. There was no operator, and I had to assume Tonks was also the lift operator now. She ushered us in and pressed the button to take us to the twenty-first floor. The door to the lift closed very fast, but the lift itself started moving excruciatingly slowly. I could almost feel the pain it was in to drag us up. Joshua seemed on edge but was silent for most of the time as usual.

The lift was moving slow enough to get me worked up. Tonks was staring at the lift ceiling and fidgeting with her blouse button. I needed to think out loud, so when Tonks turned around, I caught her attention and said, "Maybe one of our first recommendations would be to speed up the lift. Moving to the twenty-first floor mustn't feel like a bus ride."

She looked at me as if I was being a Karen about it. Her expression was clearly that of apathy. She just said, "Yeah, sure. Will pass it on to

Kobi. Just for your information, though, these elevators are hydraulic, which is why they are so slow. There are plans to make them more sophisticated with better safety measures once there is more traffic in the hotel."

For someone who is temporary, she had way more information about this hotel than I had thought would be necessary. She immediately crossed her arms and looked up, essentially telling me to back off with the questions. I did not want to challenge her at this stage. I could hear the slow pull of the elevator finally stopping with a big jerk, which almost threw me off my balance. We must have reached floor twenty-one.

Tonks opened the elevator and directed us to move out. She followed us and shut the elevator doors. As we exited the elevator, we were greeted by a pleasant smell of lavender. My feet felt different on the carpet floors. I had a weird urge to rub my feet on the carpet just to make them feel good, but I restrained myself.

There was an analog telephone at the far right of the elevator, and adjacent to this telephone was a large window extending from the floor to the ceiling. Opposite the phone, flanking the window, was a fire extinguisher that probably was never used, considering the dust that had accumulated on it. Joshua stepped to the window but wasn't impressed by what he saw. I walked towards him, and he looked at me and said, "So much for the view." I did not understand what he meant until I looked outside the window myself.

The window was completely dark, as if someone had painted the other side black. Considering that the window was common for the entire floor, it seemed a bit odd that it was pitch black. Tonks walked towards us and seemed irritated that we were paying so much attention to detail. She said irately, "There are cleaning works happening now, and so the windows are blocked by black fabric. It will be clear in an hour." I was not sure why she was trying to rationalize all our questions as if she wanted us to believe what she was saying.

Chapter 10: Is this the End?

Tonks was now beginning to give me the creeps. She was no longer that jovial, amicable lady at the diner. She had now transformed into a reclusive woman who was clearly hiding something. We walked together to the center of the corridor, and Tonks stopped at the big signboard. It read:

> *2101-2110 <-*
> *2111 -2120 ->*

It looked like Joshua and I would be staying at opposite ends of the hotel. Well, at least we were not in different floors.

The corridor was lit by a single strand of light extending all the way from the center to the last room on either side of the signboard. The lighting was minimal and disturbing. I had to squint to see what was ahead of me. As a five-star hotel, the minimum requirement I can think of was to have good lighting in the corridors and an ice-vending machine, at least.

Tonks then spoke seemingly to distract us from further observing anything else, "So Joshua, you will be in room 2110 and Sarah will be in 2120. Would you like me to take you to your room?"

Joshua nodded, and I quickly saw this as an opportunity to explore rooms without Tonks hovering around me. I said, "Alright, I will wait here while you show Joshua his room." Tonks clearly did not like the idea, but there was no way she could say no and not reveal something incriminating. Eventually, she had to accept my proposal. She and Joshua began walking down the corridor, and after getting out of their peripheral vision, I moved slowly to the first room, 2101. I considered this the best opportunity to look at all the rooms, at least on this floor. I had to devise a plan later to look at all rooms on different floors.

As I neared the door, I heard a groan. It was like a tied animal groaning at its own misfortune, almost like a bear stuck in a trap. I was sure it was from room 2101, and as I slowly tried to place my ear at the door, my head moved forward, and I almost lost balance. The door was ajar, open for my investigation.

Could it be Marko? The sound was clearer now, and I had to consider the possibility that Marko was in there and could be in trouble. I decided to investigate.

As I slowly pushed open the door to the room, I was welcomed by the smell of urine and feces. I quickly covered my nose and mouth to prevent myself from vomiting. Walking through the mini corridor was like walking into the gallows. To the left of this corridor was a wall-hugging mirror, and to the opposite was the washroom. The presence of this disgusting stink in the room made me think if the occupant really understood the use of an attached washroom. I took a detour into the washroom to make sure no one had died in there, as the bathtub was the most common location where people chose to die. Movies had almost sensitized everyone to bathtub deaths. The bathtub in this room had its curtain drawn, and I wanted to turn back and save myself, as this would be the point where the corpse gets up and devours me, but I was in too deep, so I pulled back the curtain.

No one. Thank God!

That was a relief that at least there were no dead bodies. I left the washroom and walked across the mini corridor to the wider room. The room did not have a bed. Surprisingly I couldn't see the furniture in the room itself because there was only one hanging light bulb at the center of the room. Below it was a chair, and on that chair was a boy not older than fifteen. He was not tied to the chair, but I saw blood below it on the floor along with the source of the foul stench. He was wearing torn, three-fourth shorts and a blue football jersey. His head was tilted to the side across his shoulder, and his hands were hanging down motionless. His groans were the only sign of life I could notice. I moved in closer to the boy and tried to touch him, asking him the most futile question, "Hey there, are you okay?"

Chapter 10: Is this the End?

I think the boy's senses were seriously dulled because he realized I was in the room only when I had asked him that question. The boy's head was straight now. He turned around and all I could see in place of his face were scars of burnt eyeballs and pus all over. His ears had been ripped out, explaining his lack of hearing. His face was half beaten, and his jaw was dangling to one side after consistent punching. His tongue was hanging down from his upper throat, and I could feel the extreme pain he was in, probably unable to utter any form of words. His hands were still loosely hanging, and his tibia had been shattered. He got up from his chair and limped across the room towards me.

With his limited eyesight and loose jaw, he tried to mouth, "KOBI IS A FAG!"

I was scared out of my wits, and I stumbled back to the door, which now seemed extremely far. I crawled on all fours and finally reached the door. I opened it with force and shut it with a bang. I turned around to see Tonks and Joshua waiting for me outside. Looking at Joshua made me feel a bit more comfortable, but I was breathless. I waited a while to catch my breath, and Tonks then asked me, "Sarah, why did you go into someone else's room? It's illegal to do that."

I struggled to slow down my panting and said, "Tonks, I saw a kid being tortured in there! You need to get help. Call the police and report what's going on in this room!"

Tonks responded rather calmly as if she knew already what was in the room. "Guests do not like being disturbed, Sarah. Your room is the other way. Joshua insisted on accompanying you to your room, so can we make a move now?" Joshua was standing behind her but had a grim look on his face.

"What the fuck are you talking about, Tonks? There is a boy in there who has burnt eyeballs. If you do not call the police, I will!

I began walking to the phone, and my profanity seemed to have scared her. She countered, "Okay, I will take a look and arrange for some first aid if someone is really hurt in there."

I did not care. I needed her to get the police and sort it out. The boy needed serious help. What kind of vile creature could torture a boy to that extent? Tonks opened the door and went in. I wanted to follow her but didn't want to see the boy and his disfigured face again. After almost ten minutes, she opened the room and asked us to come in.

I was surprised. Joshua had no clue what was happening, but he followed me anyway. Tonks was now brimming with anger. She escorted us through the mini corridor to the main room and what I saw was uncanny.

There was a beautifully made king-size bed at the center of the room. The lights were on, and there was a night lamp on the side, which was fluorescent blue. The room was no longer smelling of refuse but was fragrant with the same lavender from the main corridor. There was no chair or dangling light. There definitely was no tortured boy.

Tonks looked at me and asked, "Sarah, where is the boy I need to help? I don't see any tortured boy. Who should I complain to the police about?"

I was stuttering now. "He…, he was right here! It couldn't have been a dream. I saw his burnt eyelids and his broken jaw!" I turned to Joshua, "I'm not lying, Joshua. I am not crazy. He was in here!"

Joshua had one look at the room and pulled me to the side, "Sarah, I know this building is different from the others. It can adapt much faster. I don't distrust you, but there's nothing you can do now. It has adapted already."

His words stung me. Could this really be a unique building like Joshua mentioned? Tonks was losing her patience now. She said, "Sarah, please respect the hotel rules. We do not allow guests to enter other guests' rooms. Luckily, this room wasn't occupied, but you cannot keep doing this. Am I clear?"

Chapter 10: Is this the End?

I had to accept defeat for now, but I pondered over what Joshua said. The building had adapted itself when it was under threat of exposure which got me thinking, what exactly was it hiding? There was no coming back from this mentally. What I experienced was inexplicable at best and supernatural at worst, but there was clearly no proof of that scenario existing. I had to give in for now and follow Tonks to my room.

I did not speak much as we walked to my room. I felt defeated and lost. I was sure of what I saw and wondered what triggered the room to change. What exactly was this place? I was getting progressively scared, and Tonks' behavior was not reassuring. Joshua had retreated into a shell, and I was alone to deal with all these anomalies.

Tonks slowed down her pace to make sure I was not peeping into other rooms, but this time, I made no detours. We passed by a lot of other rooms, and almost all of them seemed to be occupied. Tonks being close meant I could not hear what was going on inside, but some of them were loud enough to be distinctly identified as cries of kids, women laughing, and sometimes even dogs barking.

I asked Tonks, "Are you sure these are guests? What is a dog doing inside one of the rooms?"

She replied nonchalantly, "We don't have a pet aversion, Sarah. Can we move on?"

She was clearly being a bitch about all this. Also, did she just say "we"? First the lift and now "we"? She was supposed to be part-time here, but she seems to have a lot more invested in the hotel than she's telling us.

We finally reached the room and waited for Tonks to open the door. She pushed the door open and asked me to enter. Joshua offered to enter the room first. I was planning to follow him when I heard a soft thud a couple of minutes after he went in. My first reaction was that Joshua tripped on something and fell. I immediately entered to make sure he was okay, but as I entered the mini corridor of room 2120, I could sense that there was something off. I walked into the main room and was greeted with a sweet smell of lavender on my face, but then I saw Joshua on the floor and a dead girl on the bed.

Tonks followed me shortly after, and when she saw the scene from above my shoulder, she let out a gasp. I began to become extremely sensitive of my surroundings now. I had been doing that a lot lately. My first instinct was to help Joshua.

I turned to Tonks and said, "Tonks, I need to get some water for Joshua. I don't see any drinking water around. Can you get that?" My focus was twofold, Joshua and the girl, although the girl was clearly getting all my attention

Tonks replied, "Okay, I'll call Kobi and ask him to come as well. I think as the hotel manager, he should be around to oversee what happens and how the situation unfolds." She then left the room abruptly.

My brain was processing the new information over the next couple of minutes and, at the same time, was concerned about why Tonks was taking so long. I did not feel comfortable with the way the body was arranged. Joshua was on the floor unconscious, there was a dead girl on the bed, and I had a feeling that Tonks was trying to micromanage me. Yes, I had entered a room without permission, but I didn't need babysitting. She was back a few minutes later saying, "Kobi is on his way and is bringing water."

"Why did you not just take it from one of the guest rooms, or better still, why can't I find any water here in this room?"

"We cannot disturb other guests or let this information leak out any further. I think I forgot to refill the water in this room. Anyway, let's make sure this stays within these four walls."

Chapter 10: Is this the End?

While waiting for Kobi, I began observing the environment. The girl was the center of the entire scene. Her eyes were open, and there was a peaceful pallor on her face. I couldn't say if it was surprise or sadness. Her hair was left unkempt above her head. Clips were on the floor beside her black locks. I could see her dried, lifeless lips parted to reveal her tongue, which was now blocking the path to her already putrefying throat. Her irises had decomposed, making her look almost as if she had cataracts. Rigor mortis had already set in, and the blood had most likely dried, suggesting she'd been dead for more than just a couple of hours. Below her open mouth was a curved red line with congealed blood. The open wound scared me, and I was in no way ready to look at the decomposed skin around the neck. From the distance that I was standing, it almost felt as if her neck was smiling to compensate for her not being able to. Her left hand was over her torso close to her slit throat, almost like she was trying to stop the bleeding. Her right hand extended beyond the edge of the bed. Her bra had small metal spikes on them, and she wore leather spandex. What a weird combination of clothes to die in! Her right leg was bent like a "7", and her left leg was straight. I felt a strange aversion to this girl. She fit the profile of the girl referenced by Kobi, and this girl had to be the source of the scream as well, but how could we confirm for sure?

I thought to myself, "A murder has been committed. We don't know who or why but somehow, the room was allocated to one of us." This was far from a coincidence.

I turned to Tonks and asked her, "Tonks, Kobi knew about this murder in the hotel, right?"

"That's right."

"Did you know about it?"

"I was around when the police and forensics came to gather evidence."

"How did you not know that room 2120 was the room where the girl died? Wouldn't you remember when you were walking to the room or in the corridor?"

"Actually, I was not sure which floor I was in when the police showed up. I was on some floor, most likely this one since she's in here." She pointed to the dead girl and continued, "I was going to enter one of the rooms to clean when the police barged in from the elevator and started searching all the rooms. I had provided them with cleaning services and water while Kobi was busy with the new guests, so he doesn't know about this as much, which is probably why he allocated the room number, and I honestly couldn't remember the room or the floor."

The answer was not convincing at all, especially the statement that the police used her services for cleaning, but I had nothing else to go on. Since I was waiting for Kobi to bring the water, considering Tonks was not willing to do so, I tried to find a place for Joshua to sit once he was up and awake. I looked around and noticed that the corner of the room had some chairs that could be used for Joshua to sit. I turned to the dead girl again. There were some stab wounds on her chest and exposed abdomen. I was trying to gather my thoughts when Tonks touched my shoulder.

"I'm sorry you had to undergo seeing this mess. Kobi is on his way up. She is most likely the source of the scream we heard last night. Do you, by any chance, know who she is?"

"Why would you ask me that, Tonks? What makes you think that this girl is someone I know?"

"You said your daughter was missing? Could this be her?"

"I don't know. Didn't you ask the police when they came to do forensics? They seem to have left the crime scene exactly as is." I looked at the girl again. She looked familiar, but I couldn't pinpoint the exact location where I could have met her. I did not tell this to

Chapter 10: Is this the End?

Tonks as she wasn't really being trustworthy as of now. Could this be my daughter?

"The police did not tell me anything. Why would they think they needed to be answerable to a hotel maid? Maybe we should check out some of her belongings. It might help identify her."

"No, we cannot. This is a crime scene. We need to wait for the police to come back to do their job. Why isn't Kobi here already?"

Tonks went silent and stepped back to the door to check if Kobi was arriving. She was getting impatient. I could sense it. I was now kneeling beside Joshua and saw her walking towards me. She seemed tensed about something and finally spoke, "Okay, Sarah, I'm going to be honest with you. I am a member of the police department here. I was sent here with Kobi to investigate this murder. We knew about this murder already, like Kobi had mentioned, but we needed to get more information on the identity of the girl. We have isolated this girl to be potentially related to you or Marko, and when you said your daughter was missing, we knew that you could identify her. That is why we need you to help us understand who she is and who could have wanted her dead. With Marko missing, our only inference will be that he had killed her and has gone into hiding."

My head was spinning, but my mind was now blank. Did I just hear that Kobi and Tonks were police officers and that this was a setup because they knew she was somehow related to me or Marko?

I was gradually getting my brain functions back and was trying to put two and two together. There was a dead girl, and the police did not know who she was or who killed her. They traced her identity to me and Marko and now want my help to identify her. But I don't recognize her myself. How could I help them with my current knowledge of the situation? Maybe she was related to Marko...

"Okay, where is Marko, then? Why haven't you brought him in?"

"As we stated before, Marko has fled. The last time he was seen was early this morning at the diner. He has been missing since then and is somewhere out there, but he is hiding well, and we cannot really find him. That's also why we need your help to identify the woman and then tell us why Marko would want to kill her."

I manage to croak, "So this entire charade was to get Marko and me here, to see her and identify her? So that you can track the killer and figure out his motive? Marko wouldn't kill anyone, so you have it all wrong." I made sure she was aware of my anger. I did not care that she was a police officer. To me, she was a deceitful, manipulative leech.

Tonks replied, "Unfortunately, yes. So do not worry about the police. We are the police. If you find something which can identify her, that would help us a lot."

I was hysterical now. "Then why didn't you just get us into an interrogation room and follow the usual process?"

"We tried, but we couldn't get any information. We interviewed a lot of folks, and that's how we became aware of you. We were told by our psychologist that if you or Marko saw the crime scene, you could give us information which we may have missed."

This was insane! If people kept getting witnesses to crime scenes and reliving crimes, we would be having a lot of traumatized victims and witnesses. What kind of stupid excuse was this?

Soon, Kobi came up. He seemed very calm for someone handling a crime scene in his hotel. He whispered something to Tonks, and she directed him to put water on Joshua's face and wake him up.

As Kobi walked past me to wake Joshua up, I asked him, "Don't you guys register guest details? Her identity should be in one of your registers, right?"

Kobi was surprised at my query but answered, "This is not an official stay, remember? We don't register any of the guests yet since the hotel is not public. This is more of a beta-testing." He sprinkled some water on Joshua.

"If you're police officers and this was a ploy to get us here, surely getting guests to register now shouldn't take a long time, right?"

Chapter 10: Is this the End?

It was Tonks who responded. "The plan we had executed was real, and so were the actual people who were given free stays. They still think all this is free, so we cannot change it without looking suspicious, and we do not want to alert the killer. Look Sarah, every minute you waste gives the killer time to escape. As a police officer, I give you full authority to observe or touch anything that could give us more details about the girl's identity. Could you look around and see if you can find anything that can help identify her?"

I was not ready to give up. She has clearly lied all her way up until now, and I wasn't going to trust her about the room. I ignored Tonks and turned to Kobi, "What about room 2101? Do you know who stays there?"

Kobi shot a glance at Tonks, and there was a sudden fear in his voice, "How did you open 2101? It should have been locked as there are no guests there, and we have a strict policy about guests entering rooms which are not theirs."

I replied, "It was already open. I went in, and I saw a young kid who had been tortured and was calling you a fag. When Tonks went in and came back, the room had changed, and the chair and this tortured kid were gone. How can you explain that?"

Kobi was clearly fumbling for an answer when Joshua's hands started moving. I ran to him and held his head on my lap. He opened his eyes slowly and said, "I don't know what happened. I feel weak."

"Relax, Joshua. You saw a dead body and fainted. It's not an uncommon reaction."

"No, I did not faint when I saw her. Kobi had already mentioned her at his desk earlier. I was going to see who she was when I blacked out." He sat up and looked over at the girl. "She seems very familiar."

Ignoring Kobi for now, I looked at Joshua and said, "I felt that too. Joshua, there is a chair at the far end of the room." I pointed to the chair in the corner. "Sit there for now, and we'll figure out what to do next."

Joshua said, "This is a crime scene. How can I move there? I can stand here. That's okay. Let's wait for the police."

I insisted, "It's okay." I looked at Tonks and then back at Joshua." Tonks and Kobi are police officers. They will explain later. For now, go sit there, please."

He did not seem to have the energy to argue, so he just walked to the other side of the room across the edges of the bed, narrowly grazing down at the congealed blood. He sat down on the chair and tried to catch his breath.

With Tonks in the main room, Kobi at the door, and Joshua on a chair in the other corner of the room, I thought about what had happened in the past fifteen minutes and contemplated what to do next. We found a dead body of a girl. The lady escorting us was a cop. They seem to be searching for a killer in the hotel, and both me and Joshua somehow know this dead girl.

I was hellbent on just sitting there and doing nothing. Why should I try to figure out this girl's identity? I am not even a cop, and this is not my job, but somewhere deep down, I feared that this may be my daughter. Even if it is just to confirm whether she is or not, I decided to help Tonks. I turned to her and asked, "I am not doing this for you, so don't get any wrong ideas. Are you sure I can have a look around? This will not be breaking any laws, right?"

Tonks nodded, "And the faster, the better. I'll join you as well."

Tonks and I started looking around the girl for any form of identification. Tonks was rummaging around for some information when she found the girl's black leather blouse below a three-legged stool at the left side of the bed.

"Hey, I found a blouse. This is probably what she was wearing." I had a detailed view of what she had in her hand. I don't remember the cloth or the leather material, but I had an ominous feeling that somehow my daughter was involved. This feeling was becoming more of a premonition now. I did not want to find something I knew for fear of identifying her as my daughter.

I spotted a bottle of spilled pills below the drawers. I picked them up and examined them. There were mostly pink pills, and I saw only three of them. I passed them to Tonks, and she said, "This looks like ecstasy. I cannot determine if this was used by her or brought by the perpetrator. Forensics will have to identify the substance from her bloodwork. Let's carry on."

The presence of drugs made me scared and skeptical. This girl was now involved in drugs, and she was also wearing leather spandex, which is not something you wear on normal dates or even silent getaways. What kind of twisted fantasy was this girl caught in.?

The entire atmosphere had changed now. Joshua was still gathering his wits. Kobi was being neutral at the door and not getting involved. Tonks and I continued our search for this Holy Grail of the girl's identity. We continued to the side of the bed where one of her hands extended. Something was calling out to me from below the bed. I walked towards her lifeless hands and noticed the wallet on the floor below her hand. She must have dropped it or nudged it when she was being killed. I bent down to pick up the wallet, but my hips touched her hand and disturbed another object on the bed, which fell to the floor.

It was bright and shiny and immediately caught my attention. My intention to pick the wallet was overcome by this object, and when I picked it up, I realized it was a beautiful ring. It had an opal stone engraved with "**TOGETHER FOREVER.**" No sooner had I picked it up than I was surrounded by blinding flashes of light.

*

I was now at a place with a large crowd of people frolicking around. From the looks of the decorations, this was a wedding, and I was in a church. The church itself looked old, with its dilapidated walls demanding immediate renovation. Yet its old walls and the cross at its top gave this place a charm of its own. People were busy talking to each other, probably about baseball or their next day's work. Champagne was being passed around. A band was playing melodious music on a stage. I was feeling lost when I noticed the dead girl running towards me in her wedding dress.

The girl was excited and bubbly. Her wedding dress made her look like a wild snowflake dancing in the wind on a cold morning. She looked at me and said, "Mom, Dad, what are you doing outside the church? Everyone is looking for you!" I did not know how to respond.

She then held my cheeks and kissed me. "Thanks so much for this, Mom. Paul loves you guys, and I'm happy you like him as well. He is an orphan, and all he is looking for in you are parents to love. He could not have asked for anything more. Look at this ring he got me. It's so beautiful! I cannot thank you enough. I love you!"

I was soaking it all in and admiring her beautiful face when I heard a voice from afar, "Hey Julia, are you coming over?"

She looked away towards the crowd near the center of the church and said, "Yeah, Paul. Give me a minute."

She turned towards me and said, "Got to go, but don't stay out here for long. Go meet people and let loose! Love you."

She referred to us as parents, so I wanted to have a look at Marko to make sure I remembered him well in the memory. Thankfully I did. My only daughter was getting married, and she was marrying the love of her life. She was settled now, which was more than what any parent could ask for. I couldn't remember what Paul was like, but I'm sure she selected well. I turned and looked at Marko's face. That was the face of

Chapter 10: Is this the End?

a proud father. He was as proud as I was. There was nothing in the world that could equal his love for her.

Something had changed…

*

I was transported back to the hotel room, but I knew I was not the same again. All my memories were flooding back now. I think looking at Julia brought back all my memories, but I realized how much better off I was without them. I could feel guilt and dismay flowing through my veins. My legs were shaking, and I was unable to think. Everything around me was going black. Was I phasing out? If Tonks was able to see me, she would see my eyes gorging out and staring into the void into which I wanted to lose myself.

I had just realized that this girl was indeed my daughter, making my nightmare come true. Nothing around me mattered anymore because she was murdered mercilessly, and I was culpable. I knew who killed her and why, but I did not do anything about it. All memories of her started flooding into my empty mind. I have heard this is what happens to people who are about to die, but I was glad I was seeing my memories about her and not about me. I remembered when she first fell at home and started crying. I remembered when she first got a fever. I recalled the pink dress she so fiercely loved, which she had worn for that years' Christmas party. I recalled her beautiful wedding to Paul. It was like watching my favorite movie about my daughter that I had sincerely loved. She was now dead, and I couldn't do anything about it.

A gut-wrenching scream escaped my mouth, "No! No! She's dead! This is not right! I let her down. She did not deserve this. We did not deserve this."

I did not have the willpower to continue with my life. I did not want to find out what happened because I already knew. I glanced at Joshua, then back at Tonks, and I bolted for the door. Tears were running down my cheeks and bouncing off them into the air as I ran as fast as my feet could take me. What I witnessed was my sins getting back at me. Tonks was God's messenger, and I had no intention to oppose his judgment of my scruples. I was ready to meet my Maker.

I ran outside the door and into the corridor. The dim light helped to hide my tears, which were now overflowing. I finally reached the center of the corridor, and to my left I saw the window that would be my salvation.

I took the fire extinguisher and threw it onto the window. The sound of breaking glass spread through the entire floor, but I was not interested in any of that. When I looked outside, I was spellbound. I was able to see the diner and the supermarket and even our homes. Beyond the visible land, all I could see were squares of nothingness. It was like computer pixels after our homes. There were a bunch of squares surrounding this entire world.

I thought to myself that I was right. This was a world made-up by God, and Tonks had just meted out my punishment. I got to relive my daughter's death again, but I do not want to relive it anymore. When I looked up, I couldn't see the sky, but the brightness of the sun did all that it could to prevent me from doing the inevitable. The sunlight or the source of light in the sky blinded me as I stared into it. The pain surged through my head, but it was no comparison to the pain in my heart.

"I'm sorry Julia," I whispered to myself and jumped through the window. As I plummeted to my death, I could feel the ground and all my life hitting me in my face. Thank God this will be the end…

…or was it.

Chapter 10: Is this the End?

I regained consciousness with a lot of pain. All my organs were shutting down in no specific order, but the pain was only exponentially increasing. I wouldn't even want my enemies to be in this state. I was groggy and opened my eyes. Looks like my sight was still intact with a lot of black spots in my vision, probably by staring at the sun. I couldn't hear, but I could still vaguely see. I looked down and saw my body was intact, but my legs had been shattered and were strewn across the ground. I fell from twenty-one stories, and physically, all parts of me had covered more ground than I had ever covered while I was still one piece. How could I still be alive? Oh, great Lord! Could you take me with you?

Thankfully, as if the Lord himself answered my prayers, the last image I had was a large hairy foot on my face.

My senses and me were dead.

Somewhere in Greenland

The trio entered the door, which had been opened for them by a lady in military uniform. Another gentleman was guiding them into a large viewing room. The trio had not seen anything like this before, and they had survived many tight situations in their life to live this long.

They stopped at the center of the viewing gallery, and the guide approached and faced them. His excitement was palpable. There were five people sitting on a chair dressed in normal clothes but with a large, liquid-filled helmet on their heads. The subjects were breathing, but their chests were not moving in and out, which means they were getting their oxygen from somewhere else.

"As you can see. This is going to be a revolution in interrogation. Our operatives are engaging the persons of interest with great dexterity. We are sure we will be able to glean information that could give us the needed breakthrough for this case. Our success will pave the way for groundbreaking interrogation tactics. We are now at the cusp of greatness, and you have made it possible. These people have artificial gills attached to their necks, which takes in the oxygen from the liquid around them, like a fish. We also pass them a constant dose of a sedative to make sure they stay unconscious unless pulled out explicitly by our operative."

"What about the operatives and persons of interest? Are they safe?'

"Perfectly safe. The techniques are non-invasive." The guide now allowed himself to chuckle. "It is impossible to die unless they kill themselves. The best part is the time. Would you believe that they have gone under only for around ten minutes? I am sure our operatives have probably spent ten times that time getting information."

The trio seemed to be happy. Their investment had paid off, and they were going to make millions selling this technique.

The lady who had opened the door now ran towards the guide. She seemed tense and on edge. She whispered into the guide's ears, "Commander, we're losing him. His vitals look stable, but I don't see any brain activity."

The guide was now taken aback. How was this possible? He pulled her to the side and asked her," Do you know who these people are? Why did you bring this up now?"

"But sir, we've lost him. I don't think he made it."

"How is that possible? Did he not wake up?"

"We don't know, Captain. We will have to ask our operatives once they are back. His vitals spiked for a bit and then came back to normal, but I am not getting any more feedback on the EEG. He should have woken up, but he did not!"

The guide was shocked. The electroencephalogram, or EEG for short, measured the operative's brain patterns. Why had it stopped responding? He spoke now to the lady.

"Can he talk? What about the polysomnograph? Did we get any specific external pattern which could have triggered this in him? We need to know what he saw in there, otherwise, try to contact Tonks." The polysomnograph records the brain waves, the oxygen level in your blood, heart rate, breathing, and eye and leg movements. If there was something that triggered it, we should have been able to catch it there.

"I'm not sure, Commander. He may look okay, but he's taken a major hit."

"I don't care! Try to reach Tonks."

"Commander, he's in a coma. His mind is no longer capable of basic functionality. We need to make sure what happened to him will not happen to the others."

Somewhere in Greenland

"So, try and reach Tonks ASAP, and don't question me. His mind is no longer functional, and without a mind, he is no better than a plant. Focus on the other one and do as I say."

The lady was hurt, but she left. The guide returned to the trio who were curious about what happened.

"A small bump in the road. We are in the process of fixing it. Nothing to worry about."

Unfortunately for the guide, the lady returned, this time with an apathic expression on her face. "Commander, we just lost another one. Her vitals spiked for a while as well but soon became normal, and there was no brain activity after that."

This was going to be a long day.

PERSPECTIVE
KLAUS
(King of the Jungle)

*"If you want to control someone, all you have
to do is to make them feel afraid."*

-Paulo Coelho

Chapter 11
Might Is Power

"Klaus, why are you bullying me? What have I ever done to you?" said the boy whose lunch I had just eaten.

"I'm not bullying you. I'm just reminding you that you are weak. Consider this a lesson for life and thank me later."

Yeah, I was not a very good person when I was young. Some might argue that I'm not a good person even today. I was not very good academically. I did not go to the best colleges, and I was unable to finish my higher education, so some might say I'm not that smart as well. Do you know what I am? I am a finisher, and I can get the job done. It may seem to be a skill easy to find, but this was what got me into the army.

My old man tried very hard to explain to me that bullying was the coward's way out. I couldn't relate to what he said. I had the capability to take what I wanted. Why wouldn't I? I did not want to save the world and all these weak nerds. My motto has always been "Take what I want. Do what needs to be done."

This has not been a hundred percent successful. I had had women reject me multiple times before I joined the army. They said that I am brash and aggressive and that I do not give enough in the relationship. Well, if they really wanted something from me, they needed to only ask. I was never inclined to give something for free.

The last girlfriend I had, had taken things a bit too far. She started making fun of my manhood. She said stuff like, "A real man gives selflessly; you are just a wilted willy." I did not take it seriously initially and asked her to suck it, but she started smacking me. I could smell alcohol on her breath and wasn't going to let her get away with smacking me. The next thing she remembered was being at the hospital with six stitches on her face. She sued me, and my father had to spend a major chunk of his savings hiring a costly lawyer and making this case disappear. Apparently, she was not a credible witness because she was drunk. Meh.

I don't think there's something wrong with me, but my father was one of the first people to tell me that I have a serious lack of upbringing because I did not have a mom. She died when I was born. Well, if he says there's a lack of upbringing, it's his fault, not mine. I do what needs to be done to survive.

My father got scared of leaving me to myself without supervision. He probably thought I would become a serial killer or something, so he suggested joining the army and asked me if I was interested. Initially, I was not very comfortable with letting myself be bossed around by someone else. My dad insisted and threatened to cut off my inheritance if I did not join the army. He was loaded, and I needed the money. I'm sure he figured that in the army, either I might change and become a good person or die in the line of duty. Either way, he gets rid of the current me. I chose to oblige and joined the army.

The experience was completely worth it. Never had I seen this form of brotherhood or a power-hungry bunch of men, and I was not talking about my peers but about the higher-ups. Everyone wanted to bomb everyone else, and we were just their hands and legs. The testosterone was high, and I learned a lot of good things, but the best lesson learned from the army was that there is more than one way of achieving a goal without actually using brawn. That was why I loved the army.

Chapter 11: Might Is Power

I was recruited into the 1st Battalion of the 800th Infantry regiment. With my platoon, I had served at multiple locations like Afghanistan, Syria, and most recently, Serbia. Kabul was where I learned that you don't always need to hit people with the butt of the gun to get them to give you information. Money, threats, even reason works sometimes.

In Kabul, we pursued a war criminal who was not ready to get caught, and when we finally did catch up to him, he had only one demand: to find his ex-wife. It wasn't unreasonable, and we did help him find her. She was living in a suburb in the United Kingdom, except he killed her with a handgun at first sight. We, of course, did not expect him to kill her, but he gave us what we needed.

The cost of information was always high, and there would always be collateral damage. All my operations had their share of challenges, but it was fun and also helped me develop a skill to figure out what your opponent needs and then possess the object to essentially possess them.

Alternate routes had helped me more than I had imagined in my career and as a person. I was still the same brash, narcissistic pig, but now I was a bit classier about it. I tried to avoid using force to get what I wanted. People manipulation was something I had tried to master, but I was never completely successful. I was still tending to go back to the ways of the force rather than the ways of the brain. I was so good with force and had used it creatively to succeed in so many tight situations that one day I was summoned by Commander Barnes to his chambers.

Commander Luke Barnes was a legend. He had captured an entire barrack of enemies alone with a knife and a broken leg. His war stories could be used as history textbooks or strategy lessons interchangeably. He was known to take the riskiest decisions and get the most rewards because he did not fear going against the flow. When I was called, I knew this discussion with him would be interesting.

I entered his room and gave him a salute. He was seated on his rotating chair, looking outside the window. When he turned around, I saw him speaking on the phone. I quickly saluted, and he motioned me to sit down as he continued speaking on the phone, "I won't take no for an answer, Steve. You know that. Now give me results."

I have heard of the legend but never seen the legend angry. He smashed the receiver and immediately regained his composure. That's how legends work. They can switch on and off at their will.

"Klaus. How's everything kid? I heard your last trip to Mozambique was very eventful. You brought back a snitch from the rebel ranks, right?"

I looked at him. He calmly asked me a question about my previous endeavors, but he was assessing me, measuring my response, my posture, my confidence. His clean-shaved face revealed no emotional expression. The military cap hid his neatly cut white hair. His forehead was smooth, and the lack of glabellar lines clearly revealed his aversion to show emotion. His eyes saw right through me.

"Yes, sir. It was a tough mission, but we were able to turn one of the rebel warlords to give us information. He was forced to leave his unit, and after we promised the safety of his family, he happily obliged."

He took a folder on his desk. It was a thick folder, and he flipped through some pages and stopped when he reached somewhere in the middle. He then said, "I have read your performance records and victories in the field, and I am very impressed. You have shown great persuasive skills, and I like your approach."

"Thank you, Commander." I had never expected to get praised by my hero. I was on cloud nine.

"Do you know why I have called you in today?"

"No, sir."

He stood up. The chair shifted to the back and hit the wall. He took a few steps to the side and started looking outside. "Klaus, I am

Chapter 11: Might Is Power

currently working on a project with large-scale positive implications in the surveillance space. The details of the project are on a need-to-know basis, but if you want to understand it at a high level, it is a large surveillance-enhancement project. We need you to train within certain parameters as directed by the lead scientist on the project, and you need to be able to perform certain tasks to facilitate the propagation and successful completion of this surveillance."

He then turned around, put his hands on his desk, leaned towards me, and looked me directly in the eye, "Are you with me up to now?"

"Yes, sir."

He leaned back upright and said, "You will need to put a lot of additional hours into this. Based on your psyche evaluation and your history with different operations, you have shown great physical and mental resolve and your problem solving is very good. You have the power to influence, and we need to use that. This will be nowhere like the other training you have taken part in. It's actually far from it. You will be introduced to something completely new, and your learning curve will be high." He paused here but continued in a more conversational tone. "I am confident you can do it. You will have the support of more team members, but this will be your show and your operation." He once again put his hands on his desk and leaned over at me, changing his tone to one of a commander, "Are you clear?"

"Yes, sir," I replied in a loud voice.

"Do you accept the operation and the role?"

"Without a doubt, sir. Yes, sir!" I did not need to think or reason or ask anyone else. The legend chose me, so my answer was always going to be, "Hell, yeah!"

"Good. Now go make us proud. If this works out, you will be ushering in a new era of surveillance and interrogation. Weiss will brief you later. He is the lead scientist."

*   *   *

"Later" was ten minutes after the meeting with Barnes, and later that same day, I was on a chopper to an unknown location with Dr. Weiss. We were sitting opposite each other in the chopper. He was looking outside, probably thinking about his calculus equations which he was unable to complete due to this mundane activity called travel.

His Einstein-like hair and Kepler-like beard made him almost look like a hobo, but when I heard the briefing and the training to be done, I was sure he was more than what he looks. Always dressed in a torn sweater with dark-colored pants, Dr. Weiss was the epitome of simplicity and modest living. Without a family, he had dedicated his life to neuroscience and psychology.

I asked him, "Doc, if this works, are you going to receive a Nobel Prize?"

"I'll be long dead before this works, Azubine. I hope you have what it takes to complete it by then and train the others."

Well, I'll show him. I have what it takes and more!

The chopper roared, and he turned to look outside towards the passing scenery.

From the chopper, I could see we were flying over a dark forest, and it was almost evening. The sun had set, and dusk was showering us with only limited light. As I squinted my eyes to look far into the horizon, I saw the silhouette of a building just barely visible in the limelight from the setting sun. It looked small from afar but as we closed in, it took the form of a large facility like one of the Mass Effect locations with bright lights and large complexes. It had a central tower and multiple local sites for different functions. I could see I might be spending a lot of time here.

This time Weiss looked at me and said sarcastically, "Here is where we all come to die."

* * *

Chapter 11: Might Is Power

Life, as I knew it, had changed. It did not take me long to realize my training goal. It was to build a location to intimidate a target, but it must be able to draw a crowd in. For example, if many people were being monitored, they must all be willing to enter this location. That's when I got the idea of a supermarket. It was a common building and indispensable. I even would enter a supermarket that had Pennywise the Clown if it was the only one with milk in it.

As time passed, I became clearer on the role of this supermarket. Over time it had transformed into a well-constructed location but still wasn't really a masterpiece. It took me three months to start building the supermarket, and subsequently maintaining it was substantially stressful. It was not something that would really scare me. What I had built was a supermarket, plain and simple exactly what I had initially wanted, but it did not feel like what Commander Barnes would have envisioned. My ideas for the supermarket were changing. I wanted people to be scared out of their wits, enough to tell me secrets without thinking twice.

That's when I got the idea of creating the infinite aisles, which took me more than a year to create and was possible only after Tonks had joined us. Its execution itself was a nightmare, and I was unable to maintain the aisle enough to trap people. I tried different ways of extracting energy, some from myself and some from the targets, but that did not work. That's when Tonks came in. She was new to some of the military processes, but she was a million-watt battery. She was able to help power the aisle, which gave me enough time to train and build power to fuel it myself. Tonks was gifted, and she did all this while she was building her own location, which was her diner. She was extremely powerful and strong-willed. I could say that my vision wouldn't really have come true without her.

It was inevitable that I would hit on her, but she rejected my advances, and I recused myself gracefully, but I still have feelings for her which she doesn't know. For the first time in my life, I did not pursue an interest by force. I think it was because I respected her dedication and willpower to complete her task. She helped me complete my infinite aisle while she was constructing her diner, and that was indeed commendable. It was almost like she was my equal or even superior. There would have been a time when I would have bullied her just for the heck of it, but not now. In retrospect, I felt that the operation had made me grow and mature in ways I couldn't think possible. Tonks was a good friend now, and she runs the diner, and I run the supermarket.

*   *   *

Idyllic memories were making themselves known to me on this boring morning. The scream was meant to begin the engagement with the targets. We entered the world when the sun rose and were waiting for the action to start. Our targets were Sarah Miller and Marko Flannagan. Our instructions were to keep interaction as reactive only, so we couldn't go looking for them though we knew they were here. That was the sad part of a stakeout, or as we liked to call it, minimal interaction surveillance operation (MISO). You need to wait for the action to come to you in a MISO.

I am not fond of this method and am inclined to always find out a way to bring the action here.

Chapter 12
The Infinite Problems

Memories of my training were spinning around in my mind. It was almost like watching paint dry. I was cleaning my knife and revisiting key milestones in my army career when I saw two boys walking towards the supermarket. Sensitive to the fact that our targets are fifty-year-olds, the presence of a barely post-teen and pre-teen kid surprised me. The Commander did not tell me about any boys, and I was never good with kids anyway.

The first layer of the supermarket was to instill a sense of doom in whoever entered. The air around the supermarket was dosed with fear, so anyone around the supermarket would be scared and would want to take shelter in a safe place. The kids might have reached that specific stage because now they were clearly getting a bit quirky. Considering they were kids and could get spooked easily, I decided to invite them in so that I could speak to them and understand how they reached here. That's when I realized that I did not explicitly invite them in. I needed to put up a signboard that read "Welcome All," similar to how Kobi does it, but I decided I could think more about that later. I then called out to them and asked them to come in, hoping to get some information about Marko or Sarah or how they reached here. They had to be here because they had some relation with Marko or Sarah, and I needed to know what that was.

Both the kids seemed extremely perceptive. It was understood that if one wakes up in a foreign land, one might become extra sensitive to their environment, but the smaller one saw the entrance of infinite aisles fast. The bigger one probably was looking for something specific. I needed to strategize how to extract the information from them. I was deliberating whether to separate them or to interrogate them together. I could sense they did not like me, but they might as well get in line.

I think they had almost split up, but the smaller one got a bit scared and decided to join the bigger one. I needed to wait for them to enter the aisles themselves, so I began thinking about how I had initially struggled to create the infinite aisles due to the lack of naming conventions for the aisles. It was Tonks's idea to make small changes to products and then stock them accordingly, which was brilliant. It had worked well on a lot of fellow military officials when the trials were running. Now hopefully, it would have the same effect on these kids as well.

The kids finally entered an infinite aisle, and the ball was set into motion. Both clearly sensed that something was wrong as they witnessed the ingenuity of the never-ending path, but I wouldn't intervene yet. I was spending all my energy maintaining the infinite aisles. It was relatively easy now with the years of practice. The kids, not giving much resistance, made it easy.

In the infinite aisles, the kids were probably already experiencing all the horror it could offer. The smaller one started panicking. After all, he is a kid and was not used to handling or maintaining one's cool during situations like these. I dropped everything and focused on separating the smaller one from the bigger one as I knew this would only scare him more and aggravate the situation. I saw the separation as an opportunity. I added a barrier between them so that they couldn't see each other, though physically, there were probably just a few feet apart. The bigger one was still doing okay, but the smaller one was breaking down.

Chapter 12: The Infinite Problems

I was still trying to decide whom to question about Marko and Sarah. The younger one seemed to have lesser knowledge than the older one and was almost on the verge of a meltdown. I decided that the likelihood of the older one having more information was higher, and he was relatively more stable. I freed the elder one from the infinity aisles. "Freed from the infinite aisles" means that the target now sees the exit from the aisles.

Once he was freed, he immediately saw the exit and ran towards me. As he exited the aisle, I asked him, "Kid are you okay? What exactly happened? I heard some screaming and crying. Where is the smaller one?"

He was shaken. He looked back at the aisle catching his breath, "That aisle! It's not normal! What is this place?"

"What do you mean? I don't see an issue here."

"This aisle is never-ending. I could not see the end of this aisle. Are you telling me you do not know?"

I helped him up because he was on all fours, panting and trying to catch his breath. I asked him, "You mean that end?"

I was pointing my finger towards the aisle, and when he followed its direction, he saw the other end of the aisle. There was a set of wooden boards and a mop at the other end and quite possibly a door to the warehouse.

"That's not possible! I am sure that I walked and sprinted for a long time! It cannot be. Where is my brother?"

"That's what I was asking you. I thought you guys went in together."

The kid just left without saying anything and started calling out his brother's name. How rude!! I realized his brother's name was Pogo. He was now scanning all the aisles for his brother, but he wasn't going to see anything. I made sure of that. I thought to myself that broaching any subject now while he was distraught was a bad idea. During the testing, this method had worked on many fellow military peers, and they had spilled a lot of beans, but with him, I had a feeling it wouldn't work, so I decided to allow the smaller one out as well. When both have recovered from the shock, they would probably give me more information.

I freed Pogo from the infinite aisle. The bigger one continued calling Pogo's name and Pogo soon called out back to him. The bigger one ran to the aisle where he was able to see his brother curled up into a fetal position. I think I took it a bit too far with the kid. I had obviously not tested this on kids, so this was new to me as well.

I needed to make sure this was debriefed to Barnes. I was glad he did not die, but the kid had lost a lot of his grit and energy. He called out, asking his brother to come to pick him up from where he was. The bigger one ran in and soon came back with Pogo, who had already passed out. I did not want to risk anything else with them, especially with the impact on the smaller kid, and so I thought it was best to give them some space.

The bigger one now was completely spazzed out. He did not know what to do. He came to me with anger and rage.

"What have you done to him?"

"I'm sorry, kid. I have done nothing. I am just a supervisor. I don't know what you're talking about."

"You know what's happening here. What do you want from us?"

"Nothing. I don't know what you're talking about. Do you want me to bring some water for him?" I pointed to Pogo. I could not ask him anything now while he's in this state. I needed both to calm down.

He seemed to back off and went back to his brother. I stepped to my cash desk and picked up a water bottle and passed it to him. He started dripping water onto his brother's face, which eventually woke him up. His brother was despondent and was mentioning their mother. The bigger one no longer cared. I was close by and was able to listen in on their conversation.

Chapter 12: The Infinite Problems

The kid mentioned something about water helmets and Sarah, which clearly meant that he had woken up. This was not something I had experienced, so I panicked because Pogo had clearly woken up and seen the operatives in Barnes' location. I was glad the kid did not die, but if he woke up in the real world, it means he was extremely traumatized, which was not something I had wanted to do. This was not something I was proud of, so I chose to keep this to myself and not mention anything to Tonks or Kobi. Thankfully the folks on the outside were able to save him and send him back.

I was also able to glean some information from their conversation about their mother, who left early to some location that they did not know. From the briefing, Marko and Sarah had a daughter Julia, so Sarah couldn't have been their mother. If that was true, then who was this character, and how had she entered here? More importantly, what is the relevance of these kids in this world?

The elder kid now realized that the faster he escaped, the better, so he began leading the younger one to buy what they had come for. When they gave me their bread to scan, I thought it was now or never, and this would be the best time to broach the subject. They were just out of a harrowing experience and possibly more docile than normal.

I calmly inserted their parents into an already tapering conversation. The elder one was defensive about the topic. I had expected that and tried to bring up the scream to maneuver them into the hotel so that Tonks and Kobi could then use that location to glean more information about Marko and possibly Sarah, but the kid denied hearing the scream, which was impossible. The scream was a planned encounter that every suspect here was supposed to hear, and so I was certain they must have heard it. That meant that either he was trying to avoid the question, or he was lying.

Thinking on my feet had always been my thing, and now I got had a good incentive to make them move to the hotel. I mentioned to them that their mom could have possibly been working at the hotel so they could even go explore and investigate what their mom was doing. Who can reject an opportunity for free exploration? The main motive was to get the kids to bring at least Sarah or Marko to the hotel, and I had a feeling they were somehow bound to meet.

I tried to get more information on their mother but got nothing which was disappointing, but in the end, I got the kids' names. I almost thought they wouldn't tell me, but Joshua and Pogo were not spies who needed to keep their identity secret. They were right to be skeptical; I'll give them that. On the other hand, I felt that they were also confused about this entire encounter and were trying to figure out how they reached this location and what to do next. There was nothing premeditated in their actions. They appeared just like a bunch of kids in the wrong place at the wrong time.

Joshua was adamant about leaving and was clearly not interested in the proposal to visit the hotel with an adult. From his perspective, it was right since he and his brother were just terrified out of their wits. I tried to manage the situation by explaining that the offer still stands if he changes his mind. They really did not care and just paid and left.

Overall, this was not what I had expected. I had almost killed a kid out of fright. I got little or no information about Sarah or Marko. The kids had a free stay offer that I hoped would lead us somewhere, but my masterpiece had not served its purpose as expected. I couldn't even get information about the kids' parents. The only information I got was the names, and the only thing they took away was their distrust in me.

I needed to regroup with Tonks and Kobi and try to figure out what we could do. Round One went to the kids. I was ready to wait for Round Two to begin. The bait was out, and I wanted to see if the fish would bite.

I planned to call Tonks and let her know what happened and get her thoughts on what transpired, but I decided to wait a little more and

Chapter 12: The Infinite Problems

see if something else happened before I spoke to her. Commander Barnes had warned me about this brash behavior of mine, and unfortunately, he was right. I need to focus more and make sure that I don't fuck up.

This MISO and its waiting games…sigh!! I hate it!

Chapter 13
One of Two

I was still not going to give up and was sure I would encounter at least Sarah or Marko. When testing the supermarket with peers, almost ninety percent of them had always entered the supermarket. That was the charm of a common supermarket. Its appeal to the public, irrespective of age or gender, was its alluring point.

After the kids had left, I was stuck waiting again, but this time I thought about my wife. After finishing my five years of training, I had met her in a library. I thought it was ironic that the love of my life would be a stereotype I would totally bully. She was beautiful in all senses of the word. Her face and personality were always positive. I was a changed man after the training and meeting her soon after brought an immediate desire to spend my life with her. I did not reveal to her my actual role in the military because she just thinks I am a low-fry sergeant, but she loves me nonetheless, and that is why we tick.

Before I left for this assignment, she had asked me why I had to leave for so long, and I had to lie that this was a major operation sanctioned by the president. It might have been, but I didn't know, and I did not want to lie, because she worries a lot. We had bought a small beach house with the limited savings we had, and I was always fascinated by how much time she spent on the beach than at home.

I was taken back to one of those times when she was wearing a purple bikini and reading Michael Crichton's *Westworld* on the mat at the beach. I was sitting opposite her, facing the book she was reading. She was engrossed in the book, but her maroon-edged glasses and sleek body gave me an instant hard-on. When I turned my head, I saw only one of her tanned feet, and as I turned to find the other foot, I realized that her lifted thigh had given me one of my favorite views of her. The margarita in my hand couldn't hide the pitched tent beside her, but she did not even flinch.

As luck would have it, my wet dream did not last long as I saw an older lady moving towards the supermarket. She was a little slow and podgy when walking but at that age, who wasn't? Like everyone, she wanted to come in but couldn't since I had not explicitly allowed it. As she neared the door, I realized that this was indeed Sarah Miller, so I did not want her to stand outside trembling with fear and waved out to her to let her in. I remembered her from the briefing I had with Dr. Weiss. My heart started beating fast, and I could feel my hair standing on end. Now, the game was beginning, and I had one of my main targets entering the supermarket.

As she entered, I saw her expression change to fear. She did not like the supermarket, which got me thinking that letting someone get negative vibes before entering the supermarket was probably a bad idea because they come in with a presumption that the supermarket is evil. It is essentially meant to scare, but they shouldn't feel it until they see the infinite aisles. I asked her if she was really interested in buying something. Everyone rarely was, but it was my duty, nonetheless, to ask.

She came in asking about the staycation that I had offered the boys, which confirmed two things. One was that the boys and Sarah had met somewhere. If they had met at the diner, Tonks would have called me, and if they met at the hotel, Kobi would have called me, so they must have met externally. The second was that the boys had to be related to her somehow, and everything was getting confusing now.

Chapter 13: One of Two

I mentioned to her innocently that the kids had an episode in the aisles, and she seemed to shudder at the thought. She said she thought I was scamming the kids by offering a free stay, which was justified from her perspective. I needed to convince her as an adult to make sure she tags along with the kids and their parents, and best case, bring along Marko. I gave her my usual, standard explanation as provided during training, but then I realized it wasn't going to be that easy. She began asking questions about why I extended the offer to kids and did not use fliers, etc. I was not briefed with the answers but again, thinking on my feet was my forte, so I had evaded her questions until she asked me about the reason why the hotel was reopening after such a long time. I couldn't really think of a valid answer, so I had to shift the blame to Kobi. She seemed partially satisfied with my answer and was planning to leave, but I couldn't let her go without really getting information about Marko. I did not want to leave it to chance for Marko to reach the supermarket, and if Sarah can give me information about him, that would be ideal.

This would need to be as natural as possible. She needed to feel like we knew each other, but she mustn't feel that we know too much to become a red flag. I lightly asked her if she was Sarah Miller and if she had seen Marko. It was possible that Marko was friends with me, so I did not see why she might find that disconcerting. I casually brought up Marko and was preparing for responses to questions she might ask, but as soon as she heard Marko's name, she went into a light coma.

From my training, I realized she was probably seeing a memory, but she was convulsing more than usual. This could mean that she was seeing a memory of Marko and was probably getting a large memory back. Based on how strong the memory was, she would either remember him entirely, or I would need to extract more information or triggers to get more memories out of her.

Considering the number of convulsions she was getting, I feared she might remember enough to get defensive of a foreign entity in this world, and I did not know how this information would change her personality. I was sharpening my knife earlier today and had hidden it safely below the cash register to be used in situations like this. If she transformed into something else that I could not control, I had planned to use the knife. Thankfully, I did not have to use it. When she came back to her senses, she saw me holding the knife and probably got the wrong idea, so I explained that it was just to make sure she had something to hold as it seemed she was getting seizures.

She asked me why I wanted to know about Marko, which means she got a good chunk of memory about him. I made up a story about him coming to look for rope and a meat cleaver, which gave me the motive to follow up on Marko's whereabouts. This was the closest I could think of to make it believable and at least insert a doubt in Sarah's mind about Marko. Maybe then she would tell me where he was, but she clearly did not know where he was, or she did not want to say. Either way, her conviction of Marko's innocence was strong, and I was none the wiser. Tonks will probably have to do her magic on her later.

One thing I was relieved about was that Sarah heard the scream, which means Joshua was lying and did not trust me at all. I needed to keep this in mind when engaging the kids again.

As soon as she left, I gave Kobi a call. I had hoped maybe Kobi had better luck meeting Marko. We all had analog telephones since electronic ones and mobiles couldn't be brought here. I called Kobi, and he did not seem to pick up immediately. I became tense. It was within character for Kobi to do reckless activities, but he was always ready to follow orders and was happy to be part of the team. Why would he not be at his desk? I rang again, and this time Kobi picked up.

Chapter 13: One of Two

"Kobi where were you? Why did you take so much time to pick up the call?"

"Hello, Klaus. Yeah, there was a placement issue in room 2120, so I had to fix that. I was focused on making it as real as possible so we get as much as we can later today."

"Did you speak to Tonks about what you changed?"

"No, I will let her know after this."

"Did you meet Marko today? Did he come to the hotel at all?"

"No."

"Okay, listen, Kobi. You will probably have visitors today. One lady in her fifties, who I've identified as Sarah, a twenty-something kid, and a pre-teen. Keep everything ready as planned. The pre-teen kid couldn't handle the infinite aisle and is pretty shaken up because of it. I am not sure how he will handle the room, so keep all contingencies ready."

"Yes, Klaus. That's what I specialize in – perfection and punctuality. I'm so excited, Klaus! This is my first assignment ever for something of this magnitude and importance."

God, I hate kids! Especially the over-enthusiastic ones. They tend to get excited and fuck things up. I told him, "Kobi, calm down and just make sure you follow all instructions. Okay? Once that's done, we'll call it a day, and I'll get you and Tonks a beer."

"Right, Klaus. Just follow the plan. Got it!"

I cut the call and then called Tonks. She picked up immediately and seemed relaxed. That was good. Tonks was the best among us, and she needed to be relaxed to make sure there was someone to take us home in case we screwed something up.

"Hello, Tonks. Has Marko visited you yet?"

"Hey, Klaus. No. Have you had any contacts with anyone yet?"

"Yeah, sort of. I had some developments I wanted to share. I have not seen any sign of Marko yet, which I find disturbing, but I had two kids visiting me first. One was a kid probably in his early twenties, and his name is Joshua. The other is a pre-teen, and his name is Pogo. They were brothers, as I gleaned, and I am not sure how they fit into this entire world, but I think I scared them a bit too much with the aisles."

I paused to catch a breath and continued, "To compensate, I offered them to stay at the hotel for free. I have not seen who their parents are as the kids were super defensive about that topic. They couldn't be Sarah's or Marko's kids, but they seemed to be related to them somehow because they relayed this offer to Sarah. Sarah swung by and was completely unaware of Marko until I mentioned his name. She has a good chunk of memory about him, but I had to lie about Marko, and told her he had been around yesterday at the supermarket looking for a rope and a meat cleaver.

"I am not sure if they will visit you, but if they do, maintain the lie and maybe put in some of your own to sow the seed of suspicion that Marko could be the killer. If Sarah thinks he is the killer and she has seen Marko, she may reveal his whereabouts, and we can then get him as well to the room in the hotel. If Kobi sees them first, then we will see how we can get involved."

Tonks listened carefully, "I knew your aisle thing was a bit too much. You don't need to scare everyone to get information, you know." "It's a bit too late for that, but point taken. You clear on next steps?"

"Yeah. We'll be waiting for them."

I cut the call. I knew what she meant by 'we.'"

The show must go on.

Chapter 14
I Did Not Sign Up for This

Time here was referential, which means you can say time has passed only if you take a reference. The biggest attraction of this place was the rate at which time moved forward. I had discovered it the hard way when I came back from this place to meet the Commander after my first extraction, and I was exhausted and spent mentally. I asked him if I could go have dinner, and he was surprised.

"Dinner?" He asked," You were gone for hardly an hour." I was taken aback. The fatigue was real, but it did not count for efforts in the real world. That was why this method was a great opportunity for the military. The surveillance may go on for a relatively long time which could be days, months, even years, but once you're back, it was hardly an hour or a couple of hours.

We never stretched our goals to see what one year would be like, but according to Dr. Weiss' calculations, it would be close to half a day in the real world. It saves them time, but it greatly affects the target as well as the operative's perspective of reality. After a year, how would one distinguish between the realities of this dream world and the real world? The brain now must work with two realities and carrying such a burden is not everyone's piece of cake.

It affected me for quite some time, and I just decided to avoid bothering about time because spending time within this world didn't matter. This was a place where time was plentiful. What mattered were observation and extraction of information or details that other or even the targets might have missed. This is called "passive" or "observed" information. This information is inferred rather than imparted, and we as operatives must master the art of extracting passive information.

If I take Sarah's visit as a reference, a relatively moderate amount of time had passed when Tonks called me. She seemed in high spirits and did not wait for me to respond. I assumed someone might be beside her, or she might be in a hurry.

"Hello Klaus, I don't have much time, so I will be quick with the debrief. Sarah and Joshua were here a while ago, and I believe they are onto this world. Joshua seems to have understood that the world is not normal. He observed that Kobi had built the skyscraper too close to the road. Another big news is that the smaller one, Pogo, is not his actual brother but his cousin. We know Sarah has only a daughter, so it's unlikely Joshua is related to her, but he is still here, which means he's related to either Marko or Sarah somehow. I also think I may have slipped up in conversation because he did not speak a single word throughout a major chunk of his time here."

She pondered for a bit and continued, "Sarah, though, was easy to manipulate. She may not believe that I'm her best friend, but she definitely doesn't know where Marko is. She was skeptical about the entire world as well."

I could hear some background noise and realized that she was probably multitasking. I waited for her to continue with more details, and she did, in her matter-of-fact tone, "The reason I called you was to tell you that I have identified an opportunity. Joshua, Sarah, and I are going to the hotel now, and Pogo is most likely alone at their home. This would be a good time to use some minor tactics to get some information from him or maybe even find out Marko's location. Remember, Klaus, he is a kid, so be gentle. Got to go, bye, speak to you later."

Chapter 14: I Did Not Sign Up for This

She cut the call, but at least she had made progress. We now knew that Pogo and Joshua were cousins, and that Sarah had no idea about Marko's location. I doubted that Pogo would know any more about where Marko was, but he was silent as a kid, and you never know. Silent kids are the ones who know the most. Maybe I had misjudged him in the supermarket. This was my chance to redeem myself over the previous mishap in the supermarket, but I would need to be careful as Pogo probably doesn't trust me or, worse yet, hates me. Either way, this was the time to be proactive, and I was glad I could go and do something.

I waited patiently for the right moment and finally saw Sarah, Joshua, and Tonks walking past the supermarket towards the hotel. Once they were out of sight, it was time to start the new plan B. I closed the supermarket door and headed down the grass path. I had trained with Tonks multiple times, so I knew what the diner looked like.

As I approached the empty diner, I realized that Tonks needed to be inside or at least close to the diner to be able to get the people to show up. Now that she was on her way to the hotel, I knew why the diner was deserted. We were warned against leaving the diner or supermarket unattended, but improvisations had to be made.

As I moved past the diner, two houses came into view. One of the houses was barely visible through the dense foliage around it. I was certain this was most likely the house of the kids since their parents were not around as well. The other house was too well maintained, two stories with a freshly mowed lawn. There was a clear bifurcation of the lawn, and there was no way that was maintained by the kids. Generally, adults tend to make sure that the homes they live in are in good condition. The house I was facing now clearly was not well maintained. I braced myself and went inside.

As I opened the gate, I was greeted with the rotting smell of fruits and a one-off visit from a fruit fly. I tried to find the source and saw mangoes fallen just below the mango tree, which were clearly decomposed with flies buzzing over it. I tried to create a path for myself since I couldn't find the actual path to the door, but there was grass all over the place as tall as my knees.

Walking through this grass reminded me of an operation in Bogota. It was to capture a drug lord alive or dead and bust his racket. I was a couple of operations in and was experienced in the ways of the job, but this one was especially exciting because of the change of scenery. I was used to only deserts and cities, but a jungle gave me a wild feeling. The adrenaline high when hiding in plain sight on a tree or in a shrub, was priceless.

There was no need to hide here in this house because as I knocked on the door, I received no response. I gave it a couple of more bangs and finally gave up. I sat in front of the house, thinking what to do next. I thought of moving around the house to see if there was a back door, but I did not see any such opening or entry to move to the back, so I assumed that this was the only way into the house. Even if I could actually have found a way, I wouldn't be able to get in without the explicit approval of the house owner so if no one was in there, I couldn't get in.

Since I was not really having luck with this house, I decided to move on to the other one, which I thought was definitely Sarah's. Maybe Sarah's house might have some information about Marko. She was his wife, after all. I made my way out of the grassland yard and stepped out into the grassy path. The mango tree was witness to all the activities around it. I opened the gate and entered the well-maintained lawn. The path was clearly visible, and it divided the lawn well into two halves. This had to be Marko's work, and he had to be around, at least that's what I hoped. I walked towards the main entrance, and without much hope, I rang the doorbell. I knew Sarah was gone, so my chances of getting in were at an all-time low, but I decided to give it a try anyway.

Chapter 14: I Did Not Sign Up for This

I rang the doorbell, and no one was answering. Maybe Marko was hiding inside. There was no need for him to really hide or fear me, so I knocked on the door once. There was no response. Alright, maybe he wants to play rough, so I decided that maybe a bit more aggression was okay.

I banged it a little harder, hoping he would get scared and open the door, but I still saw no one responding. Well, that was expected considering that no one was at home, and expecting Marko to be here was more of a wish I had than a reality. I was turning to leave when the door opened.

"Hey, Josh…"

His voice trailed off when he saw me. He was clearly expecting to see his brother, and when he saw me, I saw the color drain from his face. He moved his hands quickly to shut the door, but I was fast, and I stuck my foot between the door and the wall. I was still not in his house, so it did not hurt. I was surprised that this beautiful house was owned by the kids and their parents. Multiple questions were running through my head. How were two kids in the same home, and if this was their home, where was Marko's house? The world mandated that everyone here had to possess their own house, and I was now confused as to where Marko could be.

He broke into my reverie, "Let go, mister! I don't want to speak to you! What did you do to Joshua?"

"Hi, Pogo. That's your name, right? I'm sorry I turned up like this unannounced. Please just give me five minutes, and I will explain the current situation."

"No, I'm sorry, but I don't trust you. Your supermarket is evil, and so are you. You almost killed us in there. I know both Joshua and I felt the evil presence, and you were definitely aware of it too."

"Kid, trust me. I have no idea what you are talking about. Why do you think I would want to scare you? I barely even know you."

"I don't know... Maybe you just get off on seeing kids scared. I don't care. I just want you gone. Otherwise, I will call Mom."

"Your mom is not here, Pogo. Your brother told you in the supermarket, and I overheard it. Pogo, don't lie to me. It is important that you hear what I have to say. Your brother's life may depend on it."

I had no other option but to use his love for Joshua against him. I knew that he would consider listening to me if it had something to do with Joshua. I could even see a slight expression change. Fear now became concern, and he was considering the possibility that maybe he could help his brother.

The spark did not last long, and he went back into his shell. "No! I don't want to listen!" He was adamant about closing the door.

"Listen, Pogo. Your brother might be in danger. You might be the only one who can save him. There is a killer on the loose, and he has killed a girl. It was her scream you heard at night. I know you heard it, and your brother lied, but that's okay. This killer is now after anyone who tries to find out more about the girl or this place."

I continued with a grim expression, "Joshua and Sarah have now gone to the hotel to find out more, and this has put them on the killer's radar. Before going to the hotel, Joshua sent me over to tell you that he might need your help later if his life was in danger. I had to run all the way back from the supermarket to tell you this. If you still think you don't want to talk to me, I'll leave. I am going to take my foot back now."

Pogo shut the door as soon as I lifted my foot. It was a gamble I was willing to take. If he shut the door, I have nothing to go on, and I am back to square one, but one thing that the army life taught me was that life favors the brave, and bigger the risk, the higher the rewards. After a couple of seconds, he opened the door.

"Why would the killer want to kill Joshua?", he asked, "I do not see a connection."

Chapter 14: I Did Not Sign Up for This

Today's kids are so smart! When I was his age, I was literally playing with Pokémon cards. I said, "What I have told you is directly from your brother, straight from the horse's mouth. He seems to be a smart kid. Do you doubt what he thinks?"

"No, if Joshua thinks he's next, he may have a good reason. I want to help as much as I can. What can I do to help him?"

"Your brother asked me to search the house for any information about you or your family. I need to search the house to find if there's something your brother has that the killer might want. He believes that the killer may not just be killing people interested in him but may be looking for something specific, and he wants you to help me find it."

The kid thought about it. He was probably weighing in the pros and cons of believing me, but I was sure I had built a convincing lie. It felt like a sin lying to a twelve-year-old. It probably is, but what has to be done has to be done. I tried to assure him, "Let me in, and I will make sure your brother is safe."

He stepped back, opened the door, and said, "Alright, come in. The living room is to your left. You can sit on the sofa. I'll close the door and join you."

I walked in the house and immediately saw multiple points of interest. One was an orange door behind the staircase, which was most definitely the basement. A grey door was open beside it. From below, I could see a blue door on the second floor that seemingly had a lock and a green door that was also open. You did not have to be a rocket scientist to deduce that the grey and the green ones were where the kids found themselves when they got up. The orange door was most likely the basement. I did not know what the blue one was for. Maybe it was the parents'.

I saw the kitchen and the leftover pancakes on the side of the stove. I slowly walked to the living room and sat on the sofa. After a few minutes, Pogo joined me and sat down with me. He did not speak and was still thinking, probably of how he could help his brother. I felt bad taking advantage of him like this, but I knew I had no other option.

I did not want to castigate him for not opening the door on time or intimidate him into revealing anything. The kid had gone through a lot because of me at the supermarket, and I thought it might be unfair to just bombard him with questions. Instead, I started thinking about where I could start looking first.

If the kids had woken up in separate rooms, they would be surrounded by memories that they had kept close to their hearts or had traumatized them the most. Distance from where they wake up would depend on how closely they held that memory. Not having any memory object nearby when you wake up meant that there was no memory that was cherished or discarded, and it was possible that an embedded memory that was deeply rooted in the psyche might have taken shape. Either way, their rooms would most likely have their own memories. I was looking for Marko or his memories.

I asked him politely, "Hey, Pogo, do you know where your dad is?" I knew Marko couldn't be his father, but I couldn't see a connection between the kids and Marko, so I decided to start somewhere.

"I don't know. When I woke up this morning, he was not here. I'm glad he's not around, though. He beat my mom and me a lot."

From the briefing that I had received, Marko was far from a wife-beater. He was actually a very good father and fiercely loved his daughter. I believe it can be confirmed that Pogo's dad was not Marko.

The kid was almost on the verge of tears. This father of his seemed to have traumatized him a lot. I had come a long way in life, and the bully in me was long gone. I felt sad for all the times I had bullied everyone around me. This man exercised the exact same philosophy I had in life, which was to impose one's opinion on others and always take, never give. This was a man who hit his wife and kid because he could and because he felt better when he was exerting power. He was the epitome of everything one should not be. Maybe if I hadn't joined the military or met Angie, I might have been on this same path. I felt a pang of guilt, and I moved closer to him and took him in my arms.

"There, there, kiddo. I'm sorry. We don't get to choose our parents, and I know your dad may not have been a good man, but you love your mom, and she loves you, right? She will come by soon. Don't worry."

That did it for him because he hugged me back and started crying. "My mom won't come back. She is dead. I wanted to show her how well I cycle, but now she can't see that because she's dead. Father killed her and ran away."

He was wailing now, and I was patting his shoulder to make sure he knew he was not alone. I compared notes with what Tonks had told me, which means that I still needed to know who Joshua's mother was. I was not going into details yet because I did not want to leave Pogo in this distraught state.

"It's okay, Pogo. We'll save your brother and make sure you and he can live happily here. I promise." I wiped his tears and told him, "You are not alone, Pogo. We are all here for you."

"We?"

"Yeah, Joshua, me, Tonks – everyone."

"Who's Tonks?"

"You know, the lady who runs the diner."

"The diner lady?" He was sniffling now. "I had waved to her once. I don't know if she remembers."

"Yeah, she definitely remembers."

He became silent again. I pulled him closer and asked him, "Pogo, we really don't have time. If your mom or dad had to hide or store something important, where would that be? Would you know?"

He wiped his tears and thought for a while. He knew this was an important question being asked of him and his brother's life was at stake. He thought about it well and finally said, "I don't know where they would store anything, but most of the stuff that Father and Mom used would be in their room. I had once found a gun in my father's cupboard, so if you're looking for hidden items, that would be the place to look. It's the locked blue room as soon as you reach the top floor via the staircase."

"What about the orange door? You know what that is?"

"No. I have never seen it. I don't remember that door being there."

"Do you know where the keys to the rooms are?"

"No. Joshua had them in the morning, but I don't know where they are now. Maybe he took it with him."

That was going to be a roadblock. I needed to see both rooms, and I did not want to break anything in the house, but from the looks of it, I would have to break into both.

"Pogo, if I need to find out what the killer might be after, I will need to break open both the doors. Are you okay with that?"

"Yeah, if it will help Joshua, then it's okay. Could you try and fix it back before you leave, so Joshua doesn't have to do it?"

"Yes, Pogo, of course. Alright, you stay here, and I will open the doors and see if I can get any information. Alright?"

"Okay, I'll stay here."

I was happy that at least Pogo was now receptive to instructions and probably trusted me a bit more than before. I did not want to take advantage of that trust...yet.

I moved out of the living room and up the staircase. It was a sturdy staircase, and soon I reached the blue door. The door was bolted and locked shut. We did not have the keys, so I was mentally prepared to break it open. I walked all the way to the other end of the room. The green door was open, but I did not go in. I gathered myself and ran shoulder first towards the door, but not even my military training had made me strong enough to break the door. It gave way a little but recoiled back to the same position. I attempted to run into it shoulder first at least three more times, and it still did not budge. Brute force was not going to work here.

I walked down the staircase and back to the living room. Pogo was sulking on the sofa. He was still recovering from the trauma of knowing that his mom had passed away.

I hated to bother him more, but I had to. "Hey, Pogo. Do you know if there's a crowbar outside somewhere?"

"I am not sure. It might be outside the house where the tools are."

"Okay, can you tell me where those tools are? I'll go get them."

"No, I will get them. I want to help as much as I can, and every moment we waste, the killer gets closer to Joshua. Wait here. I'll bring it to you."

He got up from the sofa, sprinted to the main door, and disappeared. While waiting for him, I began to hope that all the efforts to break this door would not be in vain. I needed to get at least some information that would point to Marko's whereabouts.

Soon Pogo appeared again, and sure enough, he had found the crowbar. I thanked the lords and hugged him right there.

"Thank you, Pogo. You did good, and I am proud of you. You managed to maintain your calm and help me in this situation despite everything that's happening to you." I patted him on his head, and I could feel his sense of pride at being part of something. This time he did not sulk. He walked proudly and sat on the sofa. I left him there and walked up the staircase.

I put the crowbar between the bolt and the lock, and once it was snuggled in well, I pushed it open with all my might. It took me a couple of minutes, but the lock finally broke and fell to the ground with a loud metallic thud.

I kicked the lock aside, and it toppled and fell down the staircase. As soon as I opened the door, I was welcomed by the smell of rotting flesh. There was no light, and after essentially being rendered blind, my other senses had kicked in full force.

The room was pitch black. What scared me more was I could hear my own breath as well as another deeper breath somewhere at the far end of the room. As I moved closer, the door behind me was shrinking. I did not want to get lost in a dark room. I would hardly be able to search anything here without a flashlight and getting lost would just make matters worse. As I moved forward slowly, the breathing became louder and heavier. Each exhale released a fresh stench. My gut was telling me to turn tail and run, but I had spent too much effort breaking open this door. I was sure there would be something related to Marko here. As I slowly crept forward, I felt close to something moving in front of me.

I stopped and shouted, "Marko! Is that you? Are you in this room?"

I have seen horror films all my life, and best practices would tell you never to shout in a closed dark space, but logic goes for a toss when you're tense and desperate. Heavy breathing now turned into a slow growl followed by some chittering. A menacing presence now made itself known to me. The growls were steadying and getting closer to me, and I began to feel pure, intense fear for the first time. I stood rooted to my spot, and it was when I heard the angry roar that I realized I should be running away.

As I stepped back, I felt something sharp graze me. I couldn't see it, but I was sure it was a sword or a knife. A knife-wielding monster in a room with two kids was the last thing I was expecting when I broke open the door. As the creature drew closer, its yellow eyes illuminated the area around it, and I could see it was closing in on me.

I was not trained for situations like this and definitely not for a knife-wielding beast. From my little hunting experience, when a beast is slowly approaching you, it is most likely going to pounce at your neck straight for the jugular. This one was slow, but as it got closer, its gaze was fixed on me. Its rage multiplied as it drew closer, and its hungry, starved eyes were yearning for food.

Chapter 14: I Did Not Sign Up for This

This was not the outcome I was looking for, but unfortunately, I now had the attention of this beast. I also realized that now the door cannot be closed since I had broken it. A new wave of panic washed all over me. If the door cannot be closed, this creature would be let loose, and I have no idea how that will affect the other buildings.

I did not waste time and quickened my pace to the door. I was aware the eyes were following me, and as I neared the broken entrance, I bolted for the exit. As I exited the door, I scanned around to find the quickest way out. I looked down the stairs and saw Pogo climbing up the staircase. He was humming a tune and climbing the stairs, oblivious of the peril I had put both of us in. As he saw me exit the room, he asked me," Hey, did you find anything useful in the room?"

"No, Pogo. Why are you coming here?"

"It's been a long time since you went in, so I thought I'd come and help out."

This boy wasn't my son or little brother and wasn't in any way related to me, but after knowing what the boy had gone through, I couldn't just leave him. I was going to save both myself and him.

I was beginning to step down onto the staircase when a huge sonic boom threw me off guard, and I was flung towards the balusters. They gave way, and the next thing I remember was the handrail and me falling down to the bottom of the stairs. I used my left hand to cushion the fall, but now a sharp pain raced through my hand. I looked down and was able to see an open fracture on my lower arm. The radius was broken, and the pain was unbearable.

My head began to get groggy, and I saw Pogo helplessly standing on the stairs. He was looking at me, getting ready to rush down to help me, but then he saw the source of the disruption, and terror took over. He began screaming loudly, "Mummy! Mummy! I'm scared." He was crying hysterically, and I could see that it caught the attention of the blue silhouette behind him. I tried to shout, but only air came out. I mustered my entire energy and cried, "Pogo, run! Pogo…don't…"

My voice was too low. The creature looked at the havoc it had wreaked. Pogo's crying caught its attention immediately, and it had already turned towards him. I couldn't call out to Pogo to move. The blue creature was now clearer to my eyes as it prowled closer towards him.

It had a lupine face with bright yellow eyes focused entirely on Pogo. The knives I had felt earlier were claws as sharp as knives. This creature was well built and a little larger than a normal human, covered with dark blue hair all over. Its sharp toe-claws were biting into the treads of the staircase. For lack of a better word, it resembled a werewolf. Splinters of wood flew everywhere.

I finally shouted as loud as I could, "Pogo! Run! He's right behind you!"

That seemed to snap Pogo out of his hysteria. He turned around and was starting to sprint down when he was picked up like a crumpled piece of paper by the werewolf. The werewolf was now directly looking at Pogo.

Pogo's hysteria seemed to have gone now. His voice was still shaking when he said, "Mummy, I'm coming to meet you now."

The creature who now held Pogo in his arms started squeezing. It was torture to see Pogo struggling. I could hear his bones cracking, and I could do nothing. He screamed as the werewolf tightened his grip and wailed when he did not let go. I couldn't bear to see the kid getting tortured like this. I shouted, "You blue piece of shit! Pick on someone your own size! Leave the kid alone!"

Adrenalin was what drove all of us to decide what to do in fight-or-flight situations. Seeing Pogo getting tortured by this monster gave me enough adrenalin to shout out. What doubled it was when the monster turned its gaze towards me.

I mustered up my remaining energy and held my fractured arm, which was now bleeding all over the place. That's when I heard the pop. I looked up at the monster and saw he still had Pogo in one of his hands but Pogo was no longer wailing or screaming. He was not looking for his mom. His eyes were no longer looking for means to escape, and the dark red line below his neck was not hurtful because his head was now already at the bottom of the staircase.

As the werewolf loosened its grip, Pogo's limp body tumbled down the staircase and joined the severed head. The werewolf, of course, did not care. I glanced at the fallen head at the bottom of the stairs, and I could swear I saw a small smile. It wasn't one of those toothy smiles, but a smile, knowing that there was light at the other end of the tunnel.

I had failed Pogo. I had endangered him and myself. I needed to fix this before I endangered everyone in this world. I needed a place to chain the creature or trap it to prevent it from escaping just as it was trapped before I freed it.

I could not enter the diner now since Tonks wasn't there and taking the wolf to Kobi was not an option. He could technically get us out, but he would be bringing this werewolf with him as well, which I couldn't allow. The only other option I had was to take it to my supermarket and trap it in the infinite aisles. This was a big risk, and it posed an impending danger to my supermarket and my life itself. I had long lived for myself, and I just saw a twelve-year-old decapitated in front of me. I couldn't let this monster run loose here. This is not what I represented.

I would trap it and maintain it in the aisle until someone is here to extract me out. That was the plan, sort of. There was nothing else I could think of.

I already had the creature's attention and now that Pogo was dead it was already sprinting towards me. I held my hand and swallowed my pain. Adrenalin kicked in and I started running. First the main door and the lawn followed by the gate. I ran as fast as my body could take me. I was no longer in shock and the plan to trap the wolf was slowly taking shape.

A small ladybug was crawling on a leaf of grass in the lawn when a large foot landed on it and squished it. Hunt or be hunted was the most important rule of the jungle. I was already out and running towards the supermarket when the main door of Pogo's house flew across the lawn, and the beast took its first breath of fresh air. Its chest took large breaths, and I could feel it growing in power after it had gotten some more room to stretch.

It was over six and a half feet tall and could stand on its hind legs, but as soon as it spotted me, it looked around, picked up the lawnmower like it was a small stone in a river, and threw it in my direction. It landed somewhere opposite of the diner where I had been, but I had covered some more distance and was on my way to the supermarket.

I was running as well as keeping an eye on how close the werewolf was getting to me. When I turned around, I saw it going down on all fours to run faster. Its formidable face had anger all over it. It had ears extending inches above the head and fiery yellow eyes. Saliva dripped from its mouth, trickling down slowly from its dark red tongue. It was covered all over with dark blue hair and had a presence of a black mane, almost like a wolf that had a lion's mane over its face. My pace was just enough to allow me to reach the supermarket.

It gained on me in no time with its long strides. No sooner did I enter the supermarket than I heard a large thud at the door. It stood there, eyes fixed at me, waiting for my next move. When I just stared back, it went into a raging frenzy and started clawing the sides of the building and throwing stones at the foundation. Every stone thrown and every claw at the supermarket was a blow to me, but at least I was safe.

I was of two minds to keep it that way considering that anything destroyed by this beast can be rebuilt, but if it killed me, then there was no return. I let it stay outside and do as much damage as it pleased while I bent down to catch a breath. It will not be able to enter the supermarket without my explicit permission. The beast whacked and thrashed the walls, then picked up the rubble that was falling and threw it at the supermarket door. I realized that it would soon forget me as a target and would then turn towards the hotel, which I could not allow because there was probably a lot happening at the hotel. Our entire operation depends on it, and I believed I will be able to capture this creature and trap it at least until the operation is done.

By now a large chunk of my supermarket was being destroyed. The door was being subject to a heavy downpour of boulders and stones.

After catching my breath, I decided now was the time to let the werewolf in. It was angry and ready to charge if given an opportunity. If left unchecked, it could create much bigger problems for everyone else. This was my chance to redeem myself from all my sins. I opened the supermarket door and shouted, "Come on in, Cujo!"

That seems to have done it because now the beast came running towards the door and smashed the entrance along with the door as well. It was like a raging bull, and it charged towards me. There was no turning back now. I had to lure it into the infinite aisles and trap it there.

Luring did not seem to be a problem because this creature was now hell-bent to kill me. I ran into one of the aisles and knew that it would follow. Once it was in, I could see and even sense its exact position. It was on my turf now. I separated myself from him and ran to the other end of the aisle. I then entered the adjacent aisle and ran forward with every ounce of strength I had.

My left hand had gone limp, and all its nerves were dead. The irony was I couldn't feel my hand, but I could still feel the pain. I exited the adjacent aisle and heaved a sigh of relief when I was able to see my cash register. I limped slowly to the cash register and sat on the chair.

The creature was trapped inside the infinite aisle, and I was safe outside.

I thought about Pogo. He was a good kid. He did not deserve to die the way he did. I could have helped him or even avoided this if I had been careful. Now we have a dead kid, a broken hand, and a mad creature in this equation as well. I wouldn't call it a day well spent, but it was progress. I would live to fight another day.

The day was far from done. I now began to feel immense pressure in my head. The beast had understood what the aisle was and went into a bigger rage. It was destroying both the aisles in which it was trapped. The infinite aisle was recovering as much as it could, but the beast was fast and strong. A human has limitations on how much it can damage the aisle, but this beast was superhuman, and it was breaking the aisle at a pace much faster than the rate at which it could recover.

My mind was unable to keep up with the damage that the creature was inflicting. It was like a jackhammer, pumping my head. I was unable to maintain my balance, and I knelt on the floor. My head was blasting, and I was unable to handle the mental pressure. I had to let go of the aisle, otherwise, my brain would run the risk of getting fried.

The infinite aisles immediately reverted to normal aisles. I was no longer able to sense the beast, but I could see it now. I don't know if I saw a glint of victory in its eyes, but it was fast at finding the exit and escaping.

I spotted my knife and realized that this was not even close to a worthy weapon against this creature. Running or escaping to the hotel without killing the beast was not an option, so this was it. This was my end.

I stood my ground at the cash register while the beast was wreaking havoc in my supermarket. It was now standing on its hind legs and moving menacingly towards me. I had made up my mind, and knife in hand, I waited for the inevitable pounce. My left hand was useless and hung limply from my shoulders.

The creature tried to claw me, but I ducked and plunged the knife into the side of its chest. It seemed to have had the desired effect, and it backed off, but only momentarily. It plucked out the knife like plucking a thorn from its foot. Nothing seemed to even affect this monster.

I stood there, empty-handed and ready to meet my Maker. The werewolf closed in and took me into its embrace, similar to how it held Pogo. I could hear the crack of my spine, and the pain was unbearable as the deadly embrace tightened.

The creature tried to squeeze me, but I was more mass than it could handle, so it held me in one hand and stepped out of the gaping hole, which used to be the supermarket door. It held my front feet and lifted me above its head. My entire world was upside down, but I did not feel the blood rushing to my head because I had already lost a lot of blood.

I was not scared anymore. It threw me with all his might, and I flew through the air. The cool air hit my face hard, and somewhere amidst the pain, I felt exhilaration. That did not last long as I landed with a thud on the road opposite the hotel. This was not where I wanted to land. I did not want to lead it into the hotel, but I was too late now.

I felt a large foot on my torso, and with its bare hands, the creature ripped me apart into two pieces. It seemed to enjoy the raw carnage it was causing. My brain was numb to the pain, and as I looked at half my body below its foot, I remembered Angie, the house beside the beach, the boy I bullied for lunch money, and everyone I had ever met. He then held my head in his palm.

I was plunged into darkness, but I could still feel the pain until there was nothing, only darkness.

PERSPECTIVE
TONKS

(Don't Work Hard, Work Smart)

"Who runs the world? – Girls!"

~ Beyonce

Chapter 15
Thanks, Mom!

Sometimes I ask myself why I do what I do. Why would I willingly put myself into trouble's path? Ironically, every time I do something wrong or I lose confidence, only one face comes to mind, and that is my mother's face, the one person who should be my source of inspiration. Her scornful face is just enough to get me through whatever trouble I was in because all I needed to do was to challenge myself as my mother.

Maybe my mother was right, and I was meant to just marry a businessman and lead a normal, sedentary lifestyle. Hell no! The very thought alone that my mother could be right would set fire to my soul and bring me back from the lowest point. That was the nature of my relationship with my mother. She did not abuse me physically, but she undermined me at every step. I was her only daughter, and I'm sure she wanted a son, and all of her frustration was vented out on me. Even my dad felt it, but he did nothing because he felt it was his fault that they had a daughter. From his perspective, biology had nothing to do with it, which was stupid.

My mother did not spend time with me as a kid. I remember her expressionless face when she was summoned to school by the principal. I was caught reading pornographic novels along with another boy, and the principal had asked to see our parents. Getting caught with pornographic novels in a catholic school was a recipe for disaster.

Dad was at the office and couldn't come, so she had to come, of course, because she couldn't break her flawless reputation in society as a good mother.

As she entered the principal's room, she could see the pious sister's anger. The head mother, who was the leader of the convent managing the school and also the principal, was furious at her. The principal explained to my mother the raw nature of the contents of the novel. I couldn't help but laugh since the principal had most likely had a look at the graphic novel to be able to explain such detail. I wondered what she thought of the novel, looking at possibilities she would never achieve in this life. A smile automatically crept on my face, and damn my luck, because the principal tuned towards me and saw it. She said, "You see this insolence? She doesn't even regret it, do you?"

I was silent. The best option here was to just let it pass, but the principal went on as if she was goading me to fight with her. "This is what happens when there is no upbringing. You should pay more attention to what she does and the people she spends time with. If not, this is what will happen."

My mother looked at me and then back at her, and I knew what she was thinking. She did not care at all. She just wanted to go back home. The principal asked her to take me home for the day. My mom was silent in the taxi back.

When we reached home, I acted as if nothing had happened. I placed the bag on the couch and threw myself on my bed. She did not utter a word. It was when she was making food for dinner that she came by and said, "Try to act like a girl. I know you have no traits of being one or any shame for what you have done, but at least try and act like one when at school."

I just scowled at her and said, "Mom, you did not even ask me what happened and just assumed that I was at fault."

Chapter 15: Thanks, Mom!

"There is nothing to ask. What are you going to say? It was not your fault but someone else's? Oh, please... Don't think I'm that stupid!"

I did not want to talk to her anymore. I went to Dad and said, "Dad, let's go for a walk." Dad was always ready whenever I called him for a walk because he knew that was my code for "I need to talk."

We were walking close by the house. I felt pleasant walking with Dad, especially with the cool breeze. We walked quietly for a while. Dad never pushed me to talk because he knew I would eventually start conversing.

"Dad, do you think I'm useless?"

"Of course not, sweetie. Why would you think that?"

"Did you and Mom not want to have me?"

"Dora, where is this coming from?"

"I don't know. Today I was caught reading a pornographic novel with another boy. I tried to explain to the principal that I had nothing to do with it and that I was just passing the bags to everyone as usual, and this book fell out. I was looking to see its contents when the teacher saw us and caught me. I told her I had nothing to do with it, but she wouldn't listen. The boy did not want to take the fall alone and so kept quiet. Mom came and did not even ask me what happened. She just assumed I was at fault. Why didn't you come, Daddy?"

"I wanted to, honey, but you know how it is at the office."

"Both of you are no different. You want to have kids but don't want to handle them."

That seemed to have affected my dad. He just looked straight ahead and walked quietly. I did not mean to be vitriolic towards him. He was my only ally, but I wanted to get it all out.

"I'm sorry, Dad. That was wrong of me. Don't take me seriously; I'm only fourteen."

"Dora, your mom is different from other people. She has a different way of loving you. By being acerbic towards you, she is trying to prepare you for the world. She loves you in her own way."

"Dad, I know you feel that Mom is this obscure flower that you need to spend your entire life trying to understand, but as far as I know, she's a bitch."

"Dora, that was uncalled for! Come on, let's go back."

I did not say much. My dad may love Mom a lot, but from my perspective, she was a bitch, and she hated me. I know the feeling was mutual.

*   *   *

I still recall the time I decided to leave home. I was nineteen then and needed their signatures to get into college. I went to Dad, and he, of course, signed the papers with great pride, but when I went to Mom, she had other plans for me.

"Why do you want to go to college? Do you know what major you want to do?"

"I want to pursue cybersecurity. It is a good choice and has a lot of scope in the job market."

"An unruly child like you has no future in any job. You will not listen to any boss. Why do you want to try? Just find a good boy and get married."

My blood began to boil. I was a hot-headed teen, and this was my spiteful mom trying to set me off. How could that be unsuccessful? I lashed out, "Yeah, mom, and end up like you? Working in a kitchen unhappy with your child and marriage? Projecting your insecurities on your daughter? Yeah, that's definitely the path I want to take!"

She was fuming at my sarcasm and must have been seriously hurt by what I said because she snapped back," Yeah, I am unhappy because I got you. All I wanted was for a boy to be with me until the end. All you want is to run away."

Chapter 15: Thanks, Mom!

I couldn't believe what I was hearing. I picked up a vase and threw it to the ground. I had lost control of my emotions now. I looked her directly in the eyes and said, "If you had given me the same love that you would have given a son, maybe I would have loved you better. I am done with you, Mom! I am done with this family. I am leaving!"

I stepped over the mess I had made. I did not care. This was not my home anymore. I felt sorry for Dad, who was shocked by what just happened. He was sitting on the balcony having his tea, and now he just heard his daughter was leaving. He will now have to live with this hateful woman without any support or distraction. I was sad for him and made a note to come and check on him when possible, but for now, I needed to get away from here.

I packed some clothes and clean underwear. I put in my brush and zipped up my bag. As I left my room and went for the door, my father was in front of me, blocking the door. "Dora, there is no need to be hasty. Stay here. You know how your mom is. She will come around."

I did not say anything but turned around and looked at Mom. She was cutting the tomatoes and did not even flinch. I turned to Dad and said, "Dad, I have got my answer. I love you, and I am sorry you need to live with her, but I need to get out of here. I will reach out when I'm ready to talk." I saw my father's dejected face. I was sad that this was the face I would remember him with because that was the last time I spoke to them.

Reaching out never happened. I got into a university via a scholarship, so my studies and boarding were covered. I focussed all of my anger on my studies and completed the four years of my cybersecurity course.

After I graduated and walked past the college gate, I realized I had nowhere to go. My home was an alien location, and I did not have a lot of friends. So, I decided to pursue a master's in information security at the same college. The college was happy to have me continue my studies as I was one of their star students, and so I continued my journey into cybersecurity.

During my final year, the military had come to campus to recruit people. They usually did not see a lot of interest in general, so I'm sure they were surprised when one of the star students in the college decided to volunteer in the US military. For me, this was a boon. I had nowhere to go after my master's, and I was getting consumed by continuous study. Nothing different was happening around me. Ennui had taken over, and I wanted to feel something different. I aced their entrance exam, and they happily conscripted me into their cybercrimes division after I graduated from my master's course.

I was especially proud of myself for having gotten somewhere, contrary to what my mother believed about me. I was not just some baby-producing machine for some guy to propagate his family. I had my own individuality and was capable of living alone without any dependencies.

*   *   *

After five years in the military, I was the Head of National Cyber Defense Joint Task Force that takes care of crimes such as terrorism, espionage, financial fraud, and identity theft, which have long existed in the physical realm and are now being perpetrated in the cyber domain as well. I had captured the infamous "I love you" virus creator and had also tracked the perpetrator behind the Triton virus, which had almost crippled Ukraine. My team loved me, and I was a well-respected leader.

The best part of working in the cyber domain was creating constructs called "honeytraps." This was an intricate trap created to lure cybercriminals to try to exploit them, and when they access these honeytrap constructs, we trap them and capture locations along with their coding style and attack patterns. Once the location is in place, it's a matter of sending in troops to arrest them. I have been on many such arrests, and I deeply enjoy arresting these criminals. Creating

Chapter 15: Thanks, Mom!

constructs was almost natural to me, and this skill skyrocketed my career in cyber defense. This also brought me directly onto Commander Barnes' radar.

Five days after capturing the Triton virus creator, I was summoned to Commander Barnes' room. I entered the room, and he looked much younger than I expected with his clean-shaven face and perfect body. His presence was daunting, and he was sipping a glass of whiskey when I entered. I saluted and stood there until he motioned me to sit down.

"You want some?"

"No, sir, I'm more of a rum person, but thank you, sir."

"Suit yourself. What's with the name, though? 'Tonks' is not a common name parents give their kids."

The commander was referring to my name in the military, which I had changed. I did not want to remember anything that my parents had given me. When I was in college, a roommate had introduced me to *Harry Potter*, and I have been a fan ever since. When the time came for me to think of a name, I did not have to think further since there was already a character with the same name.

I replied with a rather animated face, "Sir, the name 'Tonks' is actually from a fantasy book series called *Harry Potter*. The name my parents gave me is 'Dora,' and I was not very happy with the name. Since there was a character in the *Harry Potter* series called 'Nymphadora,' whose name was very close to mine, I took her short name instead. She was a highly underrated character and was very crucial in the main fight against the antagonist, Lord Voldemort. 'Tonks' is just another name she had picked up. Oh, and she also married a werewolf."

The commander was hardly interested in my name. I knew he was making small talk before he asked me what he really wanted to know, but my name has been a conversation opener for most people.

"I see. I don't see an issue with Dora, but I will let that be a conversation for another day." He picked up a huge file and placed it on the desk. It was a thick file, and my mind was now racing. Did they find out something about my past? He then continued, "I called you because I am impressed with your honeypot constructs. I like the way you use them to build something in order to trap cybercriminals. I want you to use this skill in another project that I am leading. I need someone with your determination and skillset to build a place where we can safely bring people and monitor or interrogate them. This is a state-funded project, and we already have one operative who is currently in training. You will need to train with him and exchange skills. He has very good persuasion techniques, and you have very good world-building skills. Both of you together will need to build this place to be able to get information out of suspects or persons of interest. I am sure you will fit in perfectly."

He stopped for a second and sipped some more whiskey. "So, are you interested in joining this team? It needs very creative construction and design skills, which I already know that you possess."

I couldn't believe what he was saying. I was finally being acknowledged as being an expert in my field. After all the cynicism I received from my mother, I had finally made it. I wanted to jump on the chair and rock and roll, but this was Commander Barnes, and it took great efforts to be in his good book. I had no reason to think about it. I immediately blurted out, "Of course, sir! It's an honor! And thank you for considering me for the job."

"Don't thank me. You deserve every ounce of it. Speak to Weiss, and he will brief you on the mission."

* * *

I did not speak much to Dr. Weiss on my way to the facility. Klaus was not exactly what I had in mind either. I needed to stop creating this presumption about everyone, especially Klaus. He appeared a bit older than me but was agile and forthcoming. Klaus had spent a year

Chapter 15: Thanks, Mom!

in training and was still struggling with his supermarket. I could see that he was spending too much energy on powering all aspects of the building when in reality, he needed to power only some portions of it and let the rest power itself. That was how I had built my diner later. I was still in the process of thinking about where and how I would place the diner when I saw that Klaus clearly needed help. I then taught him some techniques to power his construct, but he was unable to maintain the construct since he had absolutely no energy. I then made sure whenever he was training, I would power his infinite aisle until he mastered powering techniques so that he could power the aisles himself.

In the meantime, I was planning my diner. I did not want it to be an intimidation machine like his supermarket. I wanted to build a place where people were able to offload their sorrows. In the process, if I am able to extract sensitive data, then it's a win-win situation. I was severely affected by how my mother had treated me, and I did not want to repeat it with anyone else. I also realized I was able to populate the diner and make sure people did not feel alone. I was able to create a set of dummy people who would be the background eaters in the diner while the main suspects would be within my reach. Since all these people are an extension of my construct, I could listen in on what the suspects were saying without having to be close to them. It was ingenious and kept me out of harms reach, allowing me to just eavesdrop.

I had asked Klaus if he needed his supermarket to be populated, but he declined, saying that an eerie supermarket would scare people more than a populated one. I even tried to put in an assistant supervisor in his store without him knowing but was unable to do so, which made me realize that I needed to be in the diner to be able to produce the distraction population. His loss.

Klaus grew very fond of me, and I liked him as well but obviously not as a lover. There was no space for romance in this mission. He was so enticed by me that he asked me out. It's not that he is not datable material, but I had a bigger picture in mind. Commander Barnes had chosen us as forerunners in a specific field, and I did not want to lose focus. We had the chance to change the way military and police do investigations. A professional fling was not worth it. He understood this and backed off. We have been best friends ever since.

The best part is our constructs complement each other. He is the brawn, and I am the band-aid for any hurt he has caused. He would scare and intimidate; I would preserve and comfort. One of these methods was bound to work and get the information we needed.

Essentially, I was tired of seeing people cutting fingers and electrocuting limbs to get information. Those investigation methods seemed crude and ancient. My argument and premise were that anyone will open up and give you their darkest secrets if they trust you enough and with the right incentive.

When both Klaus and I had completed our training, we had another operative joining – Kobi. Kobi seemed extremely young, and we were tasked with monitoring his progress and getting him up to speed with our knowledge. Kobi was fast, and his construct was fabulous as well, but he was raw and inexperienced, and his mistakes showed. After a tedious three years, Kobi was ready as well.

Together we were ready to take on the world.

*   *   *

My first surprise during the day was the kids. I recall waiting in the morning to see if someone would show up at the diner, and I saw the kids passing by going towards the supermarket. How had kids entered this location, and who were they? I was immediately uncomfortable. We had not tested any of these methods on kids. Their minds were not capable of handling so much manipulation and reality editing. What's worse was that they were heading straight for the supermarket where they were bound to get more scared. I was in a good mind to call Klaus and tell him to go easy, but then I assumed he would be careful. How wrong I was. The little one even stood and waved back at me when I waved to him. I felt sorry for them, but I did not interfere, fearing that I might block Klaus from getting any information.

Later, I saw an older woman going to the supermarket. I was sure she was Sarah as there were only two people who were not part of the operative team. As soon as she came back, I got the call I had been waiting for. When Klaus explained what had happened, I was so certain that this was exactly the way I would have seen it playing out. They did not get intimidated, or they just got too scared. He was not ready to take on kids, and he probably almost killed the smaller one. Thankfully, he was able to perpetuate a lie about Marko, enough to get them to hurry to the hotel. When they came into the diner, it was a pleasant surprise. Maybe they were hungry, and I was happy to get a chance to get some information from them.

Eavesdropping the suspects' conversations was the best part of the diner. They would be spilling their deepest secrets to the person they trust, thinking that no one was hearing, but here I would be, extracting information. When the bigger one spoke about Kobi and his building, I was taken aback. This kind of attention to detail was not expected from someone so young. I immediately went inside and contacted Kobi.

"Hello, Kobi. Didn't you do your research before you created the Bender?"

"Hey, Tonks. Ermm… What do you mean?"

"Kobi, cut the bullshit. Did you do your research?"

"Yeah, I did. Why do you ask?"

"Someone here has caught a flaw in the placement of the hotel. You have built it exactly at the edge of the road, which is not allowed per the law. It needs to be ten feet away from the road. How the fuck did you not catch this?"

"Silence…"

"On it now! Sorry, Tonks."

"Don't be sorry; be better."

I cut the call and went back this time, making sure I took the food to make it look natural, but that's when I heard the second interesting piece of news where this elder one was not the actual brother but the cousin of the kid. Interesting... How had these two landed in this construct when we were looking for Marko?

I don't recall what I said, but after I served them food, the elder one was completely silent. He did not say a word and ate silently. Did I spill something which gave him a hint into what the diner was? I was not sure, but I was getting no more information from him. I needed to get him or Sarah to talk. Fortunately, he asked for the restroom, and once he left, I had Sarah to myself.

I tried to lie to her about our relationship and built on the lie that Klaus had said to get more information about Marko's location, but she was clearly not aware and was seeing right through my lies. I thought it was best to just end it by asking her to let us know if there was more information. I realized later that it was actually a mistake because people expected to see a police station to make the place more believable.

The best course of action was to escort them to the scene and make sure they remembered something. I did not trust Kobi enough to let him handle it alone, but I saw a bigger opportunity now. The kid was alone at home as was confirmed by Sarah, and I thought the best course of action was to get Klaus to meet him and speak to him. This way, we could cover more ground. That was when I asked them to wait for me outside. With the excuse of leaving my apron, I asked Klaus to speak to the kid and see if we could glean some more information. I hoped Klaus would be a bit more gentle with the kid.

* * *

Kobi was getting on my nerves. Who talks about a pandemic in such a construct? I was right to stay back behind his manager's desk and listen to what he was saying because I was scared he might slip and

Chapter 15: Thanks, Mom!

give them some information. Now, watching from this vantage point, I was absolutely sure that Joshua had picked this up and was already doubting the world more than anyone else. In all honesty, I couldn't care less if Joshua figured out this is a false world because I was focussing on Sarah. She was one of our targets since the other was missing. I wanted to make sure she gets to the scene and is able to view it and replay what happened to give us more information.

I walked in and saved Kobi from any further questions and took the duo to the twenty-first floor. As we reached level twenty-one, I wanted to get rid of Joshua. Kobi had already allocated opposite rooms to both of them. Sarah volunteered to wait, so I took Joshua to his room. I was about to close the door when he said, "What about Sarah. Are you going to take her to her room?"

"Yeah, that was the plan."

"Then I'm coming as well."

"Joshua, you've had a long day. Why don't you relax for some time? Let Sarah relax as well. You can bring your brother after your freshen up and meet her later."

"No, I want to make sure Sarah is safe before I rest. I'll join as well. Do you have a problem with that?"

Yes. You are in my way of getting Sarah to see the crime scene, but I couldn't tell him that. All I could say was, "Not at all. That's okay."

When we came back, Sarah had entered one of the rooms. I believe it was room 2101. Kobi, you useless fellow! Why would you leave the door open? Sarah had probably seen one of Kobi's abominations and was already panting, saying there was someone inside who needed help. I tried to persuade her otherwise, but she threatened with non-existent police. There was no way she was going to let it go, so I had to hope Kobi was listening.

I entered the room and saw the abomination with its eyes gouged out, and its feet sliced up. It was lying on the ground motionless, probably sleeping. I looked up to the ceiling and called out, "Kobi, you moron! Can you hear me?"

"Yes, Tonks. Has Sarah seen the scene?"

"No, idiot! She entered one of the other rooms, 2101, and she saw some burnt-up kid. Can you quickly fix this room?" I was still looking at the ceiling, but I was sure Kobi could see and hear me.

"Oh, damn! That room wasn't supposed to be open."

"Tell me about it, Sherlock. Now, please fix this asap! We'll discuss this later."

Immediately the room was no longer dark and gloomy but was just like one of the other empty rooms. This was one of the best powers Kobi had, and if he did not have his powers, he was nothing but useless. Sarah was satisfied, at least for now.

*   *   *

As Sarah, Joshua and I moved to room 2120, I could sense that they were both nervous. Sarah tried to question some of the environmental anomalies, but I shot her questions down. As we reached the room, I wanted Sarah to enter first, but Joshua volunteered to enter, toppling all my best laid plans. Ironically, what happened next was a blessing in disguise.

Joshua fainted and I assumed it was because of the dead girl. I was a bit relieved that I would be able to get Sarah to focus on the crime scene of her daughter without any more distractions. I was sure she might have more insights into this than she thinks she knows, but she was adamant that this was a crime scene, and she couldn't touch it without the police.

I needed to contact Kobi again and fill him in on the current situation. I could enter one of the adjacent rooms, but I realized they were all locked. It then struck me that room 2101 was open and I could use the room to talk to Kobi, so I made my way to the room that he had just fixed. I stepped into the room and called out to Kobi.

Chapter 15: Thanks, Mom!

"Kobi, Joshua has fainted, and Sarah is not ready to touch anything, so I am going to start a lie where we are police officers and see where the lie takes us. Bring some water and play along."

I went back to the room and had to invent yet another lie that I was a police officer and that we had already taken whatever we needed from the crime scene and had brought her here to relive the crime and tell us any more information she can from the scene. Kobi had brought the water, and I asked him to wake Joshua up and then stay outside the room in case either of them tries to run out. He sprinkled some water on Joshua but was hounded by Sarah with so many questions. This was not going according to plan. I needed Sarah to calm down and look at the crime scene.

When she had indeed calmed down, and Joshua was recuperating in the corner, I thought finally we were going to make headway in the case. This was a prejudgment, and to my surprise, Sarah committed suicide after picking up her daughter's ring. It was probably an important ring, and she had gotten a pretty good memory of what had happened, but now she was dead.

I was nowhere closer to solving this mystery.

Chapter 16
Revelations

Bad luck seemed to be following me diligently. One of my prime suspects was dead now, and I was stuck with a kid who was groggy because of witnessing a dead girl. I had to think quickly because I was not sure if Joshua caught any of what had transpired, and Kobi was clearly shocked by what just happened.

I walked over to Kobi and said, "Kobi, we need to make sure Sarah is alive. With this fall, she probably has fractured her mind, but she is most likely still alive. She will not get back to her senses unless you take her through the door, so go down make sure she is alive and her mind is salvageable so that you can take her back. Debrief the Commander and then come back here. I will need you."

"Okay, Tonks. I'll check her out, but what should I do if she's dead? Should I go back and ask them to pull her out?"

"No, if she's dead, there is nothing much you can do anyway, but if she is even a bit alive, save her and come back. Understood?"

"Yup, I'm on it!"

Kobi disappeared. My only hope was that either Klaus would get some information from Pogo, or I needed to make Joshua tell me where Marko is and bring him here. I needed a strategy with Joshua. I don't know how much he heard about what I told Sarah, but since there was no other way, I decided to try the same police card with him.

I walked to the corner where Joshua sat, stunned. He was probably still in shock with what happened to Sarah. I asked him, "Joshua, are you okay?"

He was hyperventilating. "Sarah…, she… died! How?… Why?… What… has… hap…pened?"

"Joshua, calm down. I'm sorry about what happened to Sarah, but she will be okay if Kobi reaches her in time. Trust me. She will not be able to help us now, considering the mental state she will be in. I need you to tell me why you are here. How did you wake up with Pogo?"

Joshua was extremely observant and careful by nature and talking to him was like walking on eggshells. I was asking him now to tell me how he reached this world. Expecting a straight answer was almost wishful thinking. He said, "Tonks, why do you want to know that? What memory did Sarah see which made her want to die?"

I had expected this question but did not have time to divulge any more information without getting some in return. I said, "Listen, Joshua. I know this is too much to accept now, and a lot has happened. I need your help, so please focus now. I am a police officer here, and so is Kobi. We are here to investigate the death of this girl. There is a killer on the loose, and we have found that this girl may be related to Sarah or Marko. From the looks of what happened just now, I believe Sarah may have known more about her death than we thought. That is why we allowed her to access the crime scene evidence. We know that you will also…"

I was unable to complete my sentence because Joshua was suddenly covered by a blinding light. He dropped to the floor and began convulsing. Was he getting a memory of Marko? Well, that would be to my advantage because if I can connect Joshua to Marko, I can get Marko here to see the death of his daughter.

Chapter 16: Revelations

I turned towards Joshua and was concerned since he was convulsing more than usual. I was not sure if this was normal or if he was just getting a large memory. Either way, when someone is receiving a large memory, our directive is not to interfere. Finally, the light began to fade, but as the light faded, the body on the floor was no longer Joshua.

There was a well-built body on the floor wearing the same clothes that Joshua had been wearing, just tighter. It was almost hilarious to see Marko Flannagan in an Iron Maiden t-shirt. In any other circumstance I might have laughed, but here in front of me was the primary person of interest I was here to interrogate. He was now on the floor in a catatonic state.

I moved closer to him to make sure he was alive and placed my index finger on his jugular. He had a pulse and was now breathing steadily. Thank God he was alive! I was beginning to withdraw my hand when his left hand caught mine, and his right hand went straight for my neck. He slowly got up, still choking me with his right hand. He was strong for a mid-fifties-year-old and had a good hold over me now. How had we missed this? Why was Marko disguised as Joshua? Who exactly was Joshua?

Marko did not waste much time, nor did he let me think. The Iron Maiden t-shirt was doing his muscles much deserved justice. His ripped jeans were tight on his thighs and feet. In short, Iron Maiden and ripped-jeans Joshua had now changed to a more mature, self-aware Marko, who was now at my neck.

"Tonks, who killed my daughter? Why is she here dead in a hotel room?"

Straight to the point. I did not like it because he did not give me leeway to talk myself out of this. His hands were tightening around my neck, so I tried the lie again. "I am a police officer, Marko. I am here to investigate your daughter's death. Help me out. I need to know who killed her. Look around and see if something jogs your memory."

He immediately looked away and scowled, "Cut the bullshit, Tonks. This place has been giving me the creeps since the beginning. First, I saw my eight-year-old self at home, and I had to lie to him that I was his cousin. Thankfully, neither he nor I remember a lot about our past. Then I see anomalies galore. You want me to name some? For starters, this place is just five buildings. Even with the five buildings, there is no population. The people in the diner are weird and probably fake since they always say the same thing. The supervisor and you are conveniently working for this hotel, fully aware that a murder has been committed here. You say you're from the police, but I see no police station nor a patrol car. I don't see any other people, and the highway across the hotel goes nowhere. I entered a room with a dead body in it, but there was no smell considering the amount of time it had spent there. You spent too much time putting in smell and taste in the food but did not create the right environment to fake a crime scene. So, stop the nonsense and tell me what's going on; otherwise, I will not hesitate to slit your throat and find out some other way."

I realized that my time was up. I cursed the moment I trusted Kobi to create the crime scene because he clearly had not researched the hotel position or the crime scene itself. This is what we get for trusting someone who hasn't been in the field before. We had been caught with our pants down, and it was better to come clean with Marko.

Without any surprise, the room now began to stink of dead meat and decomposition. Marko left my hand free and held his nose as if he was about to vomit. I tried to use this opportunity to punch him and break free, but he was strong, and he tightened his grip around me. I managed to croak, "Marko,… let… go… of… my… neck. I… will… explain… everything!"

He loosened the grip on my neck. I fell to the ground and was on all fours trying to grasp for fresh air. He put both his hands on his nose and sat back on the chair. The smell was horrible! Thanks, Kobi, you moron, for bringing in the smell AFTER he said it was missing. I was unable to breathe.

I told him, "Let's get out. I cannot breathe." He obliged, and we stepped out of the room. I offered, "Okay, Marko, I'm sorry. I will explain everything. What do you want to know?" My strategy was to give him just enough information to overwhelm him and then ask him about the death of his daughter.

"Okay, for starters, where the fuck are we? This is definitely not real, so why couldn't you just build something more believable so that I wouldn't know this is a fake place?"

"This is a dream construct. Ideally, this is a tangible construct to assist a set of people who are lucid dreaming to move towards a certain goal. Do you know what lucid dreaming is?"

He thought for a while and said," I think I have been lucid dreaming since I was a kid. I had visited a doctor, and he had explained it to me, but I was too small to relate to it. It's a dream where the dreamer is aware of being in a dream, right?"

"Sort of... Dreams are handled by the subconscious mind. You are not actively involved in a dream. In a lucid dream, you are conscious of what's happening, and with practice, you can control the final outcome of the dream."

"Okay, so what does this have to do with us?"

"The military has been experimenting for close to eight years on using lucid dreaming to interrogate or survey people. The process is called "Hypnosis Induced Lucid Dreaming." We sedate the subjects so they cannot fully wake up from the dream unless they encounter something extremely traumatic, like dying or falling from the twenty-first floor. That's why I believe even though Sarah thinks she committed suicide, she has probably already woken up. Once they are sedated and start dreaming, we bring them into this dream construct."

Marko listened intently, so I continued, "This is not easy to create. Kobi handles the livestock in the dream, I handle the general environment, and we have another operative who created the base construct. It takes a lot of mental energy to create and maintain this world. Once we get you here, we help you lucid dream by trying to direct you towards a specific goal or outcome. Generally, the premise of the world would be targeted to something we want to investigate. In this case, for example, we want to investigate the death of your daughter."

Marko's eyes saddened at the mention of his daughter's death, and he seemed to drift away for a few seconds. But then he seemed to shake it off and refocused on what I was telling him, "You, me, Sarah, Kobi, and Klaus are in a shared dream world where all of us are sharing a lucid dream, and by influencing your viewpoint in this world, we try to make you change your current direction in the dream. We brought you here and built a premise that there was a scream and that someone was murdered. We then led you to the hotel to find the body. Yes, the methods were crude, but it was to lead you here to see the body and maybe revive a memory to tell us something we did not capture initially in the investigation. We basically were helping you construct a lucid dream to an outcome that we want."

Marko was now processing a lot of information. He seemed calm now that I was talking. I also felt somewhere down in my heart that he deserved to know. He then asked me, "So why haven't you just interrogated us normally in an interrogation room?"

"We have. I'm not sure if you remember. You probably don't want to remember. We did interrogate you and Sarah, but you both have rock-solid alibis. We couldn't find a murder weapon and so could not track any killer. The police scrubbed the entire house for fingerprints expecting to get some clue about her murderer, but they found only fingerprints of your family which includes Sarah, you, your daughter and her husband. Since Sarah had corroborated your alibi, we were not sure who killed her as all our leads became dead ends."

"So, you think I killed her and you want me to confess?"

Chapter 16: Revelations

I panicked. Yes! That was exactly what we wanted, but I did not want to spook Marko. He was beginning to become more cooperative, so I said, "No, we want to see your memories and get clues on who could have killed her. You were the only people in the house, and so we wanted to use your memory of that specific night."

"If that's the case, why don't I remember that night?"

"I don't know… I was hoping you would."

Both me and Marko were silent. He then asked, "So, are you in the military?"

"Yes, I am a Cybercrime Division lead."

"You seem to be smart. Why did you build such an unbelievable construct, as you call it?"

"The idea is to make you aware of lucid dreaming. If you continue dreaming, you won't respond to our cues. We need you to see just enough anomalies to question the world but still be motivated enough to reach the outcome we need. We need to maintain a fine balance, but I think we made it a bit too unbelievable, which is what threw you off."

"Well, what threw me off was me having to speak to myself at home. You may have worked or tested this theory with people who think something may be wrong in the world you create but are still on the fence. You had me, who was absolutely sure that the world was not real because Pogo was basically myself many years ago."

When he mentioned the anomalies initially, I did not take it seriously, but he mentioned them again now. If Pogo was his younger self and Joshua was another version of Marko, then they were all the same person. The only conclusion I could make was that Marko had a split personality disorder and all his personalities had both unique memories and some common ones. I did not want to bring this up to Marko yet, but that would explain why the kids showed up at this place instead of Marko initially.

I must have been silent for a long while because he asked me again," So how are we now exchanging information? Are you in my mind?"

"Actually, we are all here with our minds in this construct. We enter this construct when we start lucid dreaming in a safe house. That safe house is a representation of our mind. If you have memories that are close to your heart, you will have memory objects near you when you wake up. If you have traumatic experiences in the past, you wake up remembering some of them, but there may be no memory objects. Another possibility is that you had a traumatic experience, but your mind trained you to lock it away, so you don't remember it even though it was traumatic. I'm sure you might have encountered at least one memory object."

"Yeah, a couple, in fact."

"Yes, so your house is a representation of your mind and all of its memories. The owner in it is the primary driver or, in a traditional sense, the soul itself. Ideally, each mind manifests itself as a safe house in which you as a person feel safe in real life. Your house was probably a building that was close to your heart. I know Sarah had rendered the house that you two brought together because that was close to her heart. The construct allows us to share a common space and interact with each other's minds. We then lead your souls to the final goal, and you give us information based on how you react.

This was the plan. We are all now in an underground facility somewhere in Greenland. All of us are sedated, and because the lucid dream is shared, we are all opening our minds to each other so that we can look inside and gather information on possible occurrences or events which may have been repressed by our own minds. The best part is it's all in the mind. Your body is affected only if your soul is erased or cleaned, quite logically, killed."

Marko looked perplexed. "So, all of this is in my mind?"

Chapter 16: Revelations

Tonks continued, "Logically, yes, but there are a lot of things we did not understand as well. You basically entered the construct with your safe houses in raw format without any modifications. We had to make a lot of changes to ger these specific safe houses. Kobi, Klaus, and I trained for years to be able to manifest our minds the way we want. Otherwise, my safe house was my grandfather's barn. That wouldn't fit well in this construct, would it? We found Sarah in her safe house, but we did not find you. We only found the two boys, Pogo and Joshua. When you now tell me that Pogo and Joshua were just other versions of you, it answers some of the questions we had. More importantly, it explains the presence of Joshua and Pogo in this world."

"Why did you not just get into our safe houses and question us?" he asked.

"That's because one cannot enter another mind without explicit consent. That is why I always wave at my diner to allow people to enter, and that is also why Kobi needs to place a 'WELCOME' board so that he doesn't need to be at the door to explicitly allow all of you in."

A glint of realization swept across Marko's face. He then asked, "Wasn't her husband with her? I remember my daughter's marriage, and it was a beautiful ceremony." He paused for a while and then said, "Maybe her husband, Paul, did it."

I was beyond tired now. I know Marko was trying to make sense of everything, but my energy was slowly decreasing and maintaining the world was draining me as well. "Marko, Paul is also dead. Both Julia and Paul were found dead in their room in your house."

Marko was now losing it." My house? Who killed them then? Was it Sarah? She seemed to know what happened. Maybe she was complicit. Can you just sedate her and question her again?"

I replied, "No, Marko. That is no longer an option. Dying here means waking up. Our plan was to see if either of you remembers anything, and if you do, record the incident and take all of you back via the Single Exit Point Source, which was Kobi. He would open the door and gracefully take us back. You could, of course, ungracefully kill yourself, but that would leave your mind in a fragile state, not to mention that we as operatives are forbidden from doing so. You will be alive but fragile mentally."

Marko was listening intently, so I continued, "It also depends on the amount of trauma you were receiving when you died here. Sarah was under severe mental stress because she had just remembered what had happened to her daughter and was unable to handle the truth. She may take some time to heal, but she won't be fit to dive again for a while. She will be alive but only physically for now. Mentally, she will be in a coma. I really need you to focus on helping me now. We are very close, and I know you might be able to tell us who killed Julia."

Marko was now thinking and asked, "Okay, what do I do now?"

"There is one last evidence I had included in this creation which was substantial as it contained both Paul and Julia's fingerprints. It's in the upper drawer beside the bed there. Can you have a look and see if it jogs a memory?"

Marko's face turned sour." I need to go back in?"

"I'll fix that. C'mon."

We opened the door and entered the room. As we entered, I shouted," Okay, Kobi, cut the smell! We need to work. Marko knows everything." The smell subsided, and the room was habitable again. "Okay, Marko, now give me something."

Marko walked to the drawer beside the bed. He opened it and was surprised at what he saw, but he immediately was surrounded by a blinding light. Thank God! He was probably getting another memory and most likely the answer to all our questions, I thought. He was convulsing again, so it was probably a big memory.

Kobi entered the room completely shaken. I looked at him and said, "Kobi, why do you look like you've seen a ghost?"

Chapter 16: Revelations

Kobi said grimly, "I went down expecting to find Sarah and take her back but found her completely dismembered over Klaus' already decapitated body. There is a large werewolf-like creature in front of the hotel. When I went down, it was chewing the carcass of Sarah and dropping it over Klaus. I'm sorry, Tonks, I panicked. I couldn't check if they were alive, and I don't know what pain their mind is bearing now, considering that their primary driver is now in this hazardous state. If they have woken up without their primary driver, they are more or less in a coma. I was so scared I just stayed at my desk and blocked all communications until I heard about the crime scene missing its smell factor. I went blank again and could not hear anything until you called out to me again to remove the smell."

I looked at Kobi, exasperated. A monster now? I turned to look at Marko to see if he was back with his memory, and that's when he punched me.

*   *

My eyes opened, and it took a while to realize where I was. Oh damn! I woke up. Send me back! send me back! Where is Commander Barnes? I could hear the excited shouts, "Tonks is back! Extract her out!"

"No! We have Marko now. He knows something. Give me some more time!" I was shouting in my mind, but the liquid around me was not allowing me to say anything coherent.

An operative lifted my helmet after draining the gel, and before she could say anything I shouted, "Send me back NOW! Do not ask me why! If Commander Barnes asks, just say I never woke up. Do it NOW and don't waste time. GO! GO!"

The operative was clearly shaken, but thankfully she listened to what I said. I could feel the gel covering my face and the gills coming back on my neck. Commander Barnes will understand that I did what I had to do for the mission.

Marko, I'm coming for you!

*   *

Now

Kobi was sitting beside me, waiting for his next instructions with the water bottle in his hand. He probably sprinkled it on my face to wake me up. He had fucked up big time, and he knew it. He probably wished he was sitting behind enemy lines, ready to shoot someone rather than stuck on the twenty-first floor with a monster below. He was tending to his elbow. He must have been shoved by Marko before he ran.

I felt weaker now than before. Was it because I woke up and returned abruptly without recovery? We had not done that during training, so anyone's guess was as good as mine. I asked him, "How long have I been out?"

Kobi said, "Not very long. Do you want some water?"

"Yeah, and aspirin if you have any "

He felt my sarcasm but wouldn't say a word. I did need an aspirin, though, but I knew that wouldn't be available. He handed me the water, and as I sipped, he asked me, "What do we do now, Tonks? The cat is out of the bag. We do not have any further progress except that Sarah was possibly complicit in the murder, but we are nowhere closer to the actual murderer. Marko has run out of the hotel and is most likely going to be eaten. What's our game plan?"

I thought about it for a while and decided that I have had enough of this cat-and-mouse game. It has been a nightmare in itself maintaining the environment, and I was already on the verge of dropping everything and just leaving, but unfortunately, I needed Kobi to take me back unless I was willing to take the route that Sarah took. Marko knows the truth, and we just need to find him and persuade him to tell us. If we die in the process, then so be it. I was done running and had no more energy to do anything else. That's what we signed up for, and that's what we will do.

Chapter 16: Revelations

"Kobi, let's get down and see what is happening. If Marko is dead, we can just get out. If not, we'll speak to him and get more details."

Kobi was aghast, "No, Tonks! I did not sign up for this! I am not coming."

I was at the end of my patience now "Kobi, If you do not come with me now, I will report you and make sure you are discharged of all duties. I will personally kill you after that and make sure you do not return from your coma. Am I making myself clear?"

I think that worked because he said, "You go first then. If you're eaten, I don't need to worry about anything you just said."

"Fine, loser!" I just wanted this to be over. We both walked out of the room and to the elevator. We completed the long descent via the elevator and finally reached the bottom floor. We crossed the large entrance hall and reached the main door of the hotel. I was groggy and mentally exhausted.

I opened the door first and saw Marko standing opposite the dead beast. He was looking ahead of the beast onto the main highway. The creature was lying on its side, hands lifeless and tongue protruding out of its mouth. A light breeze carried a dried leaf to my feet. The silence was deafening, but it was the most beautiful sight to realize that the problem had fixed itself without us needing to interfere. I made my way out of the hotel, dropped to my knees, and closed my eyes. The stress was literally killing me.

*   *

I woke up. This time Commander Barnes was right in front of me, a grim expression on his face.

"Tonks, you should have debriefed me before descending again. Not only was it unsafe, but you also put the entire operation in jeopardy." He turned and started walking away, but then paused, turned back to me, and said,

"This is not going to end well for you."

*   *

Mindbender

PERSPECTIVE
KOBI

(The Ambitious Coward)

"A coward's courage is in his tongue."

~ Edmund Burke

Chapter 17
Serendipity

"Kobi is a fag! Kobi is a fag!"

The daily routine of getting hounded by the class bully had begun. I had just picked up a make-up set on the floor, which was dropped by some girl. I was certain I had checked twice to see no one was around, but bullies are like flies and will show up out of nowhere even if you're careful. This one was no different and had been out to get me for the last two years since he showed up at school.

"Stop it, Butch! Stop it!" It had fallen on the ground, and I picked it up to turn it in to lost and found. You know this is not mine, so why are you making fun of me?"

"Stop talking, fag, or I'll punch you!"

I was sure he would. I was not really the bravest specimen out there. I would rather settle an argument without physical violence, but Butch has been my nemesis for some time now. He was a bully even before he came to this school, and I heard that he was thrown out of the previous one because he had mentally traumatized a kid into committing suicide. I was most certainly his main person of interest. I had no capability to retaliate and was mostly a push-over from the start. His homophobic nature often revealed itself thinly disguised as comments like, "I'll punch you, fag!" or "Haven't had your daily dose of dick yet?" It was abhorrent, but there was nothing I could do.

I knew he will punch me anyway, and I was in no mind to provoke him, but I felt especially angry today. All I had done was exist. Picking up an object to hand it over to lost and found did not make me gay. The logic behind what he's trying to do I will never understand… I told him, "It doesn't matter what I say because you will punch me anyway, right?"

"Right answer!" is all I heard before I saw a closed fist flying toward my face, and a volcano of pain erupted in me. I was spread out on the floor, and he kicked my ribs. I curled into a fetal position and just closed my eyes, hoping that this onslaught would end soon.

At some deep level, I was used to the punches and the kicks physically, but I had lost my own self-respect, so I was unable to stand up for myself against common bullies. I was beaten almost every day in school, but I would come home happy and talk about all the good things that happened during the day. My mind was adept at compartmentalizing the good and the bad out of necessity. I did not want my parents to know that their kid was a loser at school. My parents weren't abusive or anything, and neither did they ignore my life. They were just not proactive enough to probe. My mother did not know I was being bullied for almost four years, and she never tried to ask me or see the visible signs. If I told her I fell from the stairs, she would just believe it.

I have been bullied since I was a kid, and in general it has affected the way I approach problem-solving. It influenced the way I isolate issues so that I could ignore some of them intentionally. Years later, when I joined my six-figure corporate job, I was on top of the world. I had landed a product manager role for a dating app software and was pretty happy where I was going in life until I met the manager. He was a divorcee and a workaholic and expected me to work overtime as well, which in some enterprises was common. Bullies sense a submissive from far. They smell the fear in them and pull them out of a crowd.

Chapter 17: Serendipity

My manager caught wind that I was a pushover. Need overtime during the festive seasons? Get Kobi to stay on. Got additional work and need someone to take over the shift? Get Kobi. A mail from him at the end of the business day would look like, "Kobi, You're doing an excellent job. Also, I need these reports in by the end of business today. Thanks."

The sad part here was that it was never a matter of incompetence. I was good at what I did but being good at what you do is nothing if you cannot have basic self-respect where you work. None of that competence will matter. I went for therapy, and the therapist asked me to take charge of what I wanted, so I went and told my boss that I needed a week's holiday. He denied my request citing resource crunches, but I had expected this. I was aware there was no such crunch, so I stood my ground, asking for the week off. He then looked at me and told me to go on a permanent holiday and fired me.

In hindsight, this was, of course, illegal. You cannot fire an employee for asking for a holiday, and I could have contested this, but he knew I wouldn't because I was a wimp.

I went back home that day and sat on my chair for a while, just contemplating. I was tired of this typecasting in every sphere of my life. I wanted a break from being picked on, so I decided to join the military. The military, from what I had seen in the films, was all about brotherhood and serving the nation, and I wanted to be able to build enough confidence and strength to fight back against the bullies in life.

As an operational strategist, my capability to break down big problems into smaller, workable issues and solve them modularly was put to the test. This was the basic principle of how Computational Thinking worked in the real world. You analyze the main objective and break it into smaller modules until these cannot be further decomposed. When you fix all these atomic problems, you achieve the main objective automatically. This was a valuable lesson I learned from my software engineering career. Breaking down bigger problems into smaller ones made them more manageable.

I had no field experience, so I was surprised when I was summoned by Commander Barnes. As I entered, he seemed animated and happy. He was reading a book and probably encountered something funny. I saluted and waited until he asked me to sit down. I had not heard much about Commander Barnes at the time, and from my perspective, this was probably just another skip-level talk. He placed the book down, regained his stoic demeanor, and said, "Kobi, do you know why you have been summoned here?"

"No, sir."

He paused for a while and took his time, "I am currently leading a government-funded project which involves building a new framework for interrogation and surveillance. You will be part of a four-member team. Two members of this team have already completed their training. You will support them and make sure that we can get information or identify specific patterns that we may not have caught through standard channels of investigation. I have seen your file, and I like your modular approach to problem-solving. This operation will not be easy and will be a much larger learning curve for you. I see you have not been in the field, so this will also be your first field experience. I am bringing you in by trusting my gut instinct but be prepared for resistance from your peers because they may not be ready to trust you without seeing your true capabilities. Are you up for this?"

I did not show any expression. In all honesty, I did not feel any special excitement. It was just another job. "Yes, sir."

"This is not how most recruits start, but we need someone with your approach to solving problems. We are close to beginning our first mission, so you will be trained and supported by the existing operatives. We might need to mobilize you soon. Speak to Weiss. He will brief you on what you need to do."

Chapter 17: Serendipity

"Yes, sir." The news still did not have any impact on me. This was basically my first assignment, and only the Lord knew what was in store for me. He seemed to pick that sentiment and said, "This is groundbreaking technology you will be working with, so do your best and make me proud, son.

$*$ $*$ $*$

After spending a few months at the training camp, I realized that this was exactly my destiny. I was a pariah for almost a month before Commander Barnes had to intervene personally with Klaus and Tonks. They were not ready to risk the mission in the accompaniment of a newbie. I briefly recall being in the same room as Commander Barnes, Tonks, and Klaus.

Klaus was flaring out," Commander, I know we are on a deadline, and we need to get another operative soon, but there are so many options out there. Why did you get this rainbow?"

"Klaus, mind your tongue. I have seen his capabilities in his previous job. He has the skillset I am looking for to complement your skillset. How can you judge him before you have even given him a chance to train?" Klaus went silent.

It was Tonks who spoke this time, "Sir, you might be right, but we are not only training him for this operation, we will also be training him with some of the basics that he was supposed to get from the field. How can we be expected to trust him with our lives?"

In all honesty, I could understand where they were coming from, and I was fully ready to go back, but Commander Barnes seemed to be losing his patience.

"I am the commander of this project, and you need to trust my instincts on this. I am sure Kobi will do well. Train him and teach him everything you know. If he doesn't cut it, I will get you someone else, but give him a chance."

Klaus and Tonks reluctantly trained me with whatever they knew and gave me a month's time to come up with a working construct for my mind. They most likely expected me to fail, but I had more than succeeded.

This was the best part. My first safe house was my parents' house. This obviously was not going to fly, so I needed something to really separate each problem or memory I had. Over the course of one month, I managed to build my skyscraper, "The Bender," and build it to near perfection. All my memories were neatly organized into the rooms. Since the entire building was my mind, I could basically see and hear everything happening in all rooms. I had always survived my childhood onslaught of Butch by mentally torturing him in my mind. This was now fleshed out in room 2101. I would spend ages every training session torturing Butch.

When I was finally done, I was proud of my work and was now excited to take on the first assignment. The milestone was still far away, of course, with a lot of testing pending, but I was satisfied with what I had created. When I called Klaus and Tonks to have a look, they were genuinely surprised. Klaus and Tonks entered "The Bender," and I was at the manager's desk to welcome them. The halls were not furnished, and there was just a chair in the right corner.

"Wow, Kobi! You did it! It took us ages to really master our mind construct. This room, though, looks a bit blank. You have seen hotel halls, right? It needs to be grand. There should be a fountain in the center at least."

I was open to criticism, of course, and this was perfect feedback. I immediately closed my eyes, and before us, there was the fountain. I focused a bit more and extended the water column across the center of the room so that there was a single file of water from the door to the manager's desk. Tonks and Klaus were spellbound. Klaus said," How did you do that?"

"Do what? I incorporated your feedback."

"How did you do it real-time?"

"What do you mean by, 'How did you do it?' Isn't that normal?"

Chapter 17: Serendipity

"Real-time manipulation of your mind construct is tough and needs a large amount of energy, but you seem to be able to do it effortlessly. I had struggled to get even a single part of my mind to change dynamically. Tonks had to support me to get the aisles to change dynamically, damn!"

Tonks now chimed in, "The same applies to me. It takes a large amount of energy to make sure there are people in the diner, and that they are animated. That's why I cannot really create dynamic people outside the diner. It takes a toll on my energy."

I was now beginning to see why this was interesting. I did not know why or what allowed me to have this ability, but I thanked Commander Barnes secretly for having trust in me even when I didn't. I told them, "Hey, you guys, go ahead and check the rooms... I'll do some more redecoration and follow you."

"Okay," said Tonks

"Where's the elevator? Or you want us to see only the bottom floor?" Klaus asked. I did not know if he was being menacing, but I pointed to the back of the desk, which led to a winding path to the elevator.

I waited, thinking about what they mentioned, and they were right. I needed to make the front hall fully believable and grand. Probably golden walls or at least some pillars that are golden. I would decide later. As I thought about home renovations, I heard Tonks trying to enter room 891, so I unlocked it. They wouldn't be able to access any of the other rooms without me explicitly allowing them. That was how I kept Butch a secret from everyone during early days of our training. She entered first, and Klaus followed. The rooms weren't as sophisticated since I had never seen or been in a five-star hotel. I hadn't even seen one in a movie or on television. As soon as they entered the room, I could hear what was happening clearly.

Tonks broke the silence, "What do you think? He seems to have a considerable aptitude for this kind of work. This tower, which he created in just under a month, is phenomenal! I like his concept as well. Each memory or each sub-construct is in a separate room and isolated from other sub-constructs."

Klaus was silent for a while. I couldn't gauge his emotion, but then he said," I agree he is a valuable asset, especially with his dynamic world-building capability, but he is still raw and has no field experience. We might need to babysit him to some extent. We cannot just leave him to extract information alone."

Tonks then said," Yeah, but we can make him our SEPS. That will reduce the load on us, and we can focus on more interrogation steps."

I recalled from my training what "SEPS" was. A "Single Exit Point Source" was a safety net that was devised to make sure no one could voluntarily exit the construct when the interrogation was taking place and while the mission was still active. All of us, even the suspects, could possibly exit a construct either by dying or getting heavily traumatized. This was called an "ungraceful exit." Alternatively, they could exit by getting pulled out after a specific time by someone external monitoring their vitals. This was called a "graceful exit." In general, the operatives monitoring health would pull us out in ten-minute intervals as it was possible for people to stay stuck in the construct for much longer time. Time as a concept was almost nonexistent or extremely slow in this world.

To make it more complex, the construct rules stated that no one could safely exit unless the mission was complete. A SEPS was created where one of the operatives creates a single point of exit and would open it only when all operatives have completed the mission and the suspects are safe to recover. Everyone would then be able to safely leave via this exit point from the inside of the construct. Of course, an operative could commit suicide, die, and wake up, but there would be a disciplinary panel waiting. Leaving a mission and waking up without completing it was equivalent to desertion.

Chapter 17: Serendipity

I personally did not like the idea considering that we were opening our minds to possible suspects and criminals, and we did not know what was in store for us. The construct worked in a fail-close model where, if something went wrong, the world locks up. This would then put all our lives in danger. Yet I did not make the rules, so I had to abide by them.

I then heard Tonks say," If he has the capability to dynamically change the environment, we can use him to move the exit point close to where we are when we need it. That would come in handy if we are stuck in impossible situations."

Klaus said," Yeah, let's talk to him about it. If he's indeed as good as he is, he is a pretty good asset to have. To begin with, he needs to fix the aesthetics of the room. This looks like my college dorm. He needs to make this look like a hotel room."

They came back after some time, and I knew they were impressed, but they did not show it. They came and said," This is good work, Kobi. It needs some tweaking, but it is pretty good work."

I was ready to take on the next level. It was exciting and scary at the same time, but I was ready for the challenge. This is by far the most I had enjoyed myself while working, and I did not want to let it go. I wanted to do much more than I thought possible. I told them," Guys, I know you have your doubts about me, but I like this job and this project. I will not let you down. Yes, I do not have field experience, but I will try my best. If you want me to become SEPS, then so be it."

Klaus and Tonks were silent for a while, looking at each other. Then Tonks said," Kobi, you can hear us in your rooms, right?"

"Yes."

"Ingenious."

"Thanks! It was a little something I needed to do to make sure I don't miss out on what's happening in the building if I am in one of the rooms.

Tonks smiled. Klaus seemed to be planning something already.

*   *   *

Steve created our base construct where Klaus, Tonks, and I bring in our minds. We never really got to talk to him since he was constantly working, but he built the world with great detail. I wanted to get him to have lunch with us once, but he seemed to be a reclusive kind of person. Maybe I might try getting him into our circle before he leaves tomorrow.

My dynamic world-building helped make the world much more believable than being a giant ghost town. Tonks would put in the foliage and environment, but I put in the moving parts. Bees, wind, smell – everything motile was part of my role in the construct. I needed more energy to maintain larger organisms, which meant I wouldn't be able to focus on the mission, so I decided that it was still believable if dogs and cats were not around. We still needed air, breeze, fragrances in flowers, rotting fruit, and so on to make sure people believed the world. I was able to bring in that pseudo-reality. People, though, were out of the question. Bringing in non-operative pseudo-people needed more manpower, and we did not have that as of now.

Over time, Klaus and Tonks mellowed out with me. They probably still were on their toes, but they considered me more as a junior partner than a noob. I wanted to make sure that I did not let them down, so I tried my best to do everything exactly as they said.

Unfortunately, nothing went as expected.

*   *   *

The final day was here, and my nerves were on edge. I was focusing on making sure I didn't make a mistake. Ironically, I was unable to focus. Klaus and Tonks had not contacted me, and I was waiting at the desk. This was something I had been briefed on already. Waiting was a key factor in MISO operations and waiting, by curbing one's urge to do something, was tougher.

Chapter 17: Serendipity

Tonks had worked with me in recreating the crime scene that we needed Sarah and Marko to see. We both had studied the crime scene and made sure every detail was in place. Initially, Tonks was not keen on using a room as the crime scene, but we did not have enough detail on Marko and Sarah's house or room to recreate it. Recreating it locally in my mind at "The Bender" would be impossible to justify without the right trigger.

We then came up with the narrative of the girl dying in the hotel and a scream being the trigger to wake them up and begin the dream construct. Tonks was overseeing the entire setup, and I was creating all aspects of the scene. I did not want to disappoint her and wanted it to be perfect. I was running through everything we had done. Was Julia's driver's license in place? The whip was there, and I had made sure her clothes and blood were the right texture to showcase the time the body would have decomposed. I tried my best but was scared that it was not enough.

I had put Butch into room 2101 as soon as I was able to create the Bender so that I could release some of my tension. Butch was my childhood bully, and I enjoyed torturing him when training went wrong or if I was upset. Over time, both Klaus and Tonks knew that I had the capabilities to hide such caricatures in each room, but they left it to me and my discretion. They knew they couldn't enter any of the other rooms but had seen me enter many locked doors after training, especially room 2101. I was glad they respected me enough to observe my privacy, but they knew I had such escapades in my construct.

On the day Marko and Sarah were brought in to commence the descent into lucid dreaming, my nerves were on high alert. I knew the only way to overcome my nervousness was to move to 2101 and ease my tension. I made my way up the elevator and navigated to room 2101. The room was locked shut, as all other rooms should be. I couldn't wait to get my hands on him. Room 2101 was basically a torture chamber. I enjoyed tying up Butch's feet and whacking them with a baseball bat until I heard bones cracking. I like to burn his eyes until they become unrecognizable from the burnt flesh around them. I liked punching holes in his hands with a nail gun. I am sure the real Butch is tucked away safely under some pillow, but the fun and catharsis I get when I perform these activities in the depths of my mind cannot be explained. I knew it might take a while for either Tonks or Klaus to call, so I spent quite some time indulging in my guilty pleasures. That was when I got the call.

I panicked, kicked fake butch to the chair and dashed out of the room. Since I could hear what was happening in all rooms, including the main desk, I was able to hear the phone. I ran to the elevator and realized the phone had stopped ringing. I did not know who it was to return the call and hoped they would call again.

Thankfully they did, and Klaus was already giving me an earful. I explained that I was checking the crime scene to make sure it was perfect. He seemed to accept that, and that was good for me, because if he knew the real reason I was not at my desk, I was done for.

Klaus gave me a forewarning that I would be getting guests, and they were a twenty-year-old, a pre-teen, and a fifty-something-old woman who was most likely Sarah. Soon after this, I got a message from Tonks as well. She admonished me for not having done my research on the placement of the hotel. I was so engrossed in making the hotel and crime scene realistic that I did not pay attention to the placement of the hotel. I quickly changed its position to make sure there was at least ten feet between the hotel and the road.

I was surprised when Tonks waltzed in with the lady in her fifties who I recognized as Sarah, and the twenty-something kid who introduced himself as Joshua. Well, it was showtime now and time to charm them into comfort.

I was rattling on about the hotel, but they had much more targeted questions. I was able to answer all of them, but somewhere down the line, while I was in the flow of answering, I mentioned the pandemic which was something we were facing in the real world. The pandemic was COVID-19, and the entire world was in its grip. Yes, it had been a couple of years after it hit, but I shouldn't have brought it up. Sarah was doing all the asking, but Joshua seemed to have picked the error up. I did not know how that would affect him when he saw the crime scene.

Later, when I got a mind message (that's what I called them) from Tonks, I was on my toes again. Tonks was angry and was bringing up yet another mistake. I could hear her biting her teeth. She reprimanded me for leaving the door to 2101 open which was careless of me. So much for making mistakes. She asked me to quickly transform the room. I could only assume it was because Sarah or Joshua had entered the room. How unlucky would I have to be for them to see the door open and get in?

I fixed the room, and after a brief amount of time, I got another mind message from Tonks to come up with some water and that she was planning to start a lie about us being police officers. I just did as I was told for fear of screwing up again but was curious why she went all the way to room 2101 to mind-message me. She could have just attempted to enter one of the adjacent rooms and I would have unlocked them. My assumption was that room 2101 was fresh in her mind after the Sarah fiasco and she was in haste to get to a room to communicate with me.

I picked some water from the desk and moved to room 2120. As I entered, I saw Joshua on the floor and Tonks and Sarah still as a statue. Tonks then asked me to put some water on Joshua and wait outside the door in case Sarah or Joshua tried to escape, but I was bombarded by more questions from Sarah. Thankfully, Joshua regained consciousness and diverted their attention, but nothing prepared me for the swift turn of events when Sarah decided to jump out of the window.

Tonks asked me to run down and check if Sarah was dead. I assumed this was to make sure she was safe on the outside. I made my way to the bottom floor via the elevator. I wandered across the hall and then opened the main door and was greeted by a large, dark blue, wolf-like creature devouring Sarah's intestines. Klaus was close by, his head missing. I was rooted on the spot, and my legs were shaking, but this is where the advice from the *Jurassic Park* movies was useful.

I moved very slowly to retreat my path to the hotel and closed the door. I might have closed it a bit too loudly because I heard a large thump on the main door, followed by many other thuds before the sounds stopped. Had the creature gone away to feed on the poor souls? I did not have the courage to go back upstairs and face Tonks' wrath, so I just stayed at my desk.

I was alone and scared, so I decided to listen to what was happening in room 2120. I heard a different sound now. It did not sound like Joshua. Whoever this was, he was clearly calling out all anomalies in the world. He even called out that the dead body in the room did not have the smell of a rotting corpse. I cursed myself for not having thought of this. I immediately changed the environment to make sure the right odor was in place. As soon as I made the change, I seemed to have lost the conversation. I decided to wait as I did not want to go up there yet without knowing who this new person was.

Soon, I got another mind message from Tonks asking me to remove the smell. I did so and ran up to the elevator. I was repeatedly pressing the 21st-floor button, hoping the elevator would go faster. Maybe fear does that to everyone, and I was scared out of my wits. My motive was to put as much distance as possible between me and the monster outside.

I reached 2120 and ran to the room only to see a well-built individual was seeing a memory, and Tonks was trying to catch a moment of solace from the entire ordeal. I explained to her what I had seen, and that both Klaus and Sarah's bodies were not salvageable to take through the SEPS. I explained my fear of the entire situation, especially what would happen to them, considering their primary driver was beyond recovery. I was scared and now did not want to have anything to do with this mission.

That was when I saw the individual getting up and punching Tonks. I caught a glimpse of his face when he ran toward me, and I was certain it was Marko from my recollection of the briefing. I tried to block him from escaping, but he shoved me to the wall and ran to the elevator. That couldn't be good because that meant that he was walking right into the face of the monster. I did not want to see how that ended. I went back to Tonks, who had passed out. I sprinkled some water and waited for her to come around.

Once she was around, I wanted to tell her to cut our losses and escape, but of course, I couldn't broach the subject so directly. When I asked her what her game plan was, she said we needed to continue with our mission, and I was aghast. We have Klaus and Sarah dead and now probably Marko too. I had no idea what happened to Pogo, and I did not want to wait to find out. I made my intentions clear that I would not have anything do to with the mission further. It was then that she threatened to turn me in for desertion. I realized that she was not here to leave. She was a veteran, and she had reached a mental state of completing the mission or die trying. I was new, and this was my first mission. I wasn't going to let this affect me. I contemplated that if she really led us down, the chances of her being eaten were higher, which would give me a window of escape.

I asked her to lead, and she was just too tired to object. We walked towards the elevator, descended, and across the hall we marched. She opened the door and probably saw the monster eating either Klaus or Sarah because she immediately dropped to her knees and closed her eyes. I'm not sure if she passed out, but as I exited and joined her outside, I saw Marko had killed the beast. The carcass of the beast disappeared, and Marko breathed in the ashes. Marko was now aware of our presence. He saw Tonks, who seemed to have passed out, so he pointed to me and asked me to leave her where she was and follow him.

* * *

I may have committed a lot of mistakes. I did not research the building; I left room 2101 open; I missed the smell of the crime scene and probably a lot more. One thing, however, I can say for certain that following Marko was the right decision to make. While I was following him, I thought about all the activities I may have screwed up.

I can say with certainty that following Marko was the right decision because this is what led to my promotion.

PERSPECTIVE
JOSHUA
(Two Is Company, Three Is a Crowd)

"Fears are nothing more than a state of mind."

~ Napoleon Hill

Chapter 18
Lost

My head hurt, and I squinted with my eyes closed. I turned my head to the left and then to the right to make sure there was blood circulation. A frown automatically formed on my face when I felt sweat trickling down my brow. A scream, who could it be? It was faint and seemed to be loud enough to get my attention and wake me up, but still distant, maybe a couple of blocks away?

I sat up, half-sleepy and trying to make sense of the scream, only to realize I was not at home. At least I was not at the asylum in a straight-jacket. I couldn't remember where I had slept last, but I did recall that it wasn't this bedroom. The last I remembered was freaking out in front of the orderlies and punching the nurse who tried to make me consume more drugs. The room and its layout looked familiar, but it wasn't ringing any bells. I tried to remember where this could be, but all I could recall was the asylum and the horrible time I had there.

Something was off about how I came to be here. I don't recall anyone bringing me here, so how did I get here? A better question was, where was "here"?

I was dressed in my favorite Iron Maiden t-shirt and ripped jeans. My friends would always make fun of the way I went around with a beanie cap on my head and loose-fitting clothes. Who cares? They don't know what I have been through. They don't know what it's like to live without a mom.

I remember that Mom was dead. It was one of the most traumatic experiences in my life to see the light leave her eyes in such a pathetic way, beaten by that monster who calls himself my father. I don't remember what happened after that, but I recall running to my mom and shaking her face to wake her up. I tried to whisper to her how she couldn't leave me alone, especially with this monster, but she was already past her earthly burdens.

I think the loneliness drove me mad because I ended up in a mental asylum. I have had episodes in the asylum and woken up at random places within the campus, either overdosed or naked, but this time the location seems different, almost premeditated.

I was alone on a bed in the center of a room that did not look like my room at all. Of course, I do not recall having a normal room for almost a decade, but this was too domestic. The quilt was not mine, and I was used to the hard blankets at the asylum. I shoved the blanket to the side and was ready to get up and investigate what exactly was happening. It did not look like morning yet, from what I could see looking out the window across the room from me.

No sooner did I get down from the bed than I stepped on something sharp. I looked down, and it was part of a broken mug. I hopped on one leg and sat on the bed. Thankfully, there was no cut. I looked around the dim-lit room, and I realized that there were a lot of orphaned, misplaced items along the bed and all over the floor. Why were there so many objects? Some origami and a small school bag lay strewn around the room. One of the most conspicuous items was a bicycle. There were no bicycles in the asylum, so this had to be from an era before. On closer observation, I concluded that this was the very bicycle I had used when I was eight years old. The green and yellow paint job was clearly visible, and the bicycle itself was sparkly clean. Why was my childhood bicycle in this room?

Chapter 18: Lost

When we see nostalgic objects like this, all of us become kids again. I wanted to feel how it was to sit on that small seat, so I walked toward the cycle and tried to put it into gear. I was immediately surrounded by a blinding flash.

*

Seconds later, I felt a cold winter breeze on my face. I was wearing a muffler around my neck and a woolen coat. I was clearly enjoying the bicycle ride. The breeze tried to oppose my speed with great vigor, but I was faster than the wind. I stood to pedal and turned around. When I did, I realized the happiness I felt was never augmented by surroundings but always increased when Mom was around. I was on a small boulevard of pine trees, and they bore witness to the comic imagery of a boy cycling away, looking back to see if his mom was still behind him. It was, of course, the lifeline of an eight-year-old boy to see his mother supporting him from behind.

"Pogo, look forward and ride your cycle. Mummy will catch up."

I knew she would, but I could never be sure. I could feel my speed picking up. Nothing was going to stop me now. I felt invincible and fast. I replied, "It's alright, Mummy, I've got eyes in the back ... Whoa!"

My shout was enough to scare my mother and quicken her pace towards me. The next moment I was flat on my back, and my feet hit the ground. My cycle had hit a large rock and toppled along with me. I remember being flung off the bike and landing on one of my legs. Searing pain shot across my right foot, confirming which leg I landed on. The trees seemed to be laughing at me and my hubris.

I was losing consciousness when I saw my mom finally catching up. I could see the fear in her eyes. She quickly called a neighboring pedestrian and requested some help to get me to the hospital. She picked up my head and placed it on her lap. My head was spinning, and the pain was unbearable.

"Honey, help is on the way. Don't be scared."

I was all groggy, and the cheesiest line I could come up with was, "Don't worry, Mom. I'm not scared if you're with me. I'll take care of you."

She smiled down at me and hugged me closer.

*

I was now back in the room. This was not normal. I have heard of phasing out and daydreaming, but this was very vivid. I do not think a dream could be this vivid. This was a memory of something that had happened pretty much more than a decade ago. Why did touching this cycle bring this memory back? What exactly is this place or specifically this room?

Questions were flooding my mind, and I was no longer able to go back to sleep. I looked down at my feet and vaguely remembered a metatarsal injury. Sure enough, at my feet was a scar showing where the stitches had been. When I thought about this injury now, I realized that it had scared Mom more than I understood at the time, but it seemed to have healed now.

I began to consider the kidnapping theory now. I couldn't have walked into this house on my own without knowing. I have blackouts, but not like this. If this was indeed a kidnapping, then I pity the kidnapper as there is no one to really give a ransom. I couldn't think of any other reason why I would be here.

While contemplating this weird situation, my attention was diverted to a cigarette butt near the window. I do not smoke, so the next obvious question was, whose cigarette was this? Were they still in the room? A shiver ran down my spine. I moved in closer to the window and was still seeing only darkness. The cigarette butts seemed to have been recently smoked and thrown on the side of the window. I moved in and picked one up.

I was greeted by another blinding light…

*

Now I was standing behind the blue door. I looked at myself and felt older. The door was ajar, and I was standing outside, contemplating whether to open it or not. I looked down at myself, and I was back to being a kid. I was loitering around the blue door aimlessly when I heard my mom's screams and a rhythmic creaking of the bed. When I slightly nudged the door, it swung slowly. I saw my father half-naked, over my mom thrusting into her. My mom had a blank look and was staring at the ceiling. I couldn't understand what they were doing, but my father seemed animated about it. At every juncture, he wouldn't miss an opportunity to beat Mom or choke her. I could feel her pain and wanted to go and stop him, but then I knew my father would skin me alive. I hated him with all my heart. After some time, I saw him slump down to the other side of the bed, but he was far from done.

"Bitch, I don't want to fuck a corpse. You don't get me excited anymore." I did not know what it meant until much later. My mom did not say anything but just acquiesced to my father's accusation. As a punishment, my father took a cigarette he was smoking and placed the burning end on my mother's hand. My mom let out a heart-rending screech that I cannot forget even today. I could see the burns on her palm and her arms, but what I could also see was her helplessness and sheer terror of this man.

"Marko! Stop, please! What did I do to deserve this?" I could hear the deep sadness in my mom's voice

"Next time, try harder," was all my father could mouth.

*

Suddenly, I was back in the bedroom and was burning with fury. This was a memory I had tried to get rid of for a very long time. My hatred of my father was catalyzed by all the atrocities he had done to my mother. He was a monster beyond doubt. I was sweating profusely and was reeking with anger when I decided to get some air. I could only imagine the plight of a ten-year-old exposed to the violence when he witnesses his parents having sex. It would be confusing but, at the same time, deeply saddening. It is not something I would want any kid to go through, but unfortunately, I did.

As I was turning to move towards the door, I saw a hilt protruding from under the bed. A hilt most likely meant a weapon, which got me interested and scared at the same time. If what I now was beginning to understand about this place is correct, if I touch that hilt, I will get another memory of when I used it.

This time, I pulled the hilt from under the bed...

*

...and I was now holding a bloody knife. The blinding lights did not surprise me anymore.

This time I was in the very room I saw my parents having sex. In the room now was me, sitting above, and below me was my father gasping for air. The white bedsheets were now rapidly becoming dyed red with his blood. I could see the knife in my hand and the slit I had made across his throat, almost as if he had a second smile below his chin. I was not done, and I swung the knife in the air and brought it down like the Hammer of God into the center of my father's chest. I could see my father was already dead, but my hands wanted to stab his heart. I could sense the fear in me that he would not be dead unless he was stabbed right through the heart. I looked at myself in the mirror and saw myself as fourteen-year-old Pogo becoming the monster I feared I would become.

I turned to the right to see my mother's lifeless corpse across the bed near the dressing table. She had been most likely beaten to death. I walked to her and placed her head on my lap. The imagery of the cycle incident was coming to my mind. I had promised my mom that I would protect her, and here was her carcass showing me up as a failure. I had never felt like such a letdown in all my life. The slap marks of my father were still fresh across her face, and I saw another set of marks on her neck. It was my mother's ill fate that she met such a depressing end at the hands of a psychopath. All I could do was scream in agony.

*

I was transported back to the bedroom now. It took me a while to get back to reality from both the memories I had just seen. These were not memories I wanted to live with, and I had probably thrown them away for a reason. Why were they here, being represented by objects?

I began to consider why these objects were now around me, and I really had no clue. I was aware that Mom was dead, but had I really killed my father? I recall harboring unimaginable hate and anger towards him, but I did not recall killing him. I am not sure what all this was or if it was even my memory, but it was definitely me in the mirror killing my father, and I know what I saw. Somewhere deep inside, I felt that he deserved it. What was scratching at the back of my brain was the question of why I was not able to remember such a crucial activity in my past.

I was tired, and I did not think I could handle another memory. This place was weird and was clearly not real. I need to figure out where I am, why I was here, and who else is here. I even considered the possibility that this house was haunted by my father's ghost!

I had heard in a commercial for a board game a catchy statement that still stuck in my mind. The ghost starts playing the board game with the main character, and then soon after, the advertisement cuts to why this specific board game was so attractive. It was banned, of course, but it went somewhat like, "What is worse than being alone in a haunted house? Not being alone in a haunted house!"

I exited my room, and I could see a staircase to my left. I immediately recognized the staircase and realized I was back in my old house when Mom and Father were alive. This was the location where I had seemingly killed my father in their own room. This means I was on the lower floor, just beside the staircase.

I saw the room I had just come from, which had an open gray door and an adjacent room behind the staircase. Its door had a bright orange color. I did not recall these rooms being present when I used to live here, so I was confused yet again on this rendition of my old house. I moved under the staircase and walked close to this door. I tried to open it, but it was clearly locked. I tried to recall where my father used to keep his keys. Either they used to be dangling from his hips, or he used to keep them on a shelf behind the TV in the living room. Since the living room was close by, I decided to get that bunch of keys.

I had no reason to believe there was anybody else in the house, so I walked to the living room and switched on the lights. The first thing I noticed was that there was no television. All electronics, including my mobile phone, were missing. This was another anomaly I did not understand. There was a big empty space in the center of the wall where the television used to be, and beside it, as expected, I could see the keys on the shelf. I picked the bunch and turned to move outside. I cast my eyes at the couch across the television space, and I could almost see my father sitting there every day watching television like the lazy moron that he was. I could swear I saw him now looking at me and laughing. With all the strange stuff happening here, I wouldn't be surprised.

There was a clean carpet at the center, and a trophy stand just near the entrance to the living room. I saw this trophy stand while leaving the room and was surprised there was only one trophy in that stand. It was the trophy I had received when I was six years old for elocution in school. I tried to read the school's name on the trophy, but there was no such thing. That's weird, because I could swear that the trophy had the school's name. I couldn't remember the school where I studied or the college I went to. Weird...

Panic was taking over. I couldn't remember the name of the asylum I had been locked in, but now the reason for me being locked up was making sense. I was probably tried in court and sent to the asylum on the grounds of mental instability for killing my father. Maybe I was mentally unstable.

I began getting curious about this selective remembrance. It was almost as if my mind was given a chance to remember some items, and it auto-selected some without asking. I was now more scared than ever.

Chapter 18: Lost

I exited the living room and moved back to the room with the orange door behind the staircase. I clasped the bunch of keys. It wasn't heavy and had close to ten keys. I tried all of them, and none of them opened this strange orange door. I was beginning to give up when I heard something fall upstairs.

My first thought was that someone tripped and fell but in retrospect it sounded more like a light item falling from a table. Either way, that meant that I was not alone in the house. With this new discovery and the possibility that there was someone to ask what was happening, I moved up the staircase.

As I climbed up, I reached the corridor with a light-blue door to my right, which I knew to be my parents' room. This was where I saw my father abuse and kill my mom, and this was where I dreamed that I had killed my father, though I have no other recollection of this act. It was locked now with a rusted lock.

I did not even want to know what could be present in this room. I was scared it might bring back memories I was not ready to revisit. I placed my ear on the door to hear if there was anyone in, and all I heard was a deafening silence. No force could get me back into that room. It was a cursed room and home to a monster who beat his wife and child. Somewhere deep inside, I was scared that if I opened the door, he would step out and beat me.

I turned and walked towards my light-green bedroom. I still had fond memories of that room. Waking up to the bright, tender rays of the sun and Mom's face ready to welcome you were some of the memories which were enough to allow me to take on the world as a kid. It's a pity I couldn't spend time here as a teenager.

I crossed the corridor and reached the door. It was ajar, and I moved it slightly to see a kid not older than twelve sleeping on my bed with his blanket over him. The room was relatively empty except for the table on the side of the bed with some plastic toys and fallen spectacles. I still saw my bookshelf with my favorite books on them.

The kid was facing the window, so I was unable to see his face, but I assumed he was important to this puzzle, and I thought it was better to let him sleep. Before leaving, I realized that since this room had some space, and my bedroom below was completely cluttered with memory items, I could move the largest memory item to this room, which was the bicycle.

I quietly tiptoed across the corridor, mindful that all this ruckus could wake the kid up. It was funny how the presence of a kid changes how we move around in the house. I looked at the closed blue door and was secretly happy it was closed. I walked down the staircase and then turned around into my bedroom. I picked up the bicycle. It wasn't very heavy. I carried it up to the corridor and dragged it into the kid's room. I did not see a safe place to put it without waking the kid, so I just opened the door a little bit and quietly rolled the cycle to the side of the wall just beside the door. Satisfied that it would not fall, I brought the door back to its original position and tiptoed down the stairs.

While going down the stairs, I began to see the first rays of sunlight entering the house from the side which faced the main road. I realized that I now had been awake for quite some time and that the sun was out. I stole a glance out the window in my bedroom. It was somehow still dark, and I saw no sign of sunshine there.

I thought about the kid and realized that he would probably need something to eat while we hopefully discussed what he and I were doing here. Logically, I decided to make breakfast.

I went into the kitchen and started looking for some bread to make toast. I couldn't find any bread, but I saw some ready-to-eat pancake mix on the side of the stove. I decided that I'll get some bread from the market later if there was one close by. I also saw a couple of eggs on the counter and so decided to make an omelet as well. If the boy woke up, he would have enough food to eat.

* * *

240

Chapter 18: Lost

I was flipping eggs when he walked in. He asked me to pass him the omelet and pancakes but addressed me as his mom.

I turned around to explain to him that I was actually a boy, but I was in for a big surprise.

Chapter 19
Am I High?

I've stared at myself in the mirror before, but this one took the cake. Looking at yourself from ten years ago was not an experience many would have had. It was like looking into the past. If I had ever thought about what I would tell my younger self when I saw him, it would be "Run!" Well, here was my chance, and I couldn't say a thing. I stood there frozen, thinking about what to say. My face clearly gave away my expression of surprise.

I was now certain that this place wasn't real. I might have doubted this before, but now after seeing myself, I could safely believe it. I kept asking myself, how was this possible? Was I in some time rift where the future me and the past me are coexisting together? My head was spinning like a centrifuge casting out all my rational thoughts. I was so astounded that I completely forgot I was making something and had the stove on. I gathered my bearings and turned around, flipped the omelet, and directed my attention to him again. I repeatedly thought in my mind, "Pogo, was that you?" I was so lost that I almost burnt the omelet.

Before I could begin the conversation, I was bombarded with questions. Apparently, as a twelve-year-old, I was exempt from social niceties of "Hi" and "How are you?" Pogo's first question was "Where's Mom?", and I had to quickly think on my feet. He was probably expecting Mom to be here, but I knew for a fact that she wasn't coming back.

My first thought was to come clean and tell him the truth, but he was too naïve to understand the implications of what happened and that I, who he sees before him, am the product of a decision he made a couple of years from his current age. I decided to lie to protect him from the fact that his mother would not be coming back. Introducing myself as a cousin was the safest way to make sure that I could remember all our memories without raising any suspicious feelers.

Looking at myself as an adult gave me a different perspective of how I was when I was young. As a pre-teen, Pogo was smart and perceptive but could get distracting and irritating with his constant questions about where his mom was and how I got into the house. Of course, I realized that making pancakes and an omelet was purely coincidental, but it was obviously my favorite, and subconsciously I had cooked it for myself without knowing it was for me. It felt weird thinking this in my mind, but that was my current view of Pogo.

Was I always this nosy? I remember when I was young and in school, I did not have a lot of friends and so I spent a lot of time with teachers, especially my English teacher, whose name I couldn't remember, but her face I could remember vaguely. The language itself fascinated me. Homonyms, antonyms, similes – everything about the language intrigued me. I started spending a lot of time with her and practicing more verbal and written speech since I was eight. At twelve, I was already participating in English essay competitions and doing well as an English language enthusiast.

The thoughts of my school haunted me again. I was unable to remember my school a while ago, and that hadn't changed. I wondered what else I couldn't remember. I was also curious why I remembered the teacher's face but not the school. There must be a pattern.

I also realized I had to build Pogo's trust up from scratch to make him believe I was real. That was the only way Pogo would help me

Chapter 19: Am I High?

help him. I remembered the memory of the bicycle in the morning and thought it would be a good point to bring up as a cousin being present when we were both together with our mom. I slightly modified the memory by mentioning that I was the pedestrian his mom called out to help. I don't know if he believed it, but it had to do for now.

I could see that he still did not believe me, so I had to bring up our father. I honestly did not want to bring up anything related to our father, but I knew that was a topic that both of us would relate to and identify with. I was helpless as I couldn't explain to him that we had the same father, but I told him that I knew about the abuse he had to undergo. Unfortunately, it backfired. Pogo lashed out, asking if I knew about the abuse, why hadn't I done anything about it?

I wanted to tell him, "Yes, Pogo. I had done something about it. You had done something about it. You killed the man who murdered your mother. You sat on your father's corpse and stabbed him seventeen times until you laughed maniacally and scared the neighbor. You were tried for murder and sent for a psych evaluation, after which you were admitted to a mental asylum. The asylum changed you. You became more friendly and finally started having a social life in the asylum with the loonies. You have worn only white for almost ten years. You may not know, but you did what you needed to do."

I couldn't, of course, tell him anything, and all I could do was be cryptic about it. He seemed to have gotten emotional about the entire situation, and I was glad we hugged it out. It was a good feeling to know that there was someone for you and that you had a shoulder to cry on. I felt that when I was young, I missed this kind of brotherly or fatherly figure. Maybe if I had one, I would have been in a much better situation in life.

As a kid, I wouldn't say I was neglected, but my parents did not let me grow up. Father never included me in anything because he saw me as a roadblock. He probably married Mom, hoping she would be just with him and would eventually abandon me, but she loved me a lot more, and the abandonment never happened. Mom, on the other hand, wanted to protect me and prevent me from exposing myself to the world. Either way, I was sure Pogo would appreciate it if I included him in the day-to-day chores because that would have made me happy when I was young. Now I was getting the hang of it. Do the same things I wanted my parents to do when I was young, and I should get along well with Pogo.

I looked outside the window near the main door and saw that the lawn was a mess, and weeds were growing across the soft grass. I thought that both Pogo and I had experienced some weird stuff, and it would be good to give our minds some space to digest all this information. I decided to mow the lawn and Pogo followed later.

When Pogo mentioned his memory retrieval, I realized that these objects were not just limited to me but to most likely everyone else in this world. For some reason, we did not have all memories, and we had to touch some of these objects to get relevant memories, almost like unlocking levels in a game. He also confirmed that he did not remember the school he studied in or the street we were in, which I still couldn't explain.

While mowing the lawn, I was paying attention to all the other buildings adjacent to ours. I noticed our neighbor's house, and it did not seem familiar. I couldn't even recall how it had looked. It was as if I had never lived here as it all seemed to be from another life. A couple of feet from the neighbor's house was a diner with a pink and blue neon light, and adjacent to it was a supermarket. A grassy path connected all these buildings, which led to a highway, and opposite the highway was a hotel. I couldn't read the name of the hotel from this distance. Pogo continued his questioning and asked all logical questions, the answers to which I had no idea.

When he asked me about our birthday, I was thinking of telling him the truth, but then, it felt simpler to maintain the lie and keep him sane rather than to break his bubble. I told him about the times we may have spent here and why we may not have celebrated our birthdays at this place. I immediately regretted it. I don't know why I said it, but I'm sure it gave me away. If I was smart enough to figure it out, I doubt that Pogo would have missed it. We had hardly celebrated birthdays because Mom was the only one who cared about me, and I knew Mom had no money. I needed to be more careful now about what I said.

I was passively listening to Pogo, but my mind was elsewhere. I was considering where the scream I heard fits into this picture. I was trying to put two and two together. Who had screamed, and where could it have happened? From the mental map I managed to create, the most logical source was the hotel since it couldn't have been any of the other buildings as they were in close proximity to me. In that case the scream would have been much louder. The scream was a factor that was as mysterious as me seeing my younger self in a house I used to live in, decades ago.

In all this fiasco, I was observing Pogo while he was speaking his mind. His eyes showed true curiosity, and for a twelve-year-old, his maturity was palpable. Here he was with someone he was just told was his cousin, and he was not at all intimidated but was brave enough to have a friendly conversation and pose relevant questions. Of course, it helps that I am him, but I still feel proud of what I used to be when I was younger. As a kid, if I hadn't killed my father, I think I may have had a completely different, even normal, life.

Sarah's entry made things a bit more complicated. As soon as I saw her, I felt obliged to protect her. I was not sure why. She was an old, middle-aged lady who probably had a husband and a kid my age to protect her, but I felt close to her. My enthusiasm was embarrassingly obvious and Pogo was sure to notice. She invited us over for cookies, and of course, I did not read anything into this and just accepted. I was interested in getting to know her more and what her story was. I'm sure she had experienced similar encounters as we had, and I wanted to know more about it.

She turned to leave, and I was a bit dejected that our meeting ended so abruptly. That's when Pogo also brought up the scream. I was in awe at how he thought exactly what I was thinking. I then realized that he was basically me, so it was only natural. I made a split-second decision to lie and was about to do so when Sarah interjected and claimed to have heard the scream as well. I tried to direct the conversation to something else by asking her about someone local, but in the end, it came down to whether I had heard the scream or not. I tried to be as equivocal as possible and recommended leaving it to the professionals, which was the right advice but was definitely not what I wanted to do. At this point my sole purpose was to shield Pogo and Sarah from any danger. They had become very important to me, and I had no idea why.

In parallel to that train of thought, I wanted to investigate the source of the scream without Pogo. I was still on the fence about including Sarah. So, the best way to distance Pogo from all of this was to introduce doubt about the authenticity of the scream, but Sarah was clearly conclusive about it, which further strengthened Pogo's trust in it. I would need to find other ways to keep Pogo out of this.

Pogo was now keen to buy a soda, so we decided to go to the supermarket. I was returning the mower when I heard keys jingling by my waist. These were the keys to multiple rooms in the house which I had picked from the living room a while ago. I did not want to be responsible for or even be the keeper of these keys. Most of all, I did not want Pogo running around opening doors in the house. I needed to get rid of these keys. I asked Pogo to wait outside and ran inside to hide the keys. I felt the best location to hide them was behind the oven. Pogo rarely investigates the kitchen, so it seemed to be a good place.

Chapter 19: Am I High?

I walked out of the house to join Pogo, and together we made our way to the supermarket.

Chapter 20
Always Running

I needed to think things through. Anomalies were piling up in my mind, and I was trying to rationalize what was happening to Sarah, Pogo, and me. The grassy path felt refreshing, and though I should have been babysitting Pogo, I felt like both of us needed some space now. Pogo was going on about where Mom was, and it was honestly getting irritating. I had to be a little harsh with him, and in doing so, I was able to relate to how Mom used to be with me.

There were many times when Mom had got angry at me because I was being difficult. She might be giving me broccoli, and I would be crying my lungs out to avoid it. Her anger had no malice, but her exasperation was becoming clearer now. Caring for a toddler was as tough as satisfying the tantrums of a pre-teen. I know it's not his fault that he doesn't know the truth, and yes, he's a twelve-year-old, but I couldn't think of anything else at the time. I was pretty sure Mom had gone through this phase with me as well. I wanted to be away from this responsibility to protect my younger self. It was not my role here to give him emotional support, but unfortunately, we are all given responsibilities we do not ask for and when we're not ready, so it takes courage and patience to make sure we fulfil them.

Something inside me felt caged and conflicted. This was not the real me. How could I think of such irresponsible things? What's wrong with me? Pogo had lagged, probably enjoying the scenery or desperately wandering, hoping that Mom would show up. I turned around, and I could see him opposite the diner waving into the air. I hope he hadn't gone full cuckoo on me.

I looked forward and realized that I was now within close vicinity of this so-called supermarket and that very approach felt ominous. Its formidable presence stopped me at the entrance. I looked to see where Pogo was and saw he was gradually catching up. I turned to my left and saw an open highway and the hotel with its name in bold, "The Bender." I noticed that this hotel was clearly in violation of so many building rules. The main one was that the skyscraper building wasn't supposed to be right adjacent to the highway road. It was supposed to be at least ten feet from the road. How had this building gotten permission to be built? I would need to discuss with Sarah and see if she has any thoughts.

Sarah... Don't even get me started with Sarah. Who was she to call us to have cookies? She seems to be a clumsy old lady who just wants to prey on young boys. I'm sure she's hiding someone in her basement with her innocent coy smile and well-mannered words. I wish Sarah and Pogo would just go away and leave me alone.

I suddenly felt an internal turmoil again. I was getting thoughts that were not in my nature. I began to contemplate some more on what these thoughts meant before I looked back at the supermarket and the door. The answer appeared to be right in front of me.

I could see the supervisor standing at the door looking but wasn't sure if he was looking at me or was just looking outside. I seemed to be getting these thoughts only after walking into the vicinity of the supermarket. There was something creepy about this place, especially the supervisor. I did not want to think about anything yet because the more I thought, the darker they became.

Pogo soon caught up, and I wondered if he felt something unnatural about this supermarket. Both of us started revealing our dark thoughts to each other, and that's when I realized it would be better to enter the supermarket than let this escalate any further. I had a gut feeling that this place was manipulating us, but there was no way to prove it.

I knew I was thinking about entering, but for some reason, we were still outside. Sometimes we walked towards the door of the supermarket, and sometimes we were closer to the highway away from the door. The supermarket seemed to be filling in the blank spaces in our minds without us knowing. Thankfully, that's when the supervisor called us inside.

As we entered the supermarket, I realized everything about this supermarket was fake. It was not directly evident, but a lot of small discrepancies were piling up. There was a discount offer on the door but no expiry date. The supervisor looked like a villain bodyguard from a James Bond film, and there was absolutely no staff. There must be at least one more person to manage inventory during the day unless this supervisor could be at two places at the same time.

Again, Pogo was silent, and I started walking forward, exploring the supermarket. I did not even remember what I wanted to buy because the aisle placement and naming conventions were all grabbing my attention to show how fake they were. Yes, it was not something everyone would see, but I have been sensitized to this world's anomalies from the time I woke up. There was something about this supermarket that did not seem right, and I was definitely close to finding out.

There were markings created on the floor starting at the cash counter, directing us to maintain social distancing, which I felt was strange considering the only population I saw were me, Sarah, Pogo, the folks at the diner, and this supervisor. The aisles themselves were not inviting at all, but some unknown force was driving me in. The trepidation was slowly building up. That's when Pogo called me and asked if I was going to get the bread and milk. I thought Pogo would go looking for the soda section, and I was of two minds to send him alone, but soon when he joined me, I realized our fear of this place was mutual and urgent.

Inevitably, we both entered the aisle and in retrospect, that was, of course, a bad idea. I was once again ahead of Pogo, and he soon couldn't catch up and asked me to slow down. The aisle was now never-ending on both sides. The bread sections were repeating like a copy-and-paste display, and I was now certain we were trapped. My focus was now to escape this aisle, but to escape it, I needed it to stop it being infinite because the more I walked, the more it extended. Should I just stop for a while?

Pogo caught up, and I explained to him what I thought. Being a kid, he went berserk. I snapped at him to let me think, but he ran off without thinking at all. I tried to shout out to him, but he had disappeared in front of me, and I was now getting scared. Pogo was a very young kid, too young to be trapped here. I was scared that something might happen to him, but I stayed where I was and was desperately trying to find a way out. I was looking left and right, each time hoping that an opening would show up and lead me to the exit.

I don't know how long I waited because now, when I turned to my left, I could see an exit – the light at the end of my tunnel. I don't know which alien dimension I would exit to, considering my rotten luck, but I had no choice. I ran towards the exit like my life depended on it. When I reached the end, there was the shady supervisor waiting to pounce at me like an eager jaguar stalking its prey. He guided me out without any facial expressions, but I could sense that he was clearly the one orchestrating all these aisles. I was catching my breath but was not planning to let him off so easily. I asked him to show me the end of the aisle to see just how much he was involved in the creation of this place, and when he showed me the end of the aisle with mops and doors, I was sure he was fully in control of what was happening at this place. I did not wait to converse with him or have a friendly chit-chat because I needed to find Pogo. I didn't know what state he might be in, and I was terrified of this place.

Maybe the supervisor sensed my fear, or he felt pity for us. I soon heard Pogo's voice responding to my calls. I had been calling out his name aimlessly across various aisles. After running for some time in all directions possible, I heard him. His voice sounded very weak. I was surprised he was even able to respond loud enough for me to hear. I was sure he wouldn't be able to make it back alone, so when he called me to pick him up from inside, I did not think twice.

Yes, there was a risk of getting trapped again, but if that had to happen, the supervisor wouldn't have brought us out. I felt this time we would not be stuck, but instead we would be able to come out faster, and I was right. When I brought him out, he had already fainted. The last time I was so scared was when my father was beating me up and berating me for using his gun.

Thankfully, Pogo woke up alive, but he was mentally fragile now and mostly incoherent. He was talking about Sarah and a water helmet and about not being able to hear clearly. The aisle had clearly taken a toll on him. He asked me if Mom was back, but she wouldn't be, which just made me sadder, because I needed to lie to him.

I was constantly weighing between telling him the truth and breaking him or continuing the lie and risking his outburst. I knew that my younger self would need much more attention. Pogo needed someone to talk to, to listen to what happened, and was beginning to recount his experience, but I stopped him knowing that this supervisor couldn't be trusted, and it would be better to talk outside the supermarket. I wanted Pogo to unload in a safe environment. Nothing in this supermarket was normal, and our debrief would have to wait. For now, my priority was to escape this place.

We walked together this time. I put Pogo's arms on my waist so that he could use me as support. We gave the bread we picked up, to the supervisor, who seemed fazed with what had happened to Pogo.

He was trying to have a friendly conversation, but I did not trust him. He had more to him than meets the eye, as if he was trying to get more information about us.

He was curious about our parents, and he tried to bring up the scream into the conversation as well. I tried to deflect most of his questions, and I could see he was getting desperate to get information out of us. He even offered a free, adult-supervised stay at the hotel.

I clearly denied having heard the scream, and I saw genuine surprise. The exact expression on his face could be roughly translated as "that's not possible. You're obviously lying," but I did not falter. When he was talking in detail about the free stay, I immediately thought of Sarah and realized I was twenty-two, so I pretty much qualified as an adult. I wondered why he was stressing about getting an adult. Didn't I look adult enough? All these charities and unsolicited offers seemed odd from the start.

His questions were focused and more information-gathering rather than real concern. He finally asked us our names, and I was in a good mind not to tell him, but I realized there was nothing much he could do with our names. Moreover, he knew Pogo's name anyway since I shouted his name while I was looking for him. I almost left without revealing our names, but I realized that technically, I couldn't prove anything that happened or his involvement in it. It might as well have been someone else using him as a puppet. I don't know why I gave him the benefit of the doubt despite having all the red flags, but as a split-second decision, I told him our names.

When I gave him the cash and asked him to keep the change, there was no reaction, almost as if he did not care about the money. Most supervisors at supermarkets would be happy about the tip, but not him. That was not expected from someone who worked in a supermarket. This only added to my presumption that he was not an actual supervisor. I paid him for the bread and left with Pogo. I could sense Pogo did not have enough energy to even say anything about it.

Chapter 20: Always Running

Outside the supermarket, we began feeling dark thoughts again, so we kept on walking until our minds felt lighter. When we looked around, we were almost in front of the diner, pretty much far away from the supermarket. As we stopped to catch our breath, Pogo mentioned that it was worthwhile to accept his offer at the hotel so we could at least find Mom considering that there was a possibility that she might be there. Yet again, I decided to avoid mentioning the truth and cautioned him about his own safety.

Our decision to meet Sarah was unanimous. We needed a calm place to think, and we were hungry post-breakfast after all the running and escaping we had to do. We needed to talk to a more affable person than the supervisor, and I thought Sarah was the right person.

Cookies could be a good excuse to understand how she fits into this puzzle, as well as to speak to her about some of the anomalies we have seen and compare notes.

Chapter 21
Nothing Is True, Everything Is Permitted

Why am I here? I was literally in a men's washroom at the diner while Sarah was alone with a bunch of strange people. I was not at all comfortable with what was happening around me. The diner seemed to be a safe space but was clearly something else. Every building here which is not our home seemed to have a significance more than just existing.

I was looking at the commode in the washroom, and it was perfectly clean. I had never seen such a clean washroom, even at home. I wondered who maintains this washroom and if people have even used it since the time it was incepted. It was just another anomaly added to the list.

I closed my eyes and recalled our visit to Sarah's. I did not want Pogo to figure out the truth about Mom, but unfortunately, he did, and his reaction was as expected. Initially, both me and him had really looked forward to visiting Sarah. We had just escaped the supermarket narrowly and were looking to start fresh and assess our current state along with Sarah.

Navigating her Amazonian front yard was not easy, but she had been expecting us. I was surprised by how sparsely populated the fauna was. There were no cats or dogs on the street. Even squirrels were missing, which was strange considering there was a large mango tree just opposite our homes. We entered Sarah's home after she invited us in and made ourselves comfortable.

One word to describe Sarah's home was "unkempt." Everything starting from the meager furnishings to the misplaced vase seemed to indicate a lack of effort in maintenance. I was not judging her but merely making an observation. I wanted to know her story and how she basically fit into this puzzle, but the initial couple of minutes were awkward, and I did not know how to really initiate a conversation. There's not much a fifty-year-old lady and a twenty-two-year-old boy have in common, to begin with. I thought the best ice breaker would be the lawn. It was a mess and needed immediate cleaning.

I offered to clean it, but she managed to divert the conversation to us being tired. Pogo had a loose tongue, and he immediately began explaining the supermarket ordeal, which I cut short. Sarah was a nice person, but we did not know enough about Sarah, so I was not comfortable telling her what we encountered. I changed the subject to make it less mild.

She, in turn, realized that the main event wasn't on the table and apologized and went to fetch the cookies. I began to consider what her role could be here. The problem that I observed was the remembrance of certain memories. In this place, it was difficult to say if we did not remember it or if it did not happen because it was now clear that we needed to interact with certain objects to trigger memories. She could have been one of our teachers at school and we had no way to confirm because we just could not remember. From the way she maintained the home, I was sure she never really had visitors.

I could sense Pogo was becoming restless, and finally, he asked me if he could get some water as he hadn't had any since the supermarket. I was thirsty as well, so I decided to go to the kitchen and check on Sarah to see what the hold-up was as she had stepped away for quite some time.

Chapter 21: Nothing Is True, Everything Is Permitted

In the kitchen, Sarah seemed to have lost the milk. Sarah and I decided to search for it, and I saw this as a good opportunity to get close to her and ask her more about the place. She offered us to stay for lunch, and I felt we were hitting it off well, so I asked her about the vase I had seen on the way in. Out of all the furniture in the room, that one seemed out of place. She said it was her husband's gift, but she clearly did not remember a lot about her husband. Could he be the one who brought us here?

I was getting tired of searching and though conversing with her was pleasant, we had just undergone a harrowing experience, and in all honesty, I just wanted to bury myself in some milk and cookies. I think she sensed it as well and asked me to go and sit with Pogo, and she'll come over. I realized I was not wrong at expressing my tiredness, and it was a bit rude, so I explained to her part of the supermarket ordeal and the free stay at the hotel that the supervisor had offered. When she brought up Father and meeting Mom with him, I felt a sudden rage which was quickly dampened by a deep sadness. I found myself explaining to her about Mom and Father. I was so desperate and sad that I almost forgot that I had spun a lie about being Pogo's cousin and had to maintain the lie with her as well. She seemed too surprised and distracted by the supervisor's offer to notice. She even asked me why we were not accepting the offer with our parents.

It all came down to our parents. It is said you cannot escape family, and, in my case, it was so true. I had to lie to Sarah and not tell her that my father had killed my mother and run away. Of course, she was not ready to hear the truth, which was that she was looking at a murderer, which would, in all likelihood, freak her out. I explained why I lied about the scream and how my priority was Pogo. She expressed her concern, but unfortunately, neither of us heard Pogo come in the room behind me.

Pogo's reaction was justified considering his perspective, and all I wanted was for him to be protected from all the meanness in the world.

When I was Pogo's age, I would feel sad that adults wouldn't treat me like one and tell me their adult secrets. Now that I am an adult, I can see what they did and why they did it. As a kid, Pogo would never understand why I did not tell him the truth or what he thinks is the truth, and I was frustrated that I couldn't gauge Pogo's reaction to his patricide.

It did not matter now because Pogo was running away again. This time he was running from me and most likely everything else. He was fragile now, and I needed to make sure he didn't do anything drastic. I explained this to Sarah and became aware of injuring her during my fall. She offered to speak to the supervisor about this free staycation while I try to fix Pogo. I could sense that she was in pain. I did not want her to strain too much but I was unable to really stay back and convince her otherwise because Pogo was not in a good place mentally and he needed me.

As I ran towards our home, my mind was pregnant with thoughts. I was thinking about myself when I was young. As soon as I witnessed my mom's death, my first reaction was to kill my father. There was no such person here and I was scared for Pogo. He had so much anger now and nowhere to channel it. I knew I had the capability of showing and storing anger, but at that age, I did not have the maturity to decide which one.

I needed to prevent myself from another meltdown. I never really had a therapist to say this, but killing my father was almost cathartic for me. I would have lived a completely different, guilty, worthless life if I hadn't killed him. If I was given a chance to go back in time, I would do the exact same things and kill him all over again. Knowing this, I needed to speak to Pogo and let him know that he's not alone and doesn't need to look for any other source to heal.

I walked into our house and up the stairs and saw him crying into his pillow. He was turned the other way, but I knew he had been crying.

Chapter 21: Nothing Is True, Everything Is Permitted

He was spewing hate toward me, which I had expected, but I explained to him what I truly felt. There was more going on in this world. He knew some of the anomalies, so he knew what I was talking about. I assured him that I would be back with more information, and he should just stay out of trouble. I was speaking to a younger version of myself here, and I was not sure if young me would stay out of trouble, but when I looked at Pogo crying after being told about Mom's death, I thought, maybe there was a path to redemption, and I did not have to end up in a looney bin again. I thought about this for a while and then left. I couldn't stand there and just do nothing. Sarah was waiting for me.

As I walked on the grassy path to Sarah's house, my mind was blank. No anomaly mattered now because I was hell-bent on understanding why we were here and possibly escape this hell. This became my primary focus even when there were so many things happening around me.

I reached Sarah's house, and the door was open. I opened it further and saw her sitting down on the sofa with her eyes closed. I wanted to make our way to the hotel quickly, so I decided to wake her up. She quickly got up and enquired about Pogo's health. Obviously, there was nothing she could really do, so I let her know he was okay. Later, she mentioned about her conversation with the supervisor and was keen to join me to the hotel. I had assumed we would go there in the evening, but Sarah was in a hurry to really understand more about this staycation offer, so I just went with the flow. She wanted to grab a quick lunch at the diner and then go directly to the hotel.

I had a lot of time to think about Pogo and Sarah. I began piecing the puzzles as I knew them. To begin with, the place here was not completely unknown. My home was real, so it was not possible this was a simulation or something. No one would have access to the home to create such an accurate replica. My neighbor was Sarah, who I do not remember, which seemed a bit odd at first, but considering I don't remember a lot of people, this added to the common anomaly of selective memory.

There was a possibility that my home was not a simulation, but then how could someone just pluck one home and slap it adjacent to another? There weren't a lot of fauna, and the most advanced beings here except for humans were insects. Apart from our homes, there were only three other buildings out of which one of them we had been to and escaped. The aisles could not be real, and this had to be some sort of black magic that was being perpetuated by the supervisor. He said his name, but I don't seem to recall. If there is magic involved, then was this another dimension? How come only a few of us got in?

There are objects in the world that can give us back our memories, but there are memories we just remember without having to think. I compared this to something like driving. I had read somewhere that tasks like driving and swimming come under procedural memory, and we do not forget them even if we forget our family. It really depends on how frequently we have been referencing the memory or doing a certain task. Maybe I remember how I looked ten years ago because it is muscle memory, and I've been seeing myself almost every day of my life. This still did not explain how the skyscraper got approval to be built just adjacent to the road.

I was so engrossed in thinking, that I did not realize I had reached the diner door. Sarah soon caught up, and we ended up sitting at the corner of the diner. I was observing the people, and they immediately did not look right. Sarah bumped into one of them, and they said something stupid like "Welcome to the diner," almost like they were programmed to say something like that. I did not like the diner. What was confusing was that the diner itself seemed to be a warm place with a perfect ambiance for gossip, but the people got my feelers up.

Soon we ordered our food and started speaking to Sarah. She revealed that the supervisor had triggered her memory of her husband somehow and that he was now last seen looking for a meat cleaver and a rope which did not sit well with the scream. She was, of course, tensed up about it but wanted to find out more about this entire fiasco, which gave her a strong motive to go to the hotel. I realized that if Pogo was to spend time with Sarah and me, she would have to follow the lie I had told Pogo initially. This was a good opportunity to make sure there were no loose ends. I glibly brought up the topic of Pogo being my cousin. It had the intended effect, and I topped it off by revealing to her about the hotel being too close to the road. She acknowledged these items but did not seem really taken aback as I was. She was surprised about Pogo being my cousin, and I wanted to leave the topic at that. The diner lady then surprised me and asked about Pogo, but as my cousin.

That was the last straw. I had just mentioned this information five minutes ago to Sarah. There was no way the diner lady knew this without eavesdropping. She most likely had bugged this seat; that's why she brought us here specifically. I was not sure how I would tell Sarah about this. The diner lady and Sarah seemed to be having an intense conversation about the scream, and I was scared that Sarah may end up giving more information. I had no way of warning her, and if I stayed back, the diner lady would most likely hear everything. The only solution I could see was to remove myself from the equation. That is how I landed here, sitting on this spotless commode. I could not gauge how much Sarah would have eaten based on the time span I was away, but I felt that I had spent enough time in the washroom. If Sarah wasn't done, we'd just have to leave it half-eaten.

When I returned to the table, there was something different, but Sarah was done, and Tonks was getting ready to take us to the hotel. She asked us to wait outside and said she would come back. I had done something similar to Pogo earlier and was sure she was not going back just to drop her apron, but why else would she want to go back inside? Later I would estimate that Tonks returned to the diner to communicate with someone else before she took us to the hotel. My best guess was that she had been announcing our arrival to someone.

The questions were just piling on with no answers in sight. I had nothing against the lady per se, but the fact that she had eavesdropped on us was a red flag. Yet here she was, escorting us to the hotel, so I felt obliged to introduce myself. She said she and Sarah had spoken about me already, which was another red flag, but now it was too late.

Tonks, Sarah, and I walked somberly towards the hotel.

Chapter 22
Welcome to the Hotel California

The entire journey was another analysis of our current state, but this time with Tonks in the equation. Tonks had walked ahead of Sarah and me as we reached the deserted highway. A "deserted highway" seems like an oxymoron, but here we were on a highway with no cars or traffic signals. Sarah seemed to have been distraught about me keeping mum about everything because she pulled me aside to confront me about it.

I explained to her some of the anomalies I had observed and asked her to figure out what had changed. When I told her that the building now had moved ten feet away from the highway, she still did not really catch what I was saying. When I explained to her the cousin scenario in the diner, that's when she realized the gravity of the situation. She explained her conversation with Tonks and the information she had shared with her, and I began to rationalize Tonks' actions. Tonks basically was part of this elaborate world but somehow was not part of the predicament we were in. I stressed that though Tonks seemed to be a nice lady, she couldn't be trusted, and we needed to always be on our toes.

If Tonks was not involved in this elaborate plan, then I wanted to test her. I asked her where the road went. I couldn't see its beginning or end, and it reminded me of the infinite aisles. She was clear that she didn't know but what struck me was the way she said it. She said she spent most of her time in the diner. If that was true, then how much time did she spend cleaning the hotel? The entire concept of moonlighting as hotel staff was not believable. Was I to believe that she ran a successful diner with NO staff, and then also had to attend to hotel rooms that needed cleaning? A hotel with almost a thousand rooms? How was this model successful?

I saw the "WELCOME" board, which also seemed a bit odd. Yes, there were small-scale hotels in the suburbs that posted welcome signs, but to put one on a five-star hotel was overkill and unheard of. Of course, when we entered, the hotel was grander than I had expected, but the lack of general population was disturbing. I accepted the lack of people in the supermarket, but how can there be no people in a hotel whose sole purpose was to house people? I began mapping out the layout in case I needed to escape from here, but I couldn't see an emergency exit.

My reverie was broken by Tonks, who introduced Sarah and me to Kobi, who was the manager. Tonks slipped away, and Kobi began his preaching about the hotel. For me, it was important to know how many types of people the hotel had used for beta testing and how extensive was the testing. When he said there were four hundred rooms being used as testing rooms, I was surprised at the scale. Catering to four hundred rooms was next to impossible without a large and hard-working housekeeping team. Tonks may be good, but in my view, it was still a huge task for one person.

Then Kobi mentioned something about a "pandemic." I recalled seeing the "Maintain Social Distance" sign at the supermarket, and now Kobi casually mentioned a pandemic. The minimum requirement for a pandemic was to have people spread a virus, and there were hardly enough people here to form a choir band. This added to the falsehoods of this place. It also means this pandemic was in another world where Kobi came from, the real one. Alternatively, there could have been a pandemic here, and we could be in a post-apocalyptic world, but if that's the case, why this elaborate plan to get us out and to this hotel? He immediately realized that he probably revealed a lot more information than he should have, but it was too late now.

Conveniently, he was posted here today and did not have any information about what happened yesterday. After some more exchanges, he asked about Pogo. Everyone seemed interested to see Pogo. It was almost like Pogo being present with us normalized everything that happening here. Nothing could change the feeling that this hotel was just like the other places. The supermarket had consumed us and lived on our fear. The diner tried to extract our deepest secrets. What had the hotel in store for us?

He offered to send Klaus, the supervisor whose name I finally remembered, to pick Pogo up when he was ready to come, but Pogo wouldn't be coming here. I wouldn't let him. He based his proposal on the fact that a scream made the area much more dangerous. I thought he was a bit naïve or maybe overconfident to bring up the scream in front of strangers. Of course, he had no way to know we had heard the scream (or so I thought).

I immediately caught this straw and pulled as hard as I could. We asked him about the scream, and he quite reluctantly revealed to us that there was a murder of a girl and that he had no idea about the details or the room number, but Tonks was present during the initial police investigation. I couldn't make sense of it because Tonks was conversing with us all about the scream as if she had no idea where it came from, and now we learn that Tonks was basically privy to the whole murder situation. Why did she act as if she knew nothing? That felt a tad suspicious.

Sarah, of course understandably, wanted to confirm if her daughter was the girl murdered and Kobi's answer that the murdered girl was around twenty years old seemed to calm her down. Before we could ask more, Tonks showed up and took us to the twenty-first floor, where the party had just begun.

Mindbender

When Sarah volunteered to stay back while Tonks showed me my room, I panicked. I had spent so much time with Sarah that I did not want to move forward alone. It was a bit selfish, but I wanted her to be around when so we could explore the hotel together. She was fragile and had probably injured herself when she fell.

I was already being led to my room while I was thinking about Sarah. Tonks opened the door and ushered me in. Considering the history of Tonks' lies and my need to be around Sarah and protect her, I insisted that I go back with her and make sure Sarah reached her room safely and has a good rest.

Tonks seemed a bit disturbed that I insisted on following her. It felt as if she was trying to get Sarah alone for some reason, and Tonks wanting someone alone was not a scenario I could push aside. She finally had to acquiesce, and I walked back with her to take Sarah to her room.

From a distance, I was unable to see Sarah, and fear kicked in again. As we neared the center of the corridor, the door to room 2101 was thrown open, and Sarah jumped out white as a ghost. She was rambling about a tortured kid who needed help. I was observing Tonks' reaction to this accusation, and her reaction was mild and not the reaction expected if you know there is someone inside one of the hotel rooms who needs help. Logically, if this was the case, she either did not believe Sarah or she already knows something is wrong in that room.

Tonks was trying to escape checking the room itself and had to be goaded with the threat of the police. When she came out sometime later, she asked Sarah whom she had to help, I knew something was wrong. It was not that I did not trust Sarah, but something like this no longer surprised me. Sarah went in to point out the boy in the chair but came out visibly shaken. She was sure there had been someone in there, and I believed her.

Chapter 22: Welcome to the Hotel California

Before she made a fool of herself, I pulled her to the side and assured her that I believed her and that I had already highlighted previously that this building was unique and could change positions and possibly room decor at will. I wasn't sure how it was doing that, but I was certain it had such a capability.

Later, as we walked towards the other side of hotel, I was getting an ominous vibe, not from here but from a distance. I could feel something bad was about to happen, but I was unable to express anything about this feeling. All I could hear were the muffled sounds coming from the neighboring rooms.

We stopped at 2120, and Tonks opened the door. I did not want Sarah or Tonks to go in first, so I offered to go in. As soon as I entered, I saw some blood already visible before even reaching the main room. From the small hallway to the main room, I could see a chair in the corner and some dried blood that had pooled at the bottom. Being in a mental asylum had desensitized me to blood, so now I was already mentally prepared to see a body. Maybe this was the room that Kobi was talking about where the girl was murdered.

As I entered, I saw a dead girl on the bed, her throat had been slit, and she had several stab wounds. She was definitely the source of the scream, and I did not want to call Sarah in yet because I wanted to have a look at the girl. There was a reason Sarah and me were brought here to this room with this dead girl, and it cannot be a happy coincidence.

I was about to move closer to the girl when I felt a sharp pain in my head. It felt as if my soul was being sucked from me. If I had to pinpoint what I felt, I would say the part of my soul that I felt leaving me was "innocence". I was unable to even stand as a large amount of energy was being sucked out of me. I dropped to my knees exactly where I had been standing beside the bed. The last thing I saw was the girl's hand sticking out across the bed.

*   *

When I woke up, I was groggy, and my eyes and face were all wet. I was not breathing through my nose but felt an attachment near my neck, allowing me to breathe. I was inside a watery gel, but I did not feel like I was floating. I looked down and realized my hands were tied, and I couldn't move. I had a helmet on my head, which covered me just up to my neck. I looked down and to the side and could see nothing specific. I looked forward, and through the water, I saw a silhouette of a woman. The feeling of being underwater was overcoming all my other emotions. I vaguely remembered what Pogo mentioned to me about seeing someone like Sarah. I felt it could be Sarah, but there was no clarity because of the gel.

I began shaking violently and tried to get out, but the metal handguard did not budge. I heard a muffled voice saying, "He's back again! His brain patterns are different, but he is waking up!"

"He cannot wake up now! We don't have Tonks or Kobi back yet. Up the dosage and make sure he goes under. We are not done with this mission yet."

I felt something entering the helmet, but I couldn't remember seeing or hearing anything because it all went blank soon...

*   *

When I woke up Kobi was sprinkling some water over me, and Tonks and Sarah were talking about looking at objects close by to identify the girl, which I felt was absolutely absurd. My body was feeling the pain of being crushed under a washing machine. My head hurt, and all I wanted to do was go to sleep. Did I just see a dream of myself being stuck in a water helmet? Was this the water helmet that Pogo saw? What did they mean by "upping the dosage"? What else was going on here with Tonks and Kobi?

Also, why weren't the police being summoned? What was the point of searching around the crime scene when we would be basically contaminating it? My mind was a mangled mess.

I heard Sarah saying something about Tonks and Kobi being police officers. My headache was intensifying by the minute now. If they were police officers, why were we here? I couldn't just stay still any longer, and I started to get up to ask what the hell was happening. Sarah came over and tried to make me feel comfortable. She thought I fainted seeing the dead body, but how could I explain to her that it was something else? I felt empty; I felt nothing except deep pain and rage.

I knew this girl, and Sarah said she knew her as well. She asked me to move to a chair and sit down and recuperate. I clearly was the only one caring about crime scene preservation. I strictly said I would not do it, but Sarah asked me to trust her with this, and due to my current state, I had to comply. I obliged and dragged myself to the other end of the room and sat on the chair.

The rest of the episode was a blur to me. I don't know how frequently I phased out, but I had lost track of what was happening. I came back to my senses when I heard Sarah's scream. Oh no… The worst I feared had happened, and someone was hurting her. I tried to look up and vaguely saw her crying. I heard the phrase, "She did not deserve it," and then the next thing I knew, Sarah was pushing past Kobi and Tonks and running outside. Then, I heard glass breaking, and I knew that the moment I dreaded had just taken place.

Tonks seemed tensed. She asked Kobi to do something, most likely to check to see what happened. After Kobi left, she walked back to me. It was fair to say I was still in shock. I could hear Tonks, and I could even hear myself talking, but I was mostly on autopilot. I couldn't believe that Sarah could have died. Tonks was explaining something about her being a police officer and investigating this murder and that this girl was related to Sarah and someone called "Marko."

I began to be surrounded by a blinding light. Did I touch something by mistake? I was not sure what triggered the memory, but most likely, it was something that Tonks said.

Mindbender

*

A church backdrop soon came into view. Julia and I were standing outside the church, waiting for our cue to enter. The atmosphere was so calming, but I was still nervous. Julia, though, seemed calm. She looked at me and said, "Dad, don't be nervous. This is one of the best moments that you will cherish."

This was true, as it was one the best memories I had of her. We finally got our cue, and we slowly entered the chapel. I was now walking down a church aisle with my beautiful daughter. The decision to make it a church wedding was mine because I knew her husband-to-be, Paul, was an orphan, and I did not want him to feel as if he was alone. I wanted the marriage and taking of vows to be in the presence of God. God was someone who was not present for a major part of my life, but I wanted him to be part of theirs. I wasn't a devout follower or anything of the sort, but it just felt right.

There were wedding pews for different folks. Our neighbors, our parents, our relatives – everyone was there. They were looking back at me and clapping, a beautiful smile on all their faces. I saw Sarah sitting in the front row. Straight down the aisle, I saw a young man with a kind face, our very own Paul, and the priest. Paul was all dressed in a gray suit and red tie. His hands were folded before him, eagerly waiting for Julia. We walked slowly and finally reached the point where she was to go be with her man.

The priest welcomed the bride and began explaining the beauty of marriage and the sacred vows that both husband and wife need to maintain. I wasn't listening to any of that but was looking at my daughter. She had grown up to be a kind, beautiful, mature woman who chose an equally kind partner. As a father, this was everything I could ask for. My biggest fear was that I would take after my father, and I am thankful to God that I did not end up like him.

Chapter 22: Welcome to the Hotel California

Before she left for Paul, she whispered into my ear, "I am proud of you, Daddy. I hope you are proud of me as well."

She went to stand with the love of her life, and I remember I cried that day. There were people who made it in life with large enterprises or businesses, but I can say for sure that I made it in life as well. After killing my father and spending close to a decade in a mental asylum, I was now a proud dad of a smart and beautiful daughter. I felt pride and happiness and thanked God for finally showing up.

*

The view of the dead girl and the crime scene came back, and that was the last time I remember being Joshua.

Chapter 23
The Cost of Anger

I was now back in the hotel room but was lying down on the ground. It felt like I had been in hibernation all this time, and a jackhammer had been hitting my head, but I tried not to show. I was not as weak as Joshua, but I was not myself either. My clothes were tighter around me, and I couldn't open my eyes entirely. My body felt stronger and toned like a new bodysuit, but mentally, I was spent.

I felt a hand making its way in front of my neck. Instinct took over, and I grasped the wrist as hard as I could and sent my other hand looking for the owner's throat. When my right hand connected to the throat, I opened my eyes and saw Tonks.

I felt a pang of anger at Tonks. From the beginning, she has been lying to us. Nothing that she said was true in any sense. Starting from the eavesdropping at the diner to the lie about not knowing the scream, she did not reveal any information about this murder or the girl, and now she was trying to feed me the lie about her being a police officer. I was done playing games and was ready to end it right here along with Sarah.

I wasn't scared of dying, but I felt Julia's death shouldn't be in vain, and I wanted to know who killed her. Tonks was the only source I had, and my hand on her neck tightened, demanding information. She tried to put her police officer façade, but I had seen right through it and was not taking any more of that bullshit. My tightening grip opened her mouth up enough to release a flood of information.

When Tonks mentioned that we are lucid dreaming, my mind immediately went to a vague memory of me punching someone and the doctor telling my mom I was capable of lucid dreaming. Tonks' explanation was foggy and probably fake considering this place, but I couldn't brush off the possibility that it was true. When she explained how we had connected with her in this world, or "construct," as she calls it, some of the anomalies made sense. It all came down to how realistic they could render the world here. If there were more sources of energy to really build this place up, it would have fooled us all.

Of course, Tonks mentioned that their motive was to make us aware that we are dreaming. It wouldn't make sense to spend so much time analyzing someone's mind when you could just get a good behavioral expert and interrogate them in the real world. I still couldn't wrap my head around why the military would spend so much time and effort to train operatives to extract information they could otherwise extract by some intimidation and brute force.

That's when she told me the reason, which frankly seemed odd. She said we had alibis for the night my daughter was murdered, but the way she said it came out wrong. It felt as if they did not believe us, and they were trying to get some unknown information that was hidden in our minds. Well, they weren't going to find anything because there was nothing to hide. I couldn't remember what happened that night, so I was most likely doing something mundane like sleeping.

Their plan to fool us and get information was viable and may have worked if it wasn't for Pogo. If I hadn't seen young Pogo, I would still have given the benefit of the doubt to this world and its anomalies, but when I saw myself, I was certain that this place was not real. It was just a matter of finding out what exactly this place was and what was the motive for bringing us here.

Chapter 23: The Cost of Anger

When she explained in detail about our minds showing up as safe houses as well as extracting memories from objects, a little more of the puzzle became clear. Some of the rules of the place also made sense, one of them being that they couldn't enter our minds without permission and vice versa. I remember Pogo and me waiting outside the supermarket with dark thoughts, still wanting to enter but unable to do so until the supervisor called us in.

Tonks was consistently bringing up hidden memories. I couldn't remember what happened that night, but Sarah had reacted very differently when she got her memory of the event. If I take Sarah's reaction as reference, why don't they consider Sarah as a possible suspect? Technically, she must have woken up from this dream and might still be alive. I asked Tonks why Sarah was not being debriefed and queried for information, but Tonks shot that down, saying Sarah wouldn't be in a good mental state to help us at this point. It now finally came down to me to help Tonks figure out who killed Julia.

She said there was one piece of evidence that was found beside Julia's body that I had not seen. I couldn't even remember my daughter's death, so I couldn't really help Tonks. She asked me to go and check it out to see maybe if it jogged a memory, so I obliged.

Tonks facilitated moving back to the room which had been filled with a rotting smell by the building after I had called it out as an anomaly. Kobi was in this building, so this was probably Kobi's mind. He seemed to have the capability to change the building as he wanted, which is probably what he did in room 2101. I did not want to bring it up as I had other issues to focus on.

Once the smell was gone, I walked to the upper drawer beside the bed. When I opened the drawer, I saw a black whip neatly wound and tied. I picked it up with my hand to witness a memory I had not expected at all.

Mindbender

*

I was in a large room with a bed in the background. I could see a swing hanging from the ceiling, and I was on my knees, sitting over the cadaver of dead Julia. At first glance, it appeared I was mourning her, but that changed when I saw the glass shard tracing an arc with my hand and landing straight at the center of her chest. I did not feel sadness or remorse, just blind rage. I witnessed blood spurting out of her neck and splattering onto my face, but I did not care. The anger fueled my hand, and I stabbed her many more times.

She was wearing the same bra with spikes and leather spandex as I had seen in the hotel room some time ago, but I wasn't thinking. I was stabbing and stabbing. From behind, I heard a small whimper, but I did not look around. I was laser-focused on ending Julia. I began phasing out and disappearing as the last stab connected on Julia's upper shoulders.

*

I then realized I was already back in the hotel room.

A sudden depressing realization swept over me. My face fell as I realized that I had ended my daughter's life. Sarah's reaction now made more sense. The beautiful girl that I had raised, whose wedding I had attended, whose life was so well sorted, was murdered by her own father. When I thought about the reason I did it, I couldn't point towards a single motive. If given a chance, I couldn't clearly say that I wouldn't do it again. Maybe I could have ended it differently or at least confronted her about why she did what she did.

A lot of things now began to make sense. I saw Pogo first in the house because he was the part of me that always believed in the good side of things. He was as naïve as kids could be until, of course, he (or I) killed Father. I don't know why my mind rendered me as Joshua first, but Joshua Flannagan was my real name. That was the name I had until I was thirty-two when I left the mental asylum all cured, though I never believed I had a problem. I just let the doctors think I did and let them cure me. What I had was a bad childhood and an abusive father which the justice system couldn't see through.

I changed my name after meeting Sarah. Sarah doesn't know my past, so she did not know my real name. She saw me and loved me as "Marko." In a way, I changed my name to make sure I did not become my father in any sense and so no one could know my past. That's why I took his name, to prove that even with his name, I can be a good man. I was running away from my past, and now it had caught up with me. This hidden anger was fueling my episodes which ended up with me killing two people.

Now I began to understand why this elaborate scheme had to be plotted. The police probably had an inkling that it was me or Sarah, but I was careful not to leave anything behind. They wanted to investigate my mind and get the information I could subconsciously reveal to them, but they were clearly not asking the right questions.

The supervisor's infinite aisle was intimidating, but there was no way I would have got this memory back there. Tonks did not have charm enough to really get me to talk, so building this crime scene was an elaborate Plan B to make me or Sarah relive the murder and reveal any details that would implicate us. It amazed me how the supervisor or Tonks would be able to train their mind to construct a trick as complex as creating an infinite set of aisles or an overarching diner with fake people. Ironically, the person I have been looking for, was me.

When I came back to the crime scene, I was done with this cat-and-mouse game. I missed my daughter yet killed her mercilessly, and I deserved to be punished. A wave of relief washed over me when all these pieces came into place, but it did not last long.

While I was contemplating surrender, Kobi barged in mentioning a monster downstairs and that Klaus and Sarah were dismembered and eaten. This did not sound familiar, but if my analysis was correct, Sarah was not the person who had anger-management issues. Klaus, Kobi, and Tonks were military variables, which left the source of the monster to be my home which was basically a representation of my mind. This was the very same monster that I am sure I had called upon unknowingly when I felt helpless, the very same which claimed the life of my father and my daughter, and it was now roaming free, here, ready to pounce on the next available soul.

I needed to fix this. I needed to make sure that this monster did not follow me back. I did not want Tonks and Kobi, or anyone else really involved in this. I needed to do this myself, but I was sure they were not really going to let me go. The only way I saw was to escape by force.

I saw an opening where Tonks was distracted with the whole monster news, and I wasted no time. I punched her face with enough force to stun her, as I did not want to hurt her, but I needed her to stay down and give me time to face the monster. Kobi was easier to shove away.

After spending so much time chasing my own tail, I realized that I was the monster. I was the source of the scream. I killed my daughter, and that led to this elaborate wild goose chase. Now I needed to end it and pay for what I had done.

My body seemed to have recovered now, and I was at least able to walk. I made my way to the elevator and descended to the main hall.

Nothing around me caught my attention except the main door. As I opened the door, the sunlight streamed in, and in the center of that light was a dark blue monolith. As I stepped into the sun, the monolith became clearer. A large, hairy werewolf was busy scraping the insides out of Sarah. I felt disgusted to see her lying there helpless. A large part of her face was missing, and the one eyeball the creature chose to leave looked back at me straight into my soul and asked me why I couldn't protect her. Why did I let this creature, which was the product of my childhood trauma, devour and manhandle her like this?

Chapter 23: The Cost of Anger

The creature seemed oblivious of its impact on the souls it was claiming, but as a product of rage, this was expected.

I walked forward slowly, clearly observing the savagery exhibited by this creature. I was expecting it to react towards me the exact same way it reacted toward Sarah and Klaus, but it clearly sensed my presence. It turned its large muzzle towards me, acknowledged my presence, and went back to chewing guts. Remnants of a large fight were visible all around me. The supermarket was crumbling down. A small piece of the ceiling fell down, and the werewolf was immediately alert, ears up and picking up the smallest sound. The deserted cash register was now visible from the hotel. Sarah's house seemed untouched, and I couldn't get a good view of my home, but for now, the only place that was severely trashed was the supermarket. Klaus had clearly got the pointy end of the dagger unfortunately.

I was now near the werewolf. It was a bit bigger than me, so I had to look up to speak to it even though it was bent down and munching away. I faced the monster now and said, "I want to say thank you. I know you were a product of my helplessness and anger, and whenever I needed you to take over, you have done your duty. Today, I know every human has a smaller version of you, but they do not feed it anger like I fed you. I needed you the first time when I felt inexplicable rage towards my father, and I unknowingly called you when I saw my daughter doing what she did. With my daughter, though, I still feel a confrontation was needed, but I strongly believe it need not have ended with you having to kill her."

I moved closer and continued, "She is dead now, but I don't blame you. The only person I blame is myself, so I want to make this right. You have done your duty in protecting me, and I want you gone. I have fed into this anger for a long time, and I do not want to do that anymore. If I let you survive, I don't know who else will be killed, and I don't want to be the reason for another murder."

The werewolf looked a little confused but continued to listen, "There is a reason I changed my name from Joshua to Marko – my father's name. I want to remind myself how bad he was and show that, in contrast, I can be a good person. I believe I was because my daughter and wife loved me. Sarah was a plain simple lady. I don't know if I loved Sarah as much as she loved me, but I had no hate for her, and I definitely loved Julia. She deserved better and did not deserve this. I am sorry it must be this way, but you must die."

The beast continued eating but shook its head. Its shiny fur gleamed in the sun. I could see its soft fur waving with the breeze. I looked up at the sky expecting to see the bright sun, but all I could see was the sky with pixelated blue blocks. I recalled Tonks had mentioned that she was part of maintaining the general environment, and considering that everything was breaking down, I wondered if something might have happened to Tonks. Sigh..., another name added to the list of casualties because of me.

The trees now were phasing between pixels and leaves. The creature now seemed to sense something was changing, and it stopped eating, closed its eyes, and laid down.

I repeated to myself that everything in my house was part of my mind – Pogo, Joshua, myself as well as this beast. I had no idea how I would be able to kill this beast, but for now, I couldn't blame it for anything it had done. It was doing exactly what my mind had created it to do.

I walked forward and placed my hand on its muzzle. Its eyes were closed, but it felt my touch. No sooner did I place my hand on it than my hand started to glow. I began to feel a lot of emotions flowing through me.

I pictured killing my father, torturing him later, and then I pictured killing my daughter. Killing seemed to be second nature to me. I remembered the moment when Father took his last breath, and his last words were, "Son of a bitch!" I remembered killing my daughter, and her last words were, "I'm sorry, dad."

I was now talking directly to her.

We could have talked about it, Julia. We could have worked it out. You were my daughter; you were not a violent person. My hatred for my father got the better of me, and I saw a part of him in you when I should have seen a part of me in you. I'm sorry, Julia. You deserved better.

The monster was now merging into me, and some of the memories I did not recall were coming back to me. After I assimilated the last life force of the werewolf, I calmed myself down, and finally, when all those emotions had been swallowed by me, the beast's lifeless hands fell to my side.

I thought it was befitting that the same emotions that made me create this monster had to be returned to me to be able to kill it. I paused for a while and looked to find a horizon, but the entire world seemed to be unstable now. Trees were disappearing, the grass was missing, and bees and insects became stationary. Had Tonks died?

As if answering my question, Tonks and Kobi came out from the hotel. I recalled Tonks saying that she had created this entire construct, and getting punched by me must have taken that last ounce of energy from her. She saw me and the dead beast and just dropped to the ground like a rag doll.

As I saw Kobi, I remembered why I did not recall any of the details relating to Julia's death. I had locked this deep inside my mind, never to be picked up or discovered. It was embedded in my psyche, and I spent so much time convincing myself of a lie that, in the end, I believed it.

I motioned to Kobi to follow me. He was scared now, but he did as I asked. We both walked across the grassy path towards my home. On the way, I saw the carnage the beast had wreaked on the supermarket up close. There was no gate, just a large gaping hole. The aisles were clearly visible but broken. No more infinite aisles for Klaus.

I hope Sarah and Klaus would make it, but considering the trauma the dismembering would have caused, I doubted that they would. The diner looked fine with negligible scratches. Sarah's home looked untouched as well, but the wall between our homes was now broken.

Our home..., my home..., itself was half broken. The walls facing the main living room were already rubble. The main door was lying opposite the house near the gate. As we opened the gate, the door slid from the side and made a loud thud. Kobi and I entered the yard as we observed trees and plants phasing out around us. It was as if the world was crumbling down. Tiles from the roof had fallen at the door, and I could see the staircase from far off. I saw a body lying at the bottom of the stairs as I entered.

Oh no!... In this entire fiasco, I completely forgot about Pogo. I entered the house, hopeful that the body was someone else's, but when I saw the lifeless body of Pogo missing a head, my voice was stuck in my throat. The head had rolled its way along the main hallway to the kitchen. I almost retched. Here was another life who deserved much more and was killed just because of me. The casualty list was increasing. A large hole had been left in my mind now. I was being torn up, and I couldn't help but walk up to Pogo's carcass and hug him with all my might. Kobi was the first to break the silence.

He said from afar, "I'm sorry for your loss Marko, I don't know if Tonks mentioned it, but I cannot enter unless you explicitly call me in."

I looked behind and couldn't find Kobi. I stepped near the door and saw him waiting outside on the porch.

I said, "Oh, yes, sorry, I know. Come on in."

I went back to the staircase and sat there with my head in my hands. I had done enough in life now to be punished many times over. I looked at Kobi and said, "Listen, Kobi. Behind this staircase is a door that is bright orange. That's the door to the basement. Go in there, and you will find an object with the memory of the murder you are looking for. I just opened it for you. I am giving you permission to view the memory object in that basement. If that doesn't work, you have my confession. Once we get out, I will confess in the real world. Let the world know my story. I killed my daughter, and I surrender to whoever is running this rig."

Kobi silently went to the back of the staircase. It was probably very dark, but after some searching, he came back with a glass shard. I don't know if he was able to see the memory, but he seemed scared and excited. Maybe he was thinking about his promotion, or maybe the prospect of just escaping this hell was good enough to put a smile on his face. He walked toward me and said, "I saw the memory, Marko. I'm sorry, but we will need to take you into custody."

"Can I stay here a while? I've surrendered already, and you don't need to worry about me escaping. This is my mind, after all, and time here is stretched. I want to spend some time here at home. I have had a lot of memories attached to this place, but I wasn't able to revisit all of them. I would like to spend some time alone, reminiscing about my family and my mom. I promise I have no reason to live, let alone escape."

Kobi obliged and went to wait outside the gate. When I was alone with Pogo, I let out a large scream which had been building up inside me for a while.

I knew this is how it ends for me.

Somewhere in Greenland

"Everyone at their stations! Kobi and Marko are back. Pull the rest out. Let the committee know."

Barnes walked briskly to Kobi and asked, "Did you find anything?"

"Yes, sir. Marko killed her. He confessed."

"That's it! We have got it! We have got the confession," Barnes announced to everyone.

There was chaos in the room. Everyone was scrambling to make sure they were able to do what the Commander wanted. No one dared to be in his bad books.

After some time, a lady in uniform walked up to the Commander and said, "Sir, Klaus, and Sarah are not responding to any stimuli. Tonks is extremely fragile and is responding very slowly. What should we do about them?"

Kobi's eyes shot up, but he did not say a word. The response from Barnes was colder than ice, "Leave them here for now and send them to a neuro-psychiatrist later to evaluate how they can be brought back."

"Sir, our in-house experts say that they may not come back and are in a permanent coma. Their mind has been torn apart beyond repair."

The commander was getting angry, "Listen, technically they are not dead, not legally, so maintain this stance. Everyone is alive, and we have got a viable confession from Marko. Kobi will give us the exact location of the murder weapon. We have enough to book Marko for homicide. This is our narrative, and this is what we need to tell the committee. Am I clear?"

"Yes, sir!"

Mindbender

She walked off, and the Commander stared at the screen. He had a parameter for measuring success, which was getting the truth. Klaus and Sarah were brain dead, and Tonks was severely strained mentally, but he had Kobi and Marko alive and kicking, along with a confession and the possible discovery of the long-missing murder weapon. In the end, the truth had won.

Did Sarah and Klaus deserve to go into coma? Was the entire mission and its repercussions worth it? In the Commander's mind, getting the truth out was always worth it.

He looked at Kobi and said, "It is imperative for your future that you keep your mouth shut about everything I just said."

Kobi looked at him and said, "I never heard anything, Commander." ...

...but then a faint smile crept across his face.

WHAT HAPPENED THAT NIGHT?

(Marko's Confession)

"Misunderstanding someone reveals how little you know about the person."

~ Samuel Zulu

Chapter 24
The Truth

I love Sarah and Julia more than anything, but my love for them is nothing at all compared to how much they love me. Sarah and I met when we were in our early thirties. She had expressed an interest in me and asked to marry me, and I had happily obliged.

I still recall our first conversation we had at a local coffee shop. We had met while volunteering for a charity run, and both of us were supposed to be delivering free bread and jam door to door. I was waiting in the common area when she joined me and said, "Hey, I think we have been paired today to distribute the bread."

She was average-looking, slim, petite, not a face that stood out, but she had a calming effect on me when we spoke. I had just been released from the asylum, and I had almost given up hope of getting a romantic interest, but here she was. She did not look too young for me, but neither did she look old. I replied, "Yeah, that's true, but unfortunately, this is my first time volunteering for bread distribution, and I am not sure where or how to begin."

"That's okay. I can help. I have been volunteering to distribute food for almost a year now."

She was amazing with the people we were delivering to. She always greeted them with a warm good morning and made sure she spent some time just chatting and listening, if they were chatty. We ended up spending an hour delivering, but in the end, I'm sure everyone that we delivered to was happy.

After our delivery was done and we reported back, she asked me, "Hey, if you're not doing anything else, do you wanna have some coffee?"

"Yeah, sure." I had nowhere to go and hadn't got a job yet. She seemed a bit forward, but I liked her.

Later over coffee, she said she was an orphan and that she had escaped from the orphanage in her early twenties. She was then adopted by a good Samaritan who ran a bakery shop close by. Now she runs his bakery shop and helps him innovate new recipes. I did not see the point of hiding the truth about me. I did not want to bring my parents or family into this conversation, but she would definitely need to know I had been in the asylum for a while. I'd rather she knows it now.

I told her I had a troubled childhood and that I had spent close to a decade in a mental institution. When she realized that I had been at a mental institution, her reaction is what struck me as something which I will never forget. She was not uncomfortable that I had spent time in an institution like most people. She said, "Golly, it must have been tough living through all that trauma. I'm glad you recovered."

That's when I knew this lady truly liked me. Maybe someday she would know the truth of my past.

As we got up to leave, she smacked her head and said, "God, I'm such a fool! My name is Sarah Miller."

I zoned out for a while and considered telling her my real name, but then I thought I wanted to start fresh, so I decided to use a new name, but the only name that came to my mind now was my father's. I could see her straining to look at me, and her next question would have been, "Are you okay?" if I had not responded with, "Hey, Sarah. I'm Marko Flannagan."

Chapter 24: The Truth

In short, she was a nice woman and a very good mother. Soon we had Julia, and our life changed entirely. We spent all our time with her. Every small change in her behavior we captured. She was a wild child, and after a certain age, she was hard to cage.

Both Sarah and I had come from very traumatic childhoods, so we decided not to enforce any of that on Julia, which allowed her to spread her wings and fly to the highest point she could. Julia especially adored me, and I always tried to be a father she deserved. She was a constant reminder of my victory over my dad's atrocities. It was proof that I was a good man, that I could build a family and not be like my father. That is also why it felt apt that I renamed myself Marko to show that not all Markos are wife beaters.

When I had married Sarah, I was a bit skeptical about what kind of husband I would be, but when I became a father, I was terrified. Would I be able to impart the right values to my child? After around twenty years, when I look at Julia and Paul, I felt proud of what I have. I was also the one who ironically ended this beautiful painting.

Paul and Julia were married for almost three years, and they had come to visit. We still did not have grandchildren, but I was okay to give them the time they needed. The night it happened, we had had a fun filled, memorable dinner. We talked about sports, Paul's bookstore, and a lot of stuff. It was fun, and we were all happy. I could see that Paul and Julia still had their spark, and I was happy for them. They seemed to enjoy each other's company, and I was glad we were together still as a family since most kids get married and just come once a year for the holidays.

Soon we retired for the day, and Sarah went to sleep early. She's been tired of late, probably due to her gastroesophageal reflux disease catching up. She had not been able to eat well and eating anything leads to stomach episodes and a possible visit to the Accident and Emergency ward at the local hospital.

Today was one such day. I couldn't get sleep, so I wandered out into our yard thinking about general stuff like the fixed deposit I had planned to get Julia for her first kid and this house, which I was planning to sign over in her name. Thoughts were brewing in my mind, and I proceeded to sit on the bench just near my daughter's room. It was a dilapidated bench and probably needed repair, but Sarah and I had spent a lot of time sitting on this bench talking and contemplating our future. This bench had witnessed too many memories which I cherish.

Our house was a huge one, and both my bedroom and Julia's room were on the ground facing either side of the yard, divided by the small pathway to the gate. My daughter's side of the lawn had a bench where me and Sarah used to sit. When Julia was born, she spent a lot of time with me on that bench. She told me about her first kiss and about the first research paper she published. She was greatly gifted, and I was planning to push her to continue her research now that both she and Paul had settled in. I was sure Paul would not have any issues with her continuing her research. She said she was researching something for sustainable farming. I was sure it was not something she just would want to drop.

I had not planned to sit there long, but I heard smacking and mild screaming coming from Julia's room. There were some smacks, and I was sure I heard whips as well. The sound of whiplash was unique, but the smacks were enough for me to get concerned to check what was going on. I got up and was going to knock on their door to ask them what happened when I saw their window was slightly open, so I opened it more. In retrospect, it was a bad idea, but at the time, I was concerned about the source of the scream. I could even hear some groaning, and every new sound had my feelers up.

Light escaped the window to the outside and illuminated the blades of grass beside the bench. The window had some broken glass placed on the side, which was probably why it couldn't be closed. I couldn't remember when this window was broken or who broke it, but I made a mental note to fix it. I slowly moved the window to the side and pushed aside the curtains, and what I saw left me in shambles.

My daughter was wearing a bra with spikes on it and a leather spandex. She had a whip in one hand, and her other hand was busy finding Paul's cheek. Paul was cowering down at her feet in his boxer shorts. From where I was standing, Paul seemed to be in danger. She was whipping him on his back, and I could see visible marks even from where I was. What was scary and depressing was that she seemed to be enjoying it. She then took her foot which had sharp-heeled shoes and placed it on his chest after which he let out a loud moan in pain.

I could see all kinds of torture items ranging from handcuffs to knives and even some sort of clips. Was she going to use all of them on Paul? I thought they were happily married. Why would Julia do this, and why was she wearing this weird costume at night? Did she bring it with her?

I had never seen this kind of behavior from her. I loved her beyond anything, but this behavior was unacceptable. In my mind, this basically proved that violence was in her genes, and she was hurting Paul, who was clearly in pain. This was exactly the behavior that I was running away from and the exact kind of beating that Father used to give to Mom. The only difference I saw was that Father did not have to wear a leather costume to beat Mom.

Rage started building inside me. She was reminding me that I could not run away from my past. I could not let this continue, and I felt the same anger I had felt when I murdered my father. A sudden urge to kill her engulfed me. I picked the nearest sharp object I could find, which was the piece of broken glass by the window, and I sneaked into the room. As I closed in on her, she picked a shoe that had a pointy wheel at the heels, similar to the ones cowboys wear to train horses. She was moving these sharp wheels on Paul's chest, and he was groaning. I couldn't stand this torture anymore!

I pulled her by the hair, and before she could say anything, I slit her throat. Blood spattered and fell on Paul, who took a while to realize what had happened.

Julia turned around and was going to react, but when she saw me, it was as if her will to live left her. Her hands that were reaching out to my neck went limp. She fell to the ground, and a pool of blood slowly formed at her neck. I saw her mouth moving, and she was clearly trying to say something, but all I could hear were muffled air sounds.

Suddenly, Paul, who just recovered from his shock, spoke up, "Marko, what have you done? What's wrong with you?" He couldn't believe what had happened! He ran to her body and started crying, "Julia! No, Julia! Come back! Marko, you sick fuck! What have you done?" He looked at Julia again and was now straining to hear what she was saying. "What are you saying, Julia?"

He finally seemed to have been able to hear and make sense of what she was trying to say because he looked at her and was almost wailing. He turned to me and said, "Marko, Do you know what she said? She said, 'I'm sorry, Dad.' She's sorry. Why did you kill her?"

I was seeing only red, so none of this was registering in my brain. "This cannot be allowed, Paul. This behavior cannot be allowed. You do not deserve to live as well, or you will become a monster like me and end up trying to kill your bully. I had spent a lot of time subduing the inner monster in me until one day, I unleashed it and killed my father. Now the same monster has killed your wife and my daughter. I need to end this cycle. I don't want you to undergo the same pain. I will end it for you."

"No, Marko. She was never a danger to me. God, do you not know what BDSM is?"

"I don't know, and I don't care. You cannot beat on someone just because you're married, even if it's something that may be common in the current times. I will not allow the propagation of a gene which leads to beating and bullying of another human, especially a family member." I did not see the need to waste any time explaining myself to him and plunged the shard into his chest.

The rage in me was not quelled yet, and I sat on Julia and stabbed her many more times before I realized that she was my daughter and I had basically killed the love of my life. Paul was sitting lifeless beside her. I had just killed my daughter and her husband and was surely going to rot in jail. Instinct took over immediately, and I decided to take the shard, dip it in kerosene, and bury it below the bench at home. That way, all the scent would be gone, and a sniffer dog would not be able to trace it. As for the prints, I would basically have been in the room pretty much a lot of times, considering it's my home. Both my wife and me would have prints on both Julia and Paul, so there would be reasonable doubt but not enough to convict. The police would just have to accept my alibi that I was sleeping since no one had seen me come out. For this to work, I would need to tell Sarah that I had done this gruesome act.

After hiding the weapon and letting the crime scene stay as is, I walked with blood on my hands and shirt into my bedroom. Sarah was already awake and waiting for me, like Hell's gatekeeper. She asked me eerily calmly," Marko, What have you done?"

"I'm sorry, Honey. I don't know what came over me, but when I gained my senses back, Julia and Paul were dead."

"What do you mean 'gained my senses back'? Did you black out?"

"No"

"Has this happened to you before?"

This was the moment when I told her about my father. I felt it was the right time, and I said, "Yes, I had killed my father in one such killing spree. I killed him and started screaming with happiness. The neighbor heard my screams and found me with a bloody shirt beside the dead bodies of my parents. I do not remember anything about that night, and all I remember are the gruesome details they kept playing on the news channels. I was sent to the asylum because of these blank spaces in my memory. I had assumed this was all over, but now I am not sure."

Either Sarah was in shock, or she did not process that her daughter was dead. She sat there expressionless. She then asked me, "Have you hidden the murder weapon?"

"Yes."

"Is the crime scene clear of any clues back to you?"

"Yes, and your alibi will decide whether I go to jail or not. I am not afraid, Sarah. If you feel I deserve it, I won't love you any less."

She looked at me and said as clear as day, "You have lived with me for almost twenty years and have never done something like this. Now you killed Julia for a reason I have no idea about. Maybe you were never cured, but you are not a bad person. I feel that keeping you in isolation was probably the best cure. I love you, Marko, and while I am enraged that you killed my only daughter, it was a risk I had accepted when I knew you had been to an asylum. I am still giving you the benefit of the doubt. Go clean yourself and come to bed." She reacted to my father's murder in such an understanding way that I was almost scared she may have done something similar.

I cleaned myself in the bathroom and came back. She then asked me, "Why did you feel such rage towards our daughter? What was she doing?"

"I saw her beating and torturing Paul. Coming from a traumatizing childhood, I couldn't accept it."

"Did Paul say he needed help?"

"No."

"Were any of them in visible pain?"

"No."

"Was she in costume? Like a leather jacket or pants?"

"Yeah, she was wearing a weird costume. How do you know?"

"Marko, you killed our daughter and her husband because they were having kinky sex. There is nothing wrong with what they were doing. You haven't been exposed to this type of encounter because you spent most of your time in the asylum. Remember this, Marko. You killed your daughter for nothing because you misunderstood her and did not trust her. You need to live with this guilt forever."

I processed this information, but my mind was blank. I stared at the ceiling, but what I saw was a bottomless pit I wanted to jump into.

As it happened, the police had indeed followed this route but were unable to pinpoint an accurate culprit. They had called it a crime of passion and closed it out.

Though I knew Sarah forgave me for the episode, we never spoke to each other and, over time, just drifted apart like most couples do. Does true forgiveness really exist?

THE HEARING

"Risk-Taking is the essence of Innovation."

~ Herman Kahn

Chapter 25
Brain Dead

Five panel members and a military judge were seated on a high table with a thick bundle of case notes in front of them at the proceeding of today's general court-martial. The judge was ready now, and all members sat down. The judge-advocate sat at the foot of the table. The accused and his attorney were present at a table opposite the military judge. There was a stenographic reporter hired to transcribe all the proceedings. The members of the court and the judge-advocate were duly sworn.

The judge began to speak, "The following hearing has been called upon for the State vs. Dr. Igor Weiss. You are hereby charged with one count of manslaughter due to unknown information which led to the death of Sarah Miller. How do you plead?"

Dr. Weiss said, "Not guilty."

"You are also charged on one count of manslaughter due to medical negligence, which led to the death of Klaus Schmidt. How do you plead?"

Dr. Weiss again said, "Not guilty."

"Judge-advocate, you may proceed."

"Thank you, judge. Dr. Weiss, can you state your name and designation for the record?"

"My name is Dr. Igor Weiss. I am the Chief Scientist in the Army Research Office. I have two Ph.Ds. in Cognitive Analysis of Dream

Patterns as well as in Neuropsychology, where my topic of research was analyzing the mind to gather suppressed information. I am also the lead consultant for Project Mindbender."

"Thank you, Dr. Weiss. Could you walk us through what exactly Project Mindbender is?"

"Sure. Project Mindbender is a state-of-the-art project where regressive hypnosis is used to create a group-hypnosis effect on certain individuals and successfully allow them to lucid dream. This is called 'hypnosis-induced lucid dreams,' or HILD in short. The operatives or "oneironauts" facilitate the dream and help the dreamers to effectively change the way the dream is progressing and, in the process, extract repressed memories. These memories can be used to gather information for surveillance or investigation of suspects.

The hypnotic trance is a state of awareness that makes a person more easily persuaded. The mind suppresses certain memories as coping mechanisms or general compartmentalization. Hypnosis helps to relax the mind to a point where it feels comfortable to bring out these oppressed memories. All oneironauts are trained to maintain a dream journal so that they can transcribe exactly what is happening in the dream.

To be able to produce the level of energy to hypnotize more than two individuals, we need a person with powerful psychic energy. These individuals are generally called "hypersensitives." Scientifically, they have increased or deeper central nervous system sensitivity to physical, emotional, or social stimuli. The three hypersensitives create a construct that is a closed boundary or scope. In our case, Steve builds the base construct; Tonks adds the environment, and Kobi dynamically adds small fauna. They then create a pseudo-real narrative for the hypnotized persons of interest to pursue. Once everyone is in the hypnotized state, we put everyone's bodies into stasis.

Stasis existed as long ago as 2006 when a Japanese climber fell down a mountain and broke his pelvis but survived because of the cold and his almost negligible metabolism. Today we have custom stasis gel that keeps the body in a pseudo rigor mortis state but keeps the brain functioning. We use this gel extensively on the head with a special helmet which adds a breath assistant gill to the operatives and suspects. This allows them to focus on sleeping and dreaming rather than necessities, like breathing. We can pump in more numbing agents or sedatives to make sure that they stay asleep if they wake up ungracefully due to a trauma."

"Thank you, Dr. Weiss. When was this project first incepted?"

"I believe the first talks happened somewhere around January 2009, way before my time, but with my research, I was able to get this vision to materialize into a viable non-invasive interrogation technique."

"Dr. Weiss, it is not really 'non-invasive'; wouldn't you agree?"

Dr. Weiss' lawyer stood up immediately, "Objection, speculative and directive."

The judge said, "Overruled. Continue, judge-advocate"

"Thank you, judge. There is a reason I call it 'invasive.' The human mind is not a tangible piece or organ which can just be a binary entry and exit. Would that be correct, Dr. Weiss? When you conduct the shared lucid dream, aren't the operatives and suspects effectively opening their minds to each other? In lieu of that action, aren't they then invading each other's mind?"

Dr Weiss was dogmatic when he answered, "When they share a lucid dream, they share brain patterns. They do not share emotions or opinions. Effectively, each mind is still intact without any invasive extraction. It is the brain which is sedated and experiencing the shared dream."

"I understand where you're coming from, Dr. Weiss, but if that were indeed the case, would you be suggesting that Sarah Miller and Klaus Schmidt committed suicide?"

"No. What I'm suggesting is that they did not land in their current state because of me or any of our research you keep blaming."

"We'll let the panel decide, Dr. Weiss. I just want the truth. Can you elaborate on why you think it is noninvasive?"

"I thought I just did, but I understand it may not be the easiest of topics to explain, so I will try again. To begin with, each mind is not tangible in your own words. That's where hypnosis comes in. We coerce the mind to manifest itself into a form that the owner of the mind is comfortable with. This is the safe house that they wake up in. In this case, for Marko, it was his childhood home, and for Sarah, it was the house she bought with Marko. It was just a coincidence that both Sarah and Marko had a fairly accurate rendering of their safe house. Tonks had a barn, and she had to train for quite some time to be able to convert it to a diner. The capability varies from person to person."

Dr. Weiss paused momentarily, and then continued, "The rendition of the safe house is complemented with 'memory objects,' as we like to call them. These are basically representations of certain memories. Consider them as metadata for your memories. Your mind creates them based on how you have compartmentalized your repressed and fond memories. Similarly, memory objects can be created and planted at specific locations for you to interact with to trigger memories for scenarios which your mind did not create a memory object. When creating memory objects for someone else, you need not have or even know the memory because the object is just a trigger to bring out memories already in your mind, which is why I compared it to metadata, which is only a description of the data and not the actual data."

Hearing no questions, Dr. Weiss continued, "This is how Tonks and Kobi had attempted to use certain objects at the crime scene to trigger memories in Sarah and Marko. The mind moves much faster than our actions. We might think about something now, and by the time it gets processed, we are already doing something else. That's how fast the mind is. Of course, memory objects are more of an abstract concept, and even certain words or names may be triggers to remember memories. Now, when someone's mind is manifested as a safe house, and there is a group hypnosis in place, all participants have access to the other minds but do not have permission to enter each other's safe house. So even if you're a suspect and I am interrogating you, I cannot enter your house, which is also your mind. You need to explicitly get permission to enter, and that's why standard military personnel cannot be recruited for this. We need personnel who can manipulate and extract information without major brute force."

"Thank you, Dr. Weiss. For the benefit of the judge, what happens if you do get access to one of these house minds?"

"If you get permission to enter, you can access any of the memories as long as the owner gives it to you or passes it to you verbally or physically. You basically become a secondary owner of that memory. It's almost like recalling a funny incident and telling it to a friend. Your memory, in a way, becomes his memory as well. I hope that makes sense. That is how in this specific case, Marko gave his memory to Kobi Takahashi, which he provided as evidence from what I have been briefed."

"Thank you, Dr. Weiss. Can you explain how this manifestation is facilitated?"

"That's where the hypersensitives come in. The hypersensitive hypnotizes the persons of interest and creates a construct where the minds materialize so that the owners of the mind find it comfortable to reveal information. They may not readily reveal information which is where the lucid dreaming comes in. When a person understands that the construct they are in is not real, they will be more open to making decisions themselves to be able to influence the end goal. The oneironauts' job is to make sure that this end goal is a common, mutual goal which will lead to more information being extracted."

"I believe from the transcripts of what happened, that was not the case here."

"Yes, that is true. One reason was because Marko suffered from multiple personality disorder, and the second reason was that Marko had a lot of suppressed memories that stemmed from his childhood trauma. I believe Tonks Patterson, Kobi Takahashi, and Steve Smith were the hypersensitives, and they had done a very good job creating the construct they were in, but the persons of interest were very resourceful, especially Marko. Klaus Schmidt had done a good job leading the team, but Marko had figured out a lot of anomalies, and essentially because of his multiple personality disorder, saw his younger self as well. This led him to discover that the world was not real, and that changed his perception of the world.

There is a world of difference between a person sure that something is false and a person having doubts." Dr. Weiss paused for a bit. The advocate was going to say something, but Dr Weiss continued, "I believe all of them did as much as they could. Creating a more believable construct with people and expanded landscape will need much more energy, which I don't think any human possesses. Recreating an entire crime scene and missing out on the minute details like the smell is completely human, and they mustn't be held accountable for that."

"Dr. Weiss, that one error may have helped Marko identify more flaws with the world and reject it, correct?"

"Yes."

"Dr. Weiss, did you know that Marko was an alias, and that his original name was Joshua Flannagan?"

"No."

"Why wasn't a background check done on them?"

"You'll have to ask Mr. Barnes for that answer."

"Coming to the multiple personality disorder, would it be accurate to say that if a person had multiple personality disorder it will materialize in some format and would have been highlighted in your medical checkup?"

"No. A person may have personalities which are extremely dormant. In this case, the monster manifestation and the child were suppressed personalities. His dominant personality was still him as Joshua because he was the most sensitive emotionally at that point. Joshua had seen the worst of life. Marko was a conscious choice he made to prove a point about his abusive father. It was not really him, and deep down, he was still Joshua. That is why we did not see Marko initially but only when he had heard his own name. This was not expected and was a learning experience for all involved."

"I wouldn't say that for Mr. Schmidt and Mrs. Miller. Dr. Weiss, what happens when a person dies in this construct? Or, to reword it, to die is to have all your cells stop functioning. What is the equivalent of death in this construct, in your opinion?"

"You cannot die in the true sense of the word as you have put it. What we are dealing with is a person's mind. The ultimate death of a person, his mind, or his personality is the destruction of where it resides, which is the brain. The manifestation of the mind is a safe house. It may take a lot of beating but as long as there is a person still there, the mind stays on. That's how people who have had mental trauma heal over time. It is that will to live and move on that keeps the mind active. When that will is gone or in any way absorbed, then it materializes as death in the construct.

Ideally, when you die ungracefully in the dream, you wake up with severe brain trauma outside the dream in the real world, which is, of course, healable. When you wake up ungracefully with severe in-construct trauma, you end up brain dead. The house is broken and stays broken because the soul owner who has the will to live is no more.

That is what happened to Sarah and Klaus. Sarah lost her will to live and jumped out a window but could still have been saved if it wasn't for the beast dismembering her soul, and the same applies to Klaus, who was basically absorbed by the beast. In the end, Marko absorbed the beast, essentially eliminating its existence."

The judge-advocate went back to his seat and picked a scribbled note from his assistant. He turned to Dr. Weiss and said, "Dr. Weiss, let me repeat two statements in your testimony. First, you stated. and I quote 'The ultimate death of a person, his mind, or his personality is the destruction of where it resides, which is the brain,' and then you said, 'When you wake up ungracefully with severe in-construct trauma, you end up brain dead.' So, can I conclude then, that with your interpretation of death, Klaus Schmidt and Sarah miller are dead?"

Dr. Weiss had not expected this. He had heard that the court room was where every word could be twisted to the advantage of any clever advocate but witnessing it in real time had shaken him. He had nothing to say and was fumbling for an answer.

"Dr. Weiss?"

"I did not kill them."

"Again Dr. Weiss, We'll let the judges decide." He turned to the judges and said "Please take note of this as it will be crucial when you make your decision, Your Honor"

He then turned to Dr Weiss and asked, "I understand that all the information you have is from Kobi, recounting the events from his transcribed dream journal, correct?"

"Yes."

"How do you validate that Kobi was not lying?"

"He is a military operative, so we have a basic level of trust in him. He also had the right location of the murder weapon. Kobi has no reason to lie."

"Retrospectively, Dr. Weiss, would you have been able to identify the personalities if you had known that Marko was suffering from multiple personality disorder?"

Chapter 25: Brain Dead

"Honestly, as you know, this was the first time we tried this method on a civilian. We have had people waking up ungracefully who are still recovering, but we have never encountered someone traumatized to such an extent in the construct. We were not prepared for what was to come."

"And this was not tested as part of your current test plans?"

"No, we did not test with individuals who suffered from MPD. Neither did we attempt to inflict serious trauma in the construct, if that's what you are implying."

"No more questions."

Chapter 26
Collateral Damage

The same panel now sat at the exact same table, but this time opposite them was Commander Luke Barnes.

The judge began to speak, "The following hearing has been called upon for the State vs. Commander Luke Barnes. You are hereby charged with one count of manslaughter due to negligence which led to the death of Sarah Miller. How do you plead?"

Commander Barnes said, "Not guilty."

"You are also charged on one count of manslaughter due to negligence which led to the death of Klaus Schmidt. How do you plead?"

Commander Barnes said, "Not guilty."

"Judge-advocate, you may proceed."

"Thank you, judge. Commander Barnes, can you state your name and your rank, please, for the record?"

Barnes was not someone to be messed with. He did not give away smiles for free. He said, "My name is Commander Luke Barnes. I am a commander in the military force, and I lead the military wing for Innovative Strategies. I am the lead personnel and operations executive of Project Mindbender."

"Thank you, Commander. Can you elaborate on your understanding and relevant stake in Project Mindbender?"

"Since its inception, Project Mindbender was solely created for information extraction and interrogation. My role was to make sure that the military had personnel who were well trained and skilled to use such a power. I was approached to find and recruit people who will be able to wield this technology and approach without breaking themselves. Klaus Schmidt had powerful, intimidating skills and was a valid candidate to lead this project but did not have enough sensitivity to be able to build something like a construct. He was raw and saw everything as binary. Tonks Patterson, on the other hand, was the exact opposite of Klaus. She wanted to make a difference and was much more sensitive to people and their emotions. Dr. Weiss confirmed that she is a hypersensitive and could create a valid construct. Steve Smith was an ad-hoc entry to the team. We had recruited him as a hypersensitive to support Tonks in the world-building as it was taking a toll on her mental stability, but that was before we found Kobi. Kobi Takahashi was the last recruit but had immense compartmentalization skills and dynamic world-building capabilities. He was also hypersensitive. He was able to help provide the right context and isolation for the suspects to be able to observe the crime scene."

Commander Barnes looked up at the judge and then continued, "The project itself has been tested with multiple other military personnel, and we had asked the police for cases where a certain degree of uncertainty was present, and police couldn't get conclusive evidence. This was the first case where the lead investigator couldn't find any proof of foul play, but he suspected that there was some involvement from the parents. Our job was to either corroborate the parents' alibi or to prove it false, which in the end we did."

"Thank you, Commander. And you believe the end justifies the means with a suspect and an operative dead?"

"Like I said, I am a soldier. I give and follow orders. So were they. They knew what they had signed up for."

"What had Sarah Miller signed up for, Commander?"

Chapter 26: Collateral Damage

"Every military operation has collateral damage. She was the collateral damage but was pivotal for Marko to go nuclear, kill the beast, and give us the proof we needed for a conviction."

"Thank you for your thoughts, Commander, but I would request you answer only when asked. Who had done the background check for Marko?"

"We do a standard, superficial background check for all suspects or persons of interest. Marko had successfully hidden his former identity, and there was no documentation to show that he had another name."

"Retrospectively, would you agree this was a mistake?"

"No. At the time, I did not feel the need to go deeper. We had a suspect, and this was the first time we were implementing this operation on people outside the military, so this was more of a trial-and-error process, but I assure you the background check done was thorough. He had hidden his old identity well, which was not in our control."

"So, you implemented a large-scale military trial run at the expense of civilians' lives?"

"There are a large number of military operations running right now. Operatives are dying, and innocents are being slaughtered. I do not see them in this court-martial room. Great innovation will need great sacrifices. If I was anywhere close to as talented as these folks, I would have gladly done it myself, but unfortunately, we need folks like them, and this time Klaus was not lucky."

"Commander, who died first, Klaus or Sarah?"

"Officially, Klaus, but it was almost together as we had sensed the changes in the brain patterns very close to the same time. Sarah had jumped from the window just as Klaus was consumed by the monster."

"Why did you not stop the operation immediately?"

"Because we still needed to find Marko, otherwise, everything would be in vain, and at this time, we did not even see Marko in any of the journals. He came afloat a couple of times, but we had nothing substantial in the journals."

"So, considering this, the argument is pursuing the truth justifies their death?"

"Nothing justifies their death, but the truth was out, and I consider that as a win."

"No more questions, your honor."

Epilogue

In other news, the double homicide at Bogtown took a new turn. Marko Flannagan, the father of twenty-one-year-old Julia, was arrested for the murder of his daughter and her husband, Paul. The military unraveled this interesting case by using an unconventional hypnotherapy-induced lucid dreaming (HILD) method. Soon you'll be seeing footage of Flannagan being arrested in a military facility in Greenland. We have our psychiatrist expert, Dr. Clive Odinson, to help us understand what was done and how this information was extracted.

Dr. Odinson, could you explain how this was achieved?

Thanks, Joley. From my sources in the military, what I know is that they used some form of group hypnosis to penetrate the suspect's mind and get information. The police had no solid leads on this except the crime-of-passion angle, and they had their suspicions about the parents. Since the parents had a solid alibi for each other, the only conclusion they could come to was that the parents murdered them and colluded in the act or that it was indeed an act of passion. This method helped sort through their suppressed memories and prove motive and means.

Thanks, Dr. Odinson. That's right. What we hear is that Marko is not his name but rather his father's name, who used to abuse him and his mother. His real name was Joshua Flannagan. Is that right? A report claimed that due to certain quirks of this process, Marko's, or in this case Joshua's wife Sarah and another operative are in a coma. We reached out to the military to comment, and they have just confirmed that the operation is no longer active, and they will regroup on another strategy.

Mindbender

In other news — How does childhood trauma lead to serial killing tendencies?

Tonks sat on her couch and watched the news. The psychiatrist was rattling away some gibberish that she wasn't even listening to. She couldn't escape the trauma that this experiment had caused her. She had not gone into a coma to make the news, nor had she got the actual confession and got a promotion. She was the actual collateral damage, with her mind destroyed, requiring years of healing. No one deserved to die like Sarah. Sarah was not a part of any of this, and her only fault was loving her husband and daughter.

Tonks had left the military, where value for life was only relevant if it did not negate your immediate superior's command. Even Marko did not deserve to be stripped bare and have all his life exposed to the public like this. There is a limit to the invasion of privacy, and Tonks was not interested in working with anyone who had a major role to play in this.

She finished her whiskey and picked her newfound love, her pet kitten.

"C'mon, Poodle, let's dream, shall we? I wanna try something new today."

Contact Information

You may contact the author directly by email at:
naisdon@gmail.com

Amazon.com

If you purchased *Mindbender* from an online bookstore, please go there and give this book a rating of one to five stars. You may also write a review or leave any comments you feel appropriate. This will be of benefit not only to the author but also to prospective readers.

About the Author

Avinash Naduvath is a Cybersecurity Architect at Cisco Systems, and *Mindbender* is his first novel.

When not designing secure networks for his customers, he loves to write. He is fond of creating complex designs, so world-building is a passion for him. He lives with his wife and son in Singapore.

His wife and brother-in-law are strong, lucid dreamers which is what triggered his interest in the subject, and *Mindbender* is the product of such interests.

Made in the USA
Las Vegas, NV
02 December 2022

60956448R00184